S0-BOH-941

SEAN D. YOUNG

With This Ring

ARABESQUE®

If you purchased this book without a cover you should be aware
that this book is stolen property. It was reported as "unsold and
destroyed" to the publisher, and neither the author nor the
publisher has received any payment for this "stripped book."

WITH THIS RING

An Arabesque novel

ISBN 1-58314-578-8

© 2006 by Sean D. Young

All rights reserved. The reproduction, transmission or utilization
of this work in whole or in part in any form by any electronic, mechanical
or other means, now known or hereafter invented, including xerography,
photocopying and recording, or in any information storage or retrieval
system, is forbidden without written permission. For permission please
contact Kimani Press, Editorial Office, 233 Broadway, New York, NY
10279 U.S.A.

All characters in this book have no existence outside the imagination of
the author and have no relation whatsoever to anyone bearing the same
name or names. They are not even distantly inspired by any individual
known or unknown to the author, and all incidents are pure invention.
Any resemblance to actual persons, living or dead, is entirely coincidental.

® and TM are trademarks. Trademarks indicated with ® are registered in
the United States Patent and Trademark Office, the Canadian Trade Marks
Office and/or other countries.

www.kimanipress.com

Printed in U.S.A.

To my mother
Mary L. Taylor

Acknowledgments

Words really can't express the gratitude I have in my heart. I've never seen such an outpouring of love and support from so many people that aren't my family.

I would like to take this opportunity to thank everyone who supported, encouraged, and promoted my first novel, *Total Bliss*. Each and every person was a blessing to me.

Tommie Ross—Uncle Tommie, thanks so much for making it possible for me to write wherever I go. I love you.

And to every seasoned author who has encouraged an aspiring writer to follow their dreams.

Chapter 1

"You may kiss the bride," the preacher announced joyfully.

Rose Hart's eyes fluttered as she watched the groom, Nicholas Damon, slowly lift the veil that covered her cousin's round face. She studied the couple as they gazed deep into each other's eyes before sharing a kiss that left them both breathless. Rose could feel the love permeating between them, and that brought a smile to her face.

She was extremely happy for Destiny, who stood at the altar in a breathtaking satin gown with a Queen Anne neckline and long illusion trumpet sleeves. Destiny had waited a long time for this day, and Rose was thrilled to stand next to her as the maid of honor.

The women had been close ever since they were chubby little girls fantasizing about all their hopes and dreams for the future. Each of them had a detailed wedding day fantasy, but unfortunately, Rose's vision of a happily ever after had been shattered years ago. Destiny's wedding would have to serve as a victory for both of them.

Rose looked up at the brass bridal arch, which she'd decorated earlier that day. She and her sisters, Violet, Lili, and Ivy, operated Hearts and Flowers, a one-stop bridal mansion that took care of all of a couple's wedding needs. Rose was responsible for the floral décor, Lili designed cakes, Violet ran the bridal salon, and Ivy took care of the general coordination of events.

Keeping with the theme of the October wedding, Rose had skillfully adorned the arch with ivory tulle that had fall flowers, leaves, and berries intertwined in it. The mixture of mango, gold, and brown colors was magnificent against the yellow flicker from the lights of the candelabras.

The thunderous applause from the audience, followed by the upbeat tempo of "The Best Is Yet To Come," brought Rose out of her daydream. Dabbing her eyes with an embroidered white handkerchief, she glanced at the women standing behind her and noticed the other bridesmaids also had to catch the tears slipping down their brown cheeks. She turned back around to find Jonathan Damon, the best man, standing with his arm extended and waiting for her to take it.

Jonathan was a devastatingly handsome man who had to be at least six feet tall. Rose had observed his good looks when she met him at the wedding rehearsal. He reminded her of a dark chocolate cover model with his cleanshaven look. "Hmmm," she grunted in appreciation, noticing that in his black one button notch lapel tuxedo, he looked like he could strike a runway pose any minute.

"I'm sorry, Jonathan, for keeping you waiting."

Jonathan took in the lush beauty standing before him. He admired the way her strapless, mango-colored gown clung to every curve of her body. Her shiny, shoulder-length black hair had been pinned into a neat French roll, which gave her an elegant appearance. He wrapped her arm over his and patted her hand.

"It's okay," he responded in a rich baritone voice as they made their way up the aisle. They walked through the church's vestibule, with the rest of the bridal party following behind them.

When they separated, Rose noticed sweat clinging to Jonathan's brow and leaned closer to him. "Are you okay?" she asked, her voice filled with concern as they entered the holding room.

"I felt fine this morning. I don't know what happened," he said hoarsely.

Rose studied him for a moment and then frowned. "You don't look so good." She guided him over to the nearest chair. "Why don't I try to get you something cool to drink?"

Jonathan pulled a handkerchief out of the inside pocket of his jacket and wiped his forehead. "I think I'll be fine, but thanks."

Rose decided to get him some water, anyway. When she returned, she found him scrunched down in the chair, with his head resting against the wall. She handed him a Styrofoam cup filled with water from the fountain in the hallway. "Here you go, sweetheart."

Jonathan pulled his long frame into an erect sitting position before accepting the cup from her. "Thanks," he said, taking a small sip.

Rose took the empty seat next to him and watched as he drank. Even though Jonathan looked sick, she noticed it did little to diminish his strikingly good looks. "Did that help any?" she asked softly.

"Yes, thank you, but I think I'm going to leave right after we take pictures. I hate to do that to Nick, but I just need to lie down for a while."

"That's probably a good idea."

Rose was watching him use his hankie to dab at the perspiration on his forehead when her sister Ivy walked into the room.

"The church has been cleared, so we're ready for our photo session," Ivy announced to the crowd. She looked down at Jonathan, and her brows creased with concern.

When the bridal party began to file out of the room, Ivy pulled Rose aside as she passed by. "Is he okay?" she asked, pointing to the best man.

"He's not feeling very well," Rose whispered, watching Jonathan sweep the now damp handkerchief across his brow again as he walked through the doorway.

She followed Ivy out of the room and into the sanctuary, where their father, Andrew Hart, had already started the photo session. As they took pictures, Rose tried to keep her eye on Jonathan, who seemed a little off balance at times. When Andrew paused to reload his camera, Jonathan took a seat on the front pew. Rose walked over to where he sat and touched his forehead once more. He was burning up.

"Jonathan, maybe you should leave now. You're starting to look kind of funny, and you have a temperature."

He looked up, piercing her with his coal black eyes. "I feel even worse, but I wanted to talk to Nick before I left." Jonathan reached into his pocket and pulled out a slip of paper. "I wrote my speech for the toast so I wouldn't forget anything. Can you have my brother read it for me?" he asked meekly.

Rose had no idea who his brother was. "Who is… Oh, never mind," she amended, seeing a fresh layer of perspiration form on Jonathan's face. "I'll talk to Nicholas. I'm sure he'll take care of everything."

Jonathan rose from his seat on shaky feet. "Thanks. Please tell him I'll catch up with him later."

Rose reached out and grabbed his hand. "Do you want someone to walk with you to your car?" she asked, watching him skeptically.

"No, it's not that serious that I can't make it to the car and drive." He squeezed her hand before releasing it. "I would kiss you for being so sweet to me, but I'm not sure if I'm contagious," he joked.

Rose smiled at the thought of his full lips descending upon hers and then realized that probably wasn't what he meant. "That's quite alright," she said, rubbing his back gently. "Just take care of yourself."

"I will." Jonathan offered her a sad smile, attempting to assure her that he was okay before he walked away.

With a shake of her head, Rose watched one of the finest men she had ever seen exit the sanctuary and then sent her attention back to the photographer. Her father was now taking a photo of both sets of parents posed with the bride and groom.

"Mr. Hart, can we get one more with the entire wedding party?" Ivy called out. She always called her father Mr. Hart when they were on a job to make things seem more professional. Quickly, Ivy looked around the church, counting the bridal party. There were nine people present when there should have been ten. "Where is Jonathan?" she asked loudly when she realized who was missing.

"He started feeling worse, so he left," Rose explained, looking down at the slip of paper Jonathan had given her. She walked to where her sister stood and handed her the paper. "He gave me this for the reception and asked if his brother could read it."

"Who is his brother?" Ivy asked, glancing at the paper, then at her sister.

Rose hunched her shoulders. "I have no idea. I told him I'd give the paper to Nicholas."

Ivy sighed heavily, trying to keep her composure. She hated when things didn't go according to plan. "I'll give it to him now and explain what happened. I hope Jonathan feels better," she added before walking away.

"Me, too," Rose mumbled, thinking of the handsome best man who'd exited her life just as quickly as he'd entered it.

After the photo session, the wedding party headed to the reception. Rose beamed when she walked into the main ballroom at the Crystal Palace, an elegant banquet facility in Taylor, Indiana. With its winding staircases, multiple fireplaces, and antique décor, it made guests feel like they were celebrating in a real palace.

The ballroom, with its countless crystal chandeliers, a marble dance floor, and high ceilings, was gracefully decorated in ivory and gold. Since Rose was part of the wedding, she'd made arrangements to go to the facility earlier to decorate. Her goal had been to bring Destiny's childhood vision of the perfect wedding to life.

Destiny had chosen raw silk, tangerine tablecloths, so Rose had designed tabletop centerpieces of deep burgundy hydrangeas, Black Magic roses, orange Leonidas roses, and calla lilies. She had also placed beautiful gold lamps on each side of the centerpieces to complete the look. Since she'd left to get ready for the wedding, the waitstaff had placed gold-trimmed china and flatware on the tables, along with beautiful antique gold frames, which housed the table numbers printed in calligraphy. Rose was proud of the outcome of her hard work, and she knew she'd accomplished her goal when she saw tears brimming in Destiny's eyes as she looked around the ballroom.

Soon, the wedding party was announced, and after the bride

and groom received their guests, everyone was prepared to eat dinner. Pastor Bobby Grayson gave the invocation, thanking God for the couple as well as the food.

Rose picked up a dainty cellophane bag next to her place setting. Chocolate leaves wrapped in gold, orange, and copper foil had been placed in the small bag. It was tied with a sheer, rust-colored ribbon. The favors had taken Lili forever to complete, but the hard work had been well worth it, Rose thought.

"Rose!"

She looked up to see Ivy, who was headed in her direction, with a panicked look on her face.

"What's wrong?" Rose asked her sister, rising from her seat. It looked serious.

"Nicholas just told me Jonathan's brother, Marc, is going to take his place," Ivy spat out, waving her hands.

Rose frowned in confusion and grabbed her sister's hands, holding them to keep them still. "What's wrong with that?" she asked calmly.

Ivy pulled a hand out of her sister's grip and took several deep breaths to calm herself. "He's going to take Jonathan's place!"

Rose crinkled her nose, puzzled. Her sister tended to be a little dramatic sometimes. It was an odd trait for a wedding planner. "Vee, you're confusing me. Why is this making you so uneasy? Why? Is he better looking than Jonathan?" she asked sarcastically. Even sick, Jonathan would be a hard act to follow.

Ivy's panicked look was replaced by the serious one she wore all the time. "You're going to have to dance with him," she stated.

"So, and…"

Ivy huffed, slowly shaking her head at her sister's inability to comprehend the dilemma. "How do you think it's going to look with all the other men in their tuxedos and this guy in a suit, *if* he's wearing one?"

Rose rolled her eyes and shook her head. "Have you even met the man?"

"No, not yet. Nicholas went to get him," Ivy said, tapping her foot on the floor as she canvassed the room. She checked her watch, then looked around some more until she spotted Nicholas. "I guess we're both about to meet him now." She pointed to Nicholas, who was walking toward them with a very tall, dark-skinned man.

Rose leaned closer to Ivy. "You should feel better now, Vee. The man has on a suit, *and* it's black," she chuckled. She didn't want to laugh and make her sister angry, but she just couldn't help it. Ivy could be so melodramatic sometimes.

As the men approached, Rose noticed the small diamond winking at her from Jonathan's brother's left ear and smiled brightly. She didn't want to stare, but this man was even finer than his brother. Of course, she thought, Jonathan was a great specimen, but his brother... Rose wondered if there were more Damon brothers she didn't know about.

"Umph, umph, umph," Rose said under her breath as she watched the dark Adonis step toward her. He was taller than Jonathan, and his hard, muscular body filled his black, double-breasted suit oh so deliciously. The man had shoulders a woman could hold on to forever. His black hair, which he wore in a tiny afro, was lined and trimmed to perfection. Rose had to make sure she kept herself together. Immediately, she smoothed the wrinkles from her dress and sucked in her tummy even farther.

"Ivy and Rose, this is my cousin Marc Damon," Nicholas began. "Marc, meet Ivy and Rose Hart."

Marc extended his hand to Rose, assessing her striking, round, dark brown face. Her seductive light brown eyes spoke volumes to him. "Let me guess, you must be Rose," he said, lifting her extended hand to his lips. "A rose of beauty is a joy forever."

Marc lowered her hand but kept it in his grasp. The softness of her hand made him imagine how soft the rest of her voluptuous body would feel against him. "It's always a pleasure to meet a beautiful woman."

Rose felt her face redden when she looked into his black eyes, which sparkled like polished onyx. Her eyes dropped to the neat, thin mustache above his full lips. A man had never affected her like this before.

"Yes, I'm Rose. It was nice of you to step in for your brother," she said politely.

"I'll make sure I thank him for this opportunity." Marc continued to admire Rose's beauty. Her strapless gown accented her ample bosom and wide, curvaceous hips. Her skin was smooth and looked velvety soft. He wondered when, rather than *if*, he would ever get the chance to touch it. For now, he'd have to settle for a handshake.

Ivy cleared her throat, and Marc's head turned in her direction. He reluctantly released Rose's hand and offered his to Ivy.

"It seems all I've been doing this evening is meeting beautiful women," he said, flashing a devastating smile and exposing perfectly straight, white teeth.

Rose couldn't help but notice the glint in his eyes as he spoke. She glanced at her sister to see her reaction to him. Ivy had given him a half-smile as she accepted his handshake.

"Nice to meet you, Marc," she said, quickly pulling her hand back. "I'd like to go over your responsibilities, so we can get started."

I knew it, Rose thought to herself. Ivy had to find Marc attractive. She was always an ice queen when it came to handsome men.

Marc's attention went back to Rose. She was unbelievably gorgeous, and he found it difficult to take his eyes off of her for even a moment. He was about to strike up a conversation with her when Ivy cleared her throat again.

"Why don't we get started with our toasts?" she suggested, heading to the podium before he could give an answer.

Stepping back, Marc extended his hand. "Ladies first," he said to Rose. As she led the way to the platform, he watched the way the fabric of her gown outlined her backside.

Rose's heart rate accelerated at the thought of Marc following her, watching her every move. She knew she looked good in her dress, so she wasn't worried that he wouldn't like what he saw; it was something else that made her uneasy. She just couldn't put her finger on what it was though. Maybe it was the way Marc's presence seemed to command her attention, or the way the huskiness in his voice or the smoky look in his eyes made her want to swoon. If she was honest with herself, she'd admit it was the entire package that unnerved her. The man was fine, plain and simple.

Once they were at the podium, Ivy handed them both a glass of champagne and signaled for Rose to begin her speech.

"Good evening, everyone. I would like you to join me in a toast to the bride and groom." Rose glanced at the bridal table, and her eyes immediately began to fill with tears. "Dez, we always talked about finding our own Prince Charming. We both knew he wouldn't look anything like the one in the fairy tale, but we wanted one. I'm so glad you found him in Nicholas. May your love for each other deepen and grow in the years to come. I wish you both all the happiness your hands and hearts can hold." She lifted her glass to the audience. "To Destiny and Nicholas, here, here."

As Rose took a sip of the golden liquid, she glanced at Marc, and their eyes met and held. He moved closer to her, placing his hand on the small of her back, and she shuddered. Nervous excitement swirled in the pit of her stomach.

Marc leaned forward to speak into the microphone, with his eyes fixed on Rose. "Wow, what can I say after such a beautiful toast? And from the most gorgeous woman in the room…besides the bride," he added quickly.

The crowd laughed at his flirtations, and he smiled at Rose, waiting for her response.

She turned slightly and playfully pinched his cheek. "He's such a sweet talker," Rose said into the microphone, giving him a teasing grin. What was it about this man that had her feeling like a schoolgirl with a crush on her teacher instead of a mature, thirty-year-old woman?

The guests erupted in laughter again.

Marc winked at her, then asked her to hold his champagne glass while he pulled the slip of paper with his brother's toast written on it from his pocket. When Rose handed his glass back to him and their fingers met, an electric spark ran up his arm. Marc stared at her a moment in stunned silence before he brought his attention back to his task.

"I'm honored to stand in for my brother, Jonathan, who couldn't be here this evening," he told the crowd. He looked over at the bride and groom and continued. "Nick, he wanted to make sure you and Dez knew exactly how he felt."

Marc glanced quickly at the paper and began to read his brother's words. "Nick, I knew from day one you'd marry Destiny. When you told me you couldn't live without her, it confirmed exactly what I'd thought. You were mesmerized by her beauty, outside and in. I'm thankful to have been a part of that special moment in your life. Keep loving her as you do today, and you'll be a happy man for the rest of your life."

Marc smiled as his eyes went to the bride. "Dez, you're the best thing that ever happened to my rockhead cousin. I'm so glad you put him out of his misery by agreeing to be his wife."

Everyone chuckled at Jonathan's words. Marc glanced at Rose, who had tears in her eyes, and he raised his glass. "The only thing left to say is congratulations. Here, here."

When the toasts were completed, Marc escorted Rose back to her seat next to Destiny at the bridal table. After he pulled out her chair and saw that she was situated comfortably, Nicholas called out to him.

"Why don't you sit with us?" he asked as he pulled out the chair next to him.

"Sure," Marc agreed, thankful for an excuse to remain close to Rose, even if he was two seats away. He embraced his cousin before taking the offered chair.

Rose watched the exchange, and the thought of Marc caused a sparkle of excitement to return. She had never been so drawn to a man so quickly. The feelings he was stirring in her were ones she thought had been gone forever.

Destiny leaned over to Rose, with her hand covering one side of her mouth. "If I didn't know any better, I would have thought you and Marc were a couple," she whispered.

Rose glanced in Marc's direction, then waved her hand at her cousin. "We were just having fun."

Destiny leaned closer. "He's the cousin I told you about a couple of weeks ago."

Rose's brows lifted in revelation. "He's the smooth-talking brotha from Boston?" she asked softly.

"The one and only," Destiny replied, smiling.

For some reason Rose felt giddy. She picked up her champagne glass and took a sip, hoping to calm her nerves. Finally, she looked at Marc again and noticed his eyes were focused on her as well, but they didn't divulge his thoughts.

Quickly, she broke the magnetic trance. "Ooo, and he's Jonathan's brother. Girl, please." She waved again at Destiny just as the server placed her entrée in front of her.

As Rose began to eat, she felt as if she was being watched. She didn't have to look in Marc's direction to know he was the observer.

A few minutes later, Nicholas assisted his bride from her chair, and they walked hand in hand over to the cake. As soon as Destiny's chair was vacant, Marc filled it.

"Are you having a good time?" he asked Rose.

"Yes, I am. How 'bout you?" Rose replied casually, hoping she appeared nonchalant even though she wasn't.

"The evening is definitely looking up. I used to think weddings were a waste of time."

"Used to think? Does that mean you've changed your mind?" she asked, trying to ignore the way his slacks strained against his muscular thigh.

"Nicholas seems happy."

"Seems? They really love each other. I'm so happy for them." There was a slight pause before Rose spoke again. "Have you checked on Jonathan since you've been here?" she asked, taking a small bite of roast beef.

Marc moved his chair closer to her. "Yes, I spoke to him on my way over. He was just pulling into the apartment complex." He smiled as he took in her feminine scent. It was a mixture of vanilla and jasmine.

His deep voice sounded so seductive. Rose slowly looked

at him, giving him a dimpled grin. "I hope he feels better after he's gotten some rest."

Marc lifted Rose's left hand and stroked it as she turned toward him. Instinctively, he observed the roundness of her heavy bosom. "It's unfortunate for him that he's not feeling well, but I wouldn't have had the pleasure of your company this evening if he was better."

Rose gave him a sidelong glance. She thought he was laying on the charm pretty thick and gently pulled her hand from his. "You shouldn't glory in your brother's illness. I'm sure he wouldn't feel that way if you were the one who was sick."

Marc felt like he'd been struck in the face. "Oh, don't get me wrong. I'd never wish my brother any harm. I love him. I was just stating a fact."

The sound of Brian McKnight's "Love of My Life" caught Rose's attention. She looked toward the dance floor as Nicholas drew Destiny into his arms for their first dance. Rose was so lost in watching the newlyweds that she didn't see Marc stand and offer his hand. He lightly touched her bare shoulder to get her attention, and she suppressed a shiver.

Rose looked up into his dark eyes and then shifted to his lips.

"They want the rest of the party to join the happy couple," he said, quoting the announcement Ivy had just made. He smiled again, and the diamond in his ear twinkled.

This man is going to drive me crazy, Rose thought. She pushed her chair back and took his hand. Marc escorted her to the dance floor and pulled her into a sensual embrace, lightly rubbing his lips against her ear as they danced.

Desire pulsed through Rose's body. Now she knew how Whitney Houston felt in the movie *Waiting to Exhale.* Slowly, she released a deep breath and relaxed in Marc's arms.

"You know you almost took my breath away," he said against her ear. His voice was husky, and the seductive tone had returned.

Rose felt a shiver again. Was she getting sick, too? Or was it the heat from the man holding her? She was acutely aware of how well she fit in the circle of Marc's arms. He held her with such delicate caution. She felt cherished, secure, and most of all, desirable.

Rose looked into Marc's eyes when he pulled back from her and thought, *I want to have this man's babies.* Immediately, she wondered where the thought had come from. Rose had never been a desperate woman, and she'd sworn off men ever since the last guy she gave her heart to took it and shattered it. Once the pain had faded, she couldn't bear to give her heart to another man ever again. She had to try to pull herself together—but not until the song ended.

Rose rested her head against Marc's shoulder as they continued to sway to the music. When the song was over, she released another sigh and attempted to take a small step backward, but realized he hadn't let her go just yet.

"Wait," Marc said, holding her for another moment before he stepped back so he could hold her at arm's length.

Rose slowly lifted her head. "Yes?"

"Thank you for the dance."

Rose chuckled. "Thank you," she said, attempting to step out of his embrace one more time. This time he released her. "We'd better get back to our seats." She turned and started to walk away from him only to feel his hand on her back as he followed her.

Confusion swarmed through Marc's mind. Rose Hart disturbed his calm. He'd just met her a little over an hour ago, and she already had him in knots. He was usually attracted to model-thin women, but this beautiful brown honey with her lush curves had changed all that in a matter of minutes. She was an exquisite female, but it wasn't the mere fact that she was beautiful. He'd known gorgeous women all his adult life and had even fallen in love with one, but there was something different about Rose....

He hadn't figured out what exactly, but now he had to decide whether he wanted to take a chance and find out.

Louvenia Hart had been mingling with some of the guests when she noticed the man dancing with her daughter.

The manner in which the young fellow held Rose, the second oldest of her four daughters, and her daughter's response piqued Louvenia's curiosity as to his identity.

Since she was the bride's aunt, she knew most of the other guests; but not him. She assumed he was a guest of the groom. She continued to watch them, and after the song was over, the handsome stranger didn't let her daughter go.

Louvenia hurried back to her table, where her daughter Violet was sitting. "Sweetie, who was that guy dancing with Rosie a minute ago?"

Violet hunched her shoulders. "I don't know." She cut another bite of her cake.

"Hmm," Louvenia said, placing her forefinger to her lips.

Lili, the youngest of the four sisters, came over to the table. "Did you see that fine man dancing with Rosie?"

Both Louvenia and Violet nodded.

"Who is he?" Lili asked.

Again Violet lifted her shoulders quickly. "Mama just asked me the same question."

"So, we have a mystery man in our midst," Lili commented, scanning the room for her oldest sister. "I bet Vee knows who he is." She walked away from the table, with her mother and sister following closely behind.

"Vee, who was that guy dancing with Rosie?" Lili asked immediately when she found her sister Ivy.

"He's Jonathan's brother," Ivy commented casually.

"Jonathan?" Violet said.

Ivy turned to her. "Yes, he got sick and had to leave. Nicholas asked his brother to step in for him."

"What's his name?" Louvenia asked.

Ivy exhaled an agitated breath. "Marc."

"Marc, huh?" Louvenia took a step back, trying to get a better look at him at the bridal table. "I don't remember Elizabeth mentioning Jonathan having a brother." She continued to stare at Marc, then glanced at Rose. A big smile appeared on her face.

Violet noticed the change in their mother's expression. She grabbed Lili's arm so she could see it, too.

"Mama, Auntie Liz doesn't know everything about Nicholas's family," Violet said, hoping her mother wasn't about to talk about her favorite subject: marriage.

Louvenia threw her hands up. "I keep coming to these things, but I'm never the mother of the bride," she commented, ignoring her daughter's words.

All three of her daughters rolled their eyes.

Lili moved closer to her. "Mama, you promised you wouldn't mention any of our names and marriage in the same sentence for one whole year. Remember?"

Violet stepped closer to them. "She's right. It was supposed to be your New Year's resolution. You were doing good, too, until Destiny announced she was getting married. We let you slide that time, hoping it wouldn't continue. Now, you're at it again."

Louvenia gave them an unpleasant stare.

Lili hugged her sister. "Violet, you better go get a man, girl, and get hitched, so your mama can shut up about the marriage thing," Lili said sarcastically.

"Oh, she's *my* mama now. Look, I've been there and done that, baby girl. I don't plan on doing it again," Violet said adamantly.

Louvenia looked at Violet. "Yeah, you did it, but you couldn't keep him, so you're in the same boat as the rest of them."

Violet balled her fist, then released it, trying to calm herself down. "I'm not going to discuss that. It's your turn, anyway, Lili." She chuckled, trying to hide her hurt feelings from her mother's comment.

Lili pointed to herself. "Me. I don't *think* so." She walked over to Ivy, who had moved farther away from them. Louvenia and Violet followed.

"Maybe Vee will be the lucky one and make Mama proud." Lili smiled, showing all her teeth.

Ivy held her hand up in front of her baby sister's face. "The closest I'm getting to a wedding gown is to help one of our clients into one."

"That's my job, Vee," Violet said, laughing.

"Precisely my point." Ivy sighed. "Look, I think you guys are making something out of nothing. The man only danced with her."

"That's not what I saw," Lili said.

"I've got work to do," Ivy said, walking away.

Lili leaned over and whispered to Violet. "I don't care what the Ice Queen says; I think Rosie is going to be the one to finally make Mama the mother of the bride."

Violet shook her head in agreement, and they both watched Louvenia watch Rose.

Chapter 2

"All single females to the dance floor," the DJ announced.

"Why don't you girls go on out there?" Louvenia suggested. "Maybe you'll catch the bouquet," she said, with a tinge of hopefulness in her voice.

Violet and Lili walked in the other direction as if their mother hadn't said a word.

"Let's go," Destiny said, pulling Rose from her chair.

Rose grabbed the small collection of orange-colored hydrangeas she'd created for the throw away. "Don't forget your bouquet," she said, handing it to her cousin.

As the rock group Queen's popular song "Another One Bites the Dust" boomed through the air, Destiny took her place in front of the eager bunch of women. She began to swing the flowers over her head to the beat of the music as if she was about to throw them on the DJ's count.

"One, two," the DJ drawled out. "Three," he said quickly.

Destiny made one final forward motion but didn't release the flowers. You could hear the moans of disappointment from the women who were anxiously anticipating catching the bouquet and maybe becoming the next one to walk the white carpet to wedding bliss.

"Let's try this again," the DJ said. "On my count, one, two, three," he said quickly.

This time Destiny turned and walked toward the back, where Rose stood, and handed her the bouquet.

Some of the women were not happy. As they left the floor, both Rose and Destiny laughed. They came together to have their picture taken for Destiny's photo album, standing cheek to cheek, smiling wide for the camera. After her father took the photo, Rose turned to her cousin.

"Why did you do that?"

Destiny's bright smile returned. She hugged Rose to her. "I just want you to be as happy as I am."

Tears sprung in Rose's eyes as she gently pulled away. "Don't worry about me. This day belongs to you. Enjoy *this* moment."

Rose was about to say something else when she saw Ivy coming toward them. She gripped her cousin's hand and cleared her throat to alert her.

"What kind of mess was that?" Ivy said through clenched teeth.

"Mess? What are you talking about, Vee?" Destiny asked innocently.

"You guys want to ruin this evening and my reputation." Ivy huffed.

"Lighten up, Vee," Rose said before walking back toward her table, with Destiny following her.

"We're not done yet, Destiny," Ivy called out. "Nicholas hasn't taken off the garter."

Destiny grabbed Rose's arm to stop her. Scrunching up her

nose, she looked at Ivy and said, "Okay." She straightened her nose once she saw the seriousness on Ivy's face. She waited for someone to bring a chair.

The music had changed to the funky sound of Parliament-Funkadelic's "Atomic Dog." Ivy placed a chair in the center of the dance floor as the DJ called for all single males.

Marc joined the other single men surrounding Destiny's chair so they could watch Nicholas take off her garter.

Destiny sat with her legs crossed and Ivy assisted her in adjusting her dress so that the garter could be seen.

Rose looked for Nicholas. She spotted him standing at the room entrance, dancing provocatively. Rose smiled as he came closer and dropped to his knees next to Destiny. He rubbed her legs up and down.

Rose looked around the room and noticed Ivy rolling her eyes, then spotted her Uncle Cliff sitting with his mouth open. She chuckled when her Aunt Marlene pushed it closed. She turned her attention back to Nicholas and Destiny.

Now Nicholas pulled at the garter with his teeth. Rose noticed how intently all the other men were watching, but Marc's eyes were on her. She smiled, and he gave her one in return.

Finally, Nicholas caught hold of the garter, pulling it down over Destiny's kneecap. He started to use his hands, but the guys yelled that he had to do it with his teeth.

Moments later, Nicholas jumped to his feet in triumph, clenching the white silk garter with a lacy overlay and blue ribbon between his teeth, shaking it back and forth.

He twirled it in the air before bending to place a wet kiss on Destiny's lips.

She got up from the chair, and it was removed. The men lined up so they could catch the garter.

On the DJ's count, Nicholas prepared to throw the lacy

item. At three, he threw it as far as he could, and the small scrap of material landed right in Marc's hands.

The other men gave Marc a congratulatory pat on the back. He smiled and looked across the room at Rose.

Rose watched Destiny whisper something to Ivy.

Ivy came over to Rose's table. "Destiny wants Marc to put the garter on your leg," Ivy said.

"Okay," Rose said, moving over to the middle of the dance floor. Sitting in the chair they placed there for her, she waited.

Rose was already nervous, and then the DJ began to play Marvin Gaye's "I Want You," making her stomach rumble.

She crossed her legs and looked up to find Marc watching her every move.

His eyes never left her. He bowed on one knee and gently took her left foot and its high-heeled sandal into his hands. The gesture was simple, but Rose felt it was the most erotic thing that had happened to her in all her years. Marc held her foot like it was the most precious thing in the world to him.

As he continued to move up her leg with the garter, Rose felt like he was taking forever to get it to where it was supposed to be. The gradual movement of his hands on her stocking-covered skin was getting to be too much for her to handle.

She had to exhale without showing her nervousness. It wasn't an easy feat because it seemed that the eyes of everyone in the room were on them, and Marc's voice made the mood more electrifying.

With every inch, Marc took in the most beautiful set of legs he'd ever laid eyes on and certainly had ever touched. He definitely wanted to know the woman behind the beauty.

Once he moved the garter over her knee, he motioned her to pull her dress up farther.

Rose moved her dress up slightly at the same time that the

audience broke out in applause. It seemed the audience was having a good time this evening on her and Marc's account.

Marc glanced into her honey brown eyes and grasped her hand. He pulled himself up and assisted her as well. He placed a light kiss on her cheek.

"That was fun," Rose said as they made their way back to the table, with the audience still clapping.

"Fun and dangerous," Marc mumbled under his breath as he watched her hips move as she walked.

The DJ played the "Mississippi Slide." Everyone headed to the dance floor; the party had begun.

Rose got out of bed early Sunday morning since she couldn't sleep, anyway. She walked into her bathroom across the hall from the master bedroom and stood before the lighted mirror. Pushing her shoulder-length hair off her forehead, she stared deeply into the mirror. She tried to remove the feel of Marc's lips on her skin and his touch from her memory but soon realized they were only a thought away.

She'd had so much fun last night. Her family knew how to have a good time, and party they did. They danced until well after midnight. By the time she got to bed, her mind was still jumbled with thoughts of Marc.

Rose couldn't help but think about Jonathan. She felt sorry for him and wondered how he was feeling. She hoped he was better. The more she thought about Jonathan, the more Marc Damon's smooth chocolate face came to her mind.

As she began her cleansing regimen, the telephone rang. In her haste, she quickly splashed water on her face to rinse away any residue of the mild cleanser and searched the counter of the sink for the thirsty white towel she had stacked there. She patted her face dry as she walked into her bedroom, trying to grab the telephone before her voice mail kicked in.

"Hello."

"You know, Mama was watching you last night," the caller said.

"Lili?"

"Girl, you should have seen her eyes, Rosie, while you were dancing with that guy."

"Yeah, she started singing that "why aren't you girls married" song. We couldn't shut her up and had to walk away," another voice said.

"Violet?" Rose said, smiling.

"I told Lili not to bother you," Violet said.

"All Mama talked about is never being the mother of the bride." Lili mimicked their mother, ignoring Violet's comment.

"There is nothing between me and Marc Damon," Rose insisted.

"We know. You'd have to use a hammer and a chisel to get between you," Lili said.

"Don't start, Lili," Violet warned.

"Thank you," Rose said in appreciation.

"The way that man was holding you on that dance floor," Lili continued, ignoring her sister's warning.

Rose shook her head. "We were just having a good time. Anyway, Dez said he's like that with all the ladies."

"Maybe it is true what they say."

Rose sighed. "And what's that, Lili?"

"You know. When you catch the bouquet, you're next in line to get married."

"Wrong," Rose said quickly. "I didn't catch the bouquet in the first place; Destiny gave it to me." Rose sighed once again. "Look, I'll see you two ladies at Mama's later."

"Don't get an attitude because you're going to be Mrs. Marc Damon," Lili chimed in.

"Get off my phone, both of you," Rose said adamantly, then laughed.

"Bye," they all said at the same time.

Rose shook her head as she hung up the phone, only to have it ring again. She quickly picked it up.

"Leave me alone," she yelled into the receiver.

"What is your problem?"

"Vee?"

"Yes."

"If you're calling about Marc, there is nothing going on between us." Rose spoke so quickly, there was a long pause until Ivy spoke again.

"I don't have any idea what you're talking about. You just met the man last night. The reason I called you was to find out if you've gotten the samples together for Erika Spencer. She's scheduled to come in next Tuesday."

"Oh." Rose felt bad that she jumped to the wrong conclusion. "Yes, we're all set." There was another pause before she continued. "Vee, why are you working on Sunday morning?"

"I have a business to run. I have to do things when I can. For a minute yesterday I thought we were going to have a catastrophe on our hands."

"But it all turned out well."

"Yes."

"Vee, I think you work too much. Sometimes, you should put down your notepad and relax."

"Now, you sound like Mama," Ivy reminded her.

"Oops, my bad," Rose said, laughing. "Will I see you over there later?"

"I'll be there," Ivy said casually.

"See you then."

"Bye."

Rose had never figured out why her oldest sister acted the way she did when it came to her own personal life. Ivy was such a good wedding consultant and could come up with the most romantic ideas for other people, but she never wanted to discuss romance for herself. She wondered if romance ever crossed Ivy's mind.

Marc stood in the kitchen, preparing breakfast. On the way home last night, he kept thinking about Rose Hart. There was a sweetness about her and a seductive huskiness in her voice that made him want to continue to be in her presence. He still couldn't figure out how she kept his head turning.

It was unusual for Jonathan to be ill, so when Marc got home after the wedding reception, he checked in on him and found him fast asleep.

To be on the safe side, this morning he prepared oatmeal and unbuttered toast for Jonathan, and a gourmet omelet for himself.

"Morning."

Marc looked toward the door as he slid the omelet onto his plate. "You look like death warmed over."

"Ha, ha," Jonathan said, walking into the kitchen, dropping in the first chair he could get to. "Man, I don't know what happened to me yesterday," he said, running a hand over his head. "By the time I got home, I felt like I had been hit by a Mack truck." He placed one of his elbows on top of the table and rested his head against his fist.

"You look like it, too," Marc commented as he placed the nonstick pan in the sink.

"Funny." Jonathan sat up and scooted his chair underneath

the table. "I haven't slept that soundly in ages, and after I take a shower, I'll feel like a new man." He slid the plate with the omelet on it toward him.

Marc pulled it back. "This is *not* for you, bruh. I don't think it's a good idea to eat an omelet so soon after being as sick as you described."

Jonathan tried to take the omelet back from him. "I told you I feel fine. Besides, I'm starving. I want to get something in my stomach before I go out for the day."

"Out? Out where?" Marc stared at his brother as if he'd gone crazy. "You don't even know what made you sick in the first place. What if it comes back?"

"Marc, I'm a grown man. I know when I feel good and when I don't."

"You also do things on the fly without thinking, but yeah, I agree you are grown," Marc said, moving the plate to the counter.

Jonathan's facial expression was frozen.

Marc took a small plate and a bowl from the cabinet. "I'm not completely heartless, though. I made a hearty breakfast for you." He placed a bowl of hot oatmeal and the dry toast in front of his brother.

Jonathan looked at the food, then up at Marc. "You call this hearty? You make yourself a breakfast fit for a king and feed me porridge."

Marc laughed. "I'm trying to look out for you."

"You're trying to starve me to death. Tell you what," Jonathan said, rising from his seat, "Why don't you split the omelet with me, and I'll eat the oatmeal, too."

Marc stood silently at first, staring at his younger brother.

Jonathan gave him a pleading look. "Come on, man, you know I can't cook like you, or else I would make one myself."

Marc picked up a knife from the counter and cut the omelet in half. "I don't want to hear anything from you about being sick."

"Promise." Jonathan took a small plate from the cabinet and handed it to Marc. "How was the reception?"

"Very interesting, to say the least." Marc placed half the omelet on the small plate.

Jonathan picked up his portion. "That's not telling me anything," he said, going back to his seat.

Marc took a chair across from him. "How well do you know Rose Hart?" he asked, shaking pepper over his omelet.

"She's Destiny's cousin. Why?" Jonathan looked curiously at his brother.

Marc stared back at him. "Don't look at me that way."

"Rose isn't your type." Jonathan cut a small piece of his omelet and lifted it with his fork.

"My type?"

"Ya know, she doesn't look like she has an eating disorder." Jonathan chuckled before placing the fork into his mouth.

Marc ignored Jonathan's remark. "She's a very intriguing woman. She was really concerned about you."

Jonathan chewed his food slowly before responding. "From what I can tell, she's beautiful, sweet, caring."

"I think she's beautiful, too, but that doesn't mean anything. I know a lot of gorgeous women, but when you get to know their personality, they're not so pretty. Rose didn't act like she knew she was pretty, though."

"I told you she wasn't your type," Jonathan said, taking a spoonful of his oatmeal.

Again, Marc didn't reply to his brother's comment. He thought about Rose's carefree attitude as she danced with a man who he later found out was her cousin.

Jonathan continued to stare at Marc. "I hope you aren't thinking about pursuing her."

Marc looked up. "What's wrong with that?"

Jonathan put his fork down. "Come on M. Let's be real. You haven't had a serious relationship since Andrea Walker, and we both know what happened after that fiasco."

"That was different."

"Different how? After Andrea's betrayal, you went through women like running water from a faucet."

Marc pushed his chair away from the table and snatched his plate off of it. "Andrea Walker was a selfish, conceited, spoiled, conniving, and insensitive wannabe." He threw the dish in the sink with a clatter.

Jonathan watched Marc. "Do you see all beautiful women that way now?"

Marc turned quickly. "I didn't say I wanted to marry Rose. I just want to get to know her better."

"I don't think she's the casual type, and you don't want a real relationship." Jonathan sensed his brother's frustration. He got up and lifted his dishes, taking them over to the sink. "Anyway, I've told you all I can about her," Jonathan said.

Marc turned and looked at Jonathan. "I think it's time for me to find my own place."

Jonathan stared at his brother. "I just bet you do."

"I want to get to know Rose. I can't help it if the woman is intriguing."

"You've been back in Taylor all of three months, and you're already chasing skirts." Jonathan shook his head as he watched his brother walk out of the kitchen without another word.

After the church service, Rose headed to her parents' home. As in many other families, sharing Sunday dinner had become a tradition for the Harts. It was a time they all set aside to be together to share a meal.

Rose was the last to arrive when she pulled her candy apple red Nissan Murano into the circular drive of her parents' white brick, quad-level home.

Rose got out of the car and prayed she could get through dinner without Marc becoming the main topic of conversation. But knowing Louvenia Hart, she wouldn't miss an opportunity to talk about any one of her daughters getting married.

Rose made her way up to the front door, and before she could grab the fancy gold handle, her sister Lili opened the door.

"I saw you pull up." She moved back so Rose could enter.

Rose closed the heavy door behind her and followed Lili into the kitchen.

Her mother and Violet were preparing to put the food on the table.

"I'm here," Rose said as she entered the kitchen.

"Rosie, would you please make the salad," Louvenia said as she pulled her homemade biscuits from the oven.

"It really smells good in here, Mama," Rose commented as she went about her task.

Louvenia beamed. "We're having roast pork with mushroom gravy, mashed potatoes, and string beans."

Lili pulled a large container from the refrigerator. "I'm trying a new dessert recipe. Make sure you tell me what you think."

Rose stopped to take a look at her sister's newest creation. "It looks scrumptious. What kind of cake is it?"

"It's chocolate strawberry mousse."

Louvenia walked past them with the platter containing the main dish. "Rosie, I don't want you eating too much of that. You should be watching your figure."

Rose turned around quickly only to see her mother's retreating back. She knew then that it would be a long dinner. Shaking her head, she got back to making the salad.

"Where is Vee?" Rose asked.

"She's in the family room with Daddy, talking about Erika Spencer's wedding photo package," Violet answered.

"That girl works like there's no tomorrow," Rose commented.

Lili leaned over to Rose. "You know if you say that to her face, she'll probably scratch you with her paws." She lifted her hands, forming them to look like claws. "Rrrr," she said, laughing before picking up the dessert plate and carrying it into the dining room.

Rose laughed at her youngest sister, then glanced over at Violet, who was placing the biscuits on a tray, her reaction unreadable.

Rose opened the refrigerator.

Violet came over to her. "I made some of that honey mustard dressing you like so well," she said.

"Great. Where is it?" Rose said, moving the things around inside the refrigerator.

"I've already put it on the table," Violet said, moving closer to Rose as she shut the refrigerator door. "You and Lili shouldn't make fun of Vee. I don't think she can help herself. She doesn't have anything else except for the business."

"Vee is a beautiful and intelligent woman. She has no excuse not to have a man in her life," Rose said.

"What's your excuse then?" Violet asked as she walked out of the kitchen with the tray of biscuits in her hands. "Bring the French and Ranch. We're ready to eat," she said over her shoulder.

Rose gawked at her sister. Violet was two years younger than her, but of the four of them, she had had more serious relationships.

"I'm right behind you." Rose opened the refrigerator once again, pulled out the requested items and shut the door.

Everyone had already taken their seats when Rose entered the dining room. She sat down beside Lili and across from her mother.

Andrew Hart said the prayer, and they began with the salad.

"Wasn't Destiny gorgeous yesterday?" Lili commented.

"Oh yes, she was stunning," Violet said as she poured dressing on her salad.

"I was soo happy for her," Rose commented as she waited for Violet to hand her the salad dressing. "I don't think I've ever seen her look so radiant." She poured some salad dressing on her greens.

"Why don't you have salad with your dressing, Rosie?" Louvenia said.

Here we go, Rose thought to herself, stabbing her salad with her fork. Her mother always commented on her eating habits. Even though Rose wasn't a big eater, since she was much larger than her sisters, Louvenia always watched what Rose ate.

"Mama, don't," Rose admonished.

"Don't what?" Louvenia asked. "You do want to keep that young man's attention."

All of her daughters rolled their eyes.

Louvenia sat her glass down on the table. "I don't care if any of you get an attitude. I just don't understand it. All of my friends' children are married. Even the mayor's daughter is getting hitched. Here I am the mother of four beautiful young women. I don't see why something you love so much can't be a part of your personal life. Your business is all about love, marriage, and happily ever after, yet none of you want to be married."

Ivy dropped her fork and leaned forward so her mother could see her. "Mama, not being married is our choice."

"Yeah," Rose interrupted. "Most of your friends' children have been married more than once. I wouldn't want my child to keep getting married if he or she wasn't happy."

"I'm not saying marry the first guy you lay your eyes on. Each one of you is very special, and I just think there is someone out there that would appreciate that." She reached across the table to grab her husband's hand. "I want all of you to be happy like me and your father," Louvenia continued, looking at her husband, Andrew, who still hadn't said anything.

Louvenia sighed, then focused her full attention on Rose. "I watched you last night with that handsome young man, swaying back and forth on the dance floor."

"And?" Rose said, waving her hand so her mother would hurry up and get to the point.

"I asked your Aunt Liz to tell me what she knew about him."

All the young women sat up straight in their chairs.

Rose's eyes grew larger. "Mama, please tell me you didn't discuss Marc with Aunt Liz." Her voice filled with panic. "She's the Walter Cronkite of our family. She'll spread untruths," Rose said in disappointment.

"Don't say things like that," Louvenia said as she stuck a forkful of salad into her mouth.

"Mama, you know Rosie's right. All Aunt Liz does is gossip," Violet said.

"Hold up a minute, Violet. Let's hear what Mama found out," Lili said.

Rose frowned. "Lili." She didn't want her sister encouraging her mother.

Her baby sister shrugged. "What? Aren't you the least bit interested?" Lili glanced at her other two sisters.

"Mama, you are a trip." Violet chuckled.

"I am no such thing." Louvenia leaned forward slightly. "He's been back in Taylor for a little over three months. He and his brother are renovating the old banquet facility on Sixty-first and Broadway."

"That used to be Queen's, right?" Lili asked.

Louvenia waved her hand anxiously. "Yes, now let me finish. I haven't gotten to the good part," Louvenia said, giving them all a big smile. "Anyway, he's single and has no kids."

"Why did he move back?" Violet asked.

"Well, Liz said it was because he and his brother were going into business together, but I say it's a sign."

Now everyone was rolling their eyes.

"A sign, Mama?" Rose spoke up.

"Yes, it's a sign that you two were destined to meet."

"Mama," Lili warned.

"What?"

Ivy sighed loudly. "Mama, which one of the mayor's daughters is getting married?" She didn't want to hear her mother's love theory any longer.

Rose knew Ivy had her own reasons for changing the subject, but she appreciated the reprieve.

Louvenia continued to talk. "Liz said that she was in the beauty shop yesterday morning, getting her hair done for the wedding, and Dianna highfalutin Hawkins came in. She overheard Dianna telling some other woman that her baby daughter was marrying some real estate developer from Chicago."

"You sure her parents didn't set it up?" Lili said.

"I don't know, but Liz said she heard Dianna say they were going to stop by the estate and check you girls out."

"Not without an appointment, she's not," Ivy insisted before picking up her glass, taking a sip of lemonade.

"Why not? I think it would be good for business to have serviced the mayor's family," Louvenia said, looking at Ivy, then at her other daughters.

"I've heard Dianna Hawkins is an obnoxious customer," Violet said.

"You've dealt with difficult clients before, Violet."

"This is true, but Marguerite Thomas, who owns the art gallery, told me she ordered an original painting for Dianna. Dianna took one look at it and changed her mind right on the spot, telling Marguerite that she'd ordered the wrong one."

"Maybe it was."

"Mama, I don't think we need that kind of a head-ache."

Ivy held up her hand. "Let's wait and see what happens. We'll just have to be on alert."

"You won't have any problems then, Vee. Your radar is always on," Lili giggled.

Ivy huffed and picked up her knife and fork to cut into her roast pork.

Rose tried to relax. If they could finish their meal without talking about Marc, she would be home free. He'd been on her mind all morning, including while Pastor Donaldson was bringing the message.

Chapter 3

Marc and Jonathan arrived at Magic Moments, the banquet facility they were renovating, to meet with Rob Mason, the site foreman, to get an update on his progress. It had already been three months, and they hoped that they were coming to the homestretch.

Marc had been skeptical about the business venture at first, when Jonathan called to tell him about it.

He had agreed to listen to his brother's proposal and actually liked what he heard. Jonathan had even sent him a hard copy for him to study. The idea of being part owner of a business really excited Marc. He'd worked in several well-known restaurants and at a banquet facility in Boston, but always under the management of someone else.

Once Jonathan told him he'd already secured financing, Marc was really impressed with his brother's foresight and determination. He knew Jonathan had the knowledge but hadn't tackled a business venture this large, so Marc wasn't so sure his brother could handle it.

As they walked through each of the four banquet rooms with Rob, Marc thoroughly investigated and commented, while Jonathan took notes.

Marc suddenly stopped at the opening to the massive kitchen. Wrinkles surfaced on his forehead. His dark eyes focused on the mess in front of him.

Dust, debris, dry wall, plaster buckets, tools, and other things were everywhere. He quickly turned around to face the foreman, with a scowl on his face.

Marc touched his forehead with his finger. "If I remember correctly, you told us the kitchen would be completed in the next three weeks." He walked farther into the spacious room, scanning the area. "It looks like you've just started demolition."

Rob looked between the two brothers. "Well, this part of the project is going to take longer than we expected," he said, with a nervous voice.

Marc's right eye began to twitch, a sign that Rob had become familiar with, and one that meant he was about to lose his temper. "We told you we wanted the kitchen completed first," Marc said rapidly.

Rob opened his mouth again to speak, but this time Marc cut him off.

"Can you realistically say you will have this kitchen completed in three weeks?" His brow arched.

Rob removed his baseball cap and scratched his short black hair. "That's the plan. I don't have an excuse as to why we haven't gotten further than we have, except to say I've been shorthanded the last couple of weeks," he said nervously.

Jonathan stepped forward. "We wanted to give you a chance. I hope you don't botch this job, because my brother and I will come after you," he said sternly.

Rob glanced at both men. He knew right away that Jonathan Damon was the more understanding of the two.

"No, Mr. Damon, if my workers have to work twenty-four-hour shifts, we'll get the job done right and on time as promised," Rob said with confidence, replacing his cap.

Marc shook his head. "Why do I feel like I just heard a television commercial?"

Rob's eyes widened. "I promise both of you; I'm a man of my word."

Marc glared at him. "So am I." He knew he was making the skinny man nervous, but he felt Rob shouldn't have taken on such a big project if he didn't have the resources to get the job done.

The ringing of Marc's cell phone caught his attention. He pulled it from his belt clip. "Damon."

"What's up?" the voice on the other end said.

Marc raised a finger to Jonathan and Rob as he walked away to take his call.

"So, you've finally decided to come back from Fantasy Island?"

"We actually got back last week," Nicholas said.

"Oh, now that you've tied the knot, I guess you can't hang out with a brotha anymore."

"I was taking care of my business. If you know what I'm saying." Nicholas laughed.

"I hear ya, bruh. What can I do you for?" Marc asked.

"Destiny wants to have a little get-together at our new place."

"I heard about the new house. Congrats."

"Thanks, man. I was calling because we wanted you to prepare the spread for our little affair."

"Say the word and I'm there. When is it?"

Nicholas paused before answering. "Friday night."

"Friday? Look, man, I'm good, if I do say so myself, but I'm not a miracle worker," he said as he heard Nicholas laughing on the other end.

"Do you think you could drop by and talk about it?" Nicholas asked.

Marc glanced at his watch. "Sure, I can spare an hour. Give me your address." He pulled out his checkbook register and a pen to write the information down. "I'll swing by in about forty-five minutes."

"Cool."

Marc ended the call and walked back into the kitchen, where he found Jonathan pointing at the floor.

Jonathan spotted Marc coming toward them. "I want to do a walk-through once a week until it's completed," Jonathan said.

Marc looked at the foreman, then at his brother. "I'll go along with it for the next two weeks, but if I don't see significant progress, we're going to get someone else to finish the job. We want to open this place before the Thanksgiving holiday."

"I agree," Jonathan said.

"Everything will be completed according to the specifications in the contract," Rob said, readjusting his cap.

Marc pulled Jonathan to the side. "Listen, can you handle everything from here?"

"You know you're scaring the hell out of Rob, man," Jonathan said.

"I'm not scaring him; I'm giving him a reality check. Owning your own business means taking responsibility for everything that goes on in your company," Marc said.

He pointed to Jonathan's chest. "You'd better get used to it now, little bruh, because very soon it could be our clients talking to us."

"I know," Jonathan said, shoving his right hand in his pocket. "Where are you going?" Jonathan glanced at his watch.

"Out to Nick's new place. He and Destiny want to have a get-together for the wedding party."

"I hope I'm invited." Jonathan smiled.

"I'm sure you are."

Marc walked back over to Rob. "The next time I come in this place, I want to see progress and not dust." He walked away, then turned around again. "Jonathan, call me on my cell if you need me," Marc said, then walked away.

Marc had no problem finding Nick's house. He pulled his black Lincoln LS into the driveway. He climbed out and walked to the front door. After punching the doorbell with his finger, he looked around the neighborhood. It was a new housing development, so there were only two houses next to Nick's house and one being built across the street. The landscaping was meticulous, and the houses were even more impressive.

Destiny greeted him. "That was fast," she said, opening the glass door.

"I was close by," Marc said.

"Come on in," Destiny said, holding the door open for him.

Marc walked into the foyer and could see the house looked empty.

Nicholas galloped down the staircase.

They embraced each other.

"Man, how are you going to have a party on Friday with no furniture in here?" Marc said.

Nicholas scanned the room.

"We haven't needed anything so far except a bed," he said, glancing sheepishly at Destiny. "And we really didn't use *it*."

Marc laughed as he watched Destiny's face redden.

Nicholas hugged her to his side and pressed his lips to her forehead before turning back to Marc. "No, seriously, we'll have the furniture before the end of the week."

"Well, show me the place," Marc said, looking up at the vaulted ceiling.

"Wait. Before you do that," Destiny began. "Bay, I wanted to go see Rosie at the shop, so can we talk about the menu, and then you two can visit?" Destiny said.

"How is Rose?" Marc wanted to know. The brown-skinned beauty crossed his consciousness several times a day since they'd met. As he stared at Destiny, waiting for her answer, he got the feeling she mentioned Rose on purpose.

"I haven't spoken to her since the reception. I thought I'd go see her today," she said, looking at him curiously.

"Let's go in the kitchen. We do have a table and some chairs in there." Destiny led them into the kitchen.

For the next thirty minutes, they discussed the plans for the small gathering for Friday evening. Marc shared his ideas for the meal and suggested they serve hors d'oeuvres while everyone watched the wedding video. The meal would be served afterwards in the dining room.

Destiny and Nicholas agreed with all his ideas and asked him to oversee everything. Now, all Marc had to do was hire servers for the evening. An old gentleman friend of their family came to mind.

Destiny got up and walked over to Marc. "Thanks for your help," she said, placing a kiss on his cheek. "I'll make sure I tell Rosie you said hello."

Marc gave her a lopsided grin when he noticed the smirk

on Destiny's sweet face. "Tell her I look forward to seeing her on Friday evening."

Destiny giggled. She walked over to her husband, who had stood, and gave him an openmouthed kiss.

Nicholas's hands began to roam over her large behind. Destiny leaned into him and gently pushed his hands down to his sides. "Bay, not in front of company," she whispered, holding his hands in her grip.

"Hmmm," Nicholas moaned before looking over at Marc. He released her and watched as she turned and walked from the room.

Marc's eyes filled with longing as he witnessed the couple's passionate exchange. He hadn't had that feeling in years.

Once Destiny was out of sight, Nicholas turned to Marc, biting his fist.

Marc chuckled. "Looks like marriage agrees with you."

"Man, I love my big bay," Nicholas responded affectionately as he glanced at the space his wife had just left.

"I hear ya, man," Marc replied. His thoughts went to Rose.

Nicholas walked to the threshold of the door. "Let's take that tour now, because I think I'm going to be busy a little later."

Marc shook his head as he got up from his chair and followed Nicholas out of the room. From the look in Nicholas's eyes, it was evident he really loved his wife.

"I should be so lucky," he said to himself.

Rose had just finished the samples she'd been working on when she heard the chime. Before she could get out of her seat, Destiny walked into her work area.

"What's up?" Destiny said, mimicking the comedian Martin Lawrence.

Rose got up and quickly rounded her worktable to embrace her favorite cousin. "When did you guys get back?" she asked, stepping away to study Destiny's face.

"Girl, we've been back," Destiny replied as she pulled away.

"I bet Hawaii was beautiful," Rose commented.

"The honeymoon was even better." Destiny laughed as she dramatically pulled off her navy blue leather gloves.

Both women laughed. Destiny removed her coat and placed it on the brass coatrack in the corner.

Rose went back to her seat, and Destiny sat across from her.

"If the honeymoon was so great, why did you guys come back so early?" Rose asked.

Rose watched as her cousin pulled out a green, plastic photo wallet and handed it to her.

"Dez, these aren't rated X?" Rose asked as she accepted them.

"I'm not that kinky. They're pictures of my new house."

Rose's mouth fell open as she retrieved the photos. She looked down at them, "It's beautiful." She flipped through them, then she came around the table and hugged her cousin. "I'm so happy for you. You didn't tell me you were buying a house." She handed the photos back to Destiny.

"I didn't know. He surprised me on the way home from the airport."

Rose's eyes began to fill. "See you got the castle to go along with your prince." She gave a generous smile.

"Aw, Rose, your prince is coming, too. I just know it," Destiny said, her voice quivering. "Speaking of your prince, I just left Marc at the house. He told me to tell you he's looking forward to seeing you again."

Rose went back to her seat. "Oh yeah."

Destiny leaned forward to get closer and waved a finger in front of Rose. "You can act all nonchalant and play that game with Aunt Luv and your sisters, but it's me, girl, you're talking to."

Rose looked away, and Destiny tried to move even closer to her. "Let's not pretend you're not interested. I saw the chemistry between you two. Girl, it was almost combustible." Destiny laughed.

Rose got up from her seat and walked over to the window.

Destiny rose to her feet as well and walked over to her, placing her hands on Rose's shoulders. "You don't have to buy to window-shop, ya know," she whispered.

Rose turned to face Destiny, and a smile grew on both their faces. "Just don't go with money in your pocket," they both said at the same time.

Rose's smile faded before she spoke again. "I don't want you to worry about me. You're married now. My love life, or lack thereof, is strictly my problem."

Destiny eyed Rose at first; then she spoke. "I was kind of thinking that maybe you and Marc would get together."

"Listen at you. Now you sound like Mama," Rose said as she walked back to the table.

Destiny raised a perfectly arched brow. "You aren't dead, Rosie, so I know you've noticed how handsome he is."

Rose opened the lid on the see-through box on the worktable. "Of course, I have. The man is past fine…he and his brother." She lifted a floral arrangement and placed it inside the box, relieved the bride liked it.

Destiny quickly moved back over to the worktable. "See. Now we're getting somewhere."

Rose glared at her cousin. "Dez," she warned, placing the lid on the box.

Destiny raised her hands in surrender. "Okay, okay, I'll back off. Listen, Nick and I are having a dinner for the wedding party on Friday. I want you to make a couple of center-pieces for the table."

"You know I'll do anything for you," Rose said, smiling. "What are your colors?"

"We're using gold and cinnamon."

"Nice. Why don't I stop by tomorrow after I get off work so I can see the house and get an idea for centerpieces?"

"Sounds great. Maybe you can give me some decorating tips, too," Destiny said as she picked up her coat and slipped it on.

She then picked up her gloves and leaned to kiss Rose on her cheek. "I'll see you tomorrow evening," she said as she walked out the door.

After her cousin left, Rose thought about their conversation. Sadness overtook her as she thought about the sheer happiness that radiated from Destiny. Rose wasn't jealous, but in her heart, she wished she could experience that same magic. From the looks of things, it didn't seem to be in her future.

Chapter 4

Rose left work an hour early on Friday afternoon in order to get dressed for Destiny's party. After taking a quick shower, she walked into the second-floor extra bedroom she'd set up as her dressing room.

One of Rose's favorite pastimes was decorating her home. The Victorian-style house was decorated beautifully with a different theme for each room. The eclectic mix blended well, but Rose always found ways to change things around when she came up with a new idea.

She called her dressing room A Touch of Romance because of its romantic allure. She'd chosen ivory filigree, semisheer lace curtains with an elegant boucle weave pattern for the window treatments. The scarf-style valances featured fringed ends. She'd found a decorative ivory and gold resin cherub to place directly in the middle of the carved gold rods.

The skillfully engraved brass bed in the room was covered with delicate linen that matched the window treatments. Rose loved all the little trinkets and sconces she'd placed in the room, but her favorite piece was her dressing table. She'd found the antique piece at an estate sale several years ago. As soon as she saw it, she knew she had to have it.

Flicking the light switch, she walked into her closet and browsed through the many skirts, blouses, and outfits. Rose liked to shop and always loved a bargain.

As she moved the wooden hangers across the steel bars, she wondered what combination would be perfect for the evening. After pulling out several garments and looking at them against her body in the full-length antique mirror, she still wasn't satisfied.

Finally, she pulled out a pair of rust-colored cuffed slacks and a matching angora sweater. Opening the many shoe boxes she had, she retrieved her brown leather high-heeled mules with a leaf design carved into the heel.

Rose walked over to the dressing table and pulled open the bottom drawer to retrieve her gold hoop earrings.

After laying the outfit across the bed, she placed a few curls in her already bouncy, dark brown, shoulder-length hair. She loved changing her hairstyles as much as her clothes. Tonight she wanted her hair to be loose and free.

Rose slipped on her clothes and assessed herself carefully in the mirror. Satisfied with the results, she applied her makeup. After outlining her lips with her favorite brand of Patti LaBelle liner, she swabbed them with a champagne-tinted, shimmering lip gloss, then smacked them together. After putting her earrings in her ears, Rose walked across the hall to the bathroom. Staring at herself in the lighted mirror, she said, "Rosie, girl, you are too cute."

After she washed and dried her hands, she applied cocoa-scented cream from a dispenser. She thought about all the time she took to get dressed. She had always been concerned about the way she looked and tried to dress to impress, if for no one but herself, but tonight she had to be honest. Marc would probably be at the party, and she wanted him to notice her.

Rose checked herself once more before she turned off the lights on her way out of the bathroom. She moved down the staircase and picked up her coat and purse on her way out the door.

As Rose drove her Nissan Murano through the gates of Briar Ridge Estates, she was impressed all over again with the surroundings. Following tree-lined Briar Ridge Avenue, she continued until she saw Woodale, an enclave that hadn't been fully developed.

Rose pulled up to the curb in front of Destiny's house. It was already dark, and even though she'd been there earlier in the week, she was relieved that the glow from the attractive yard lights illuminated the sprawling brick structure.

She got out of her SUV and went around the back to open the hatch. She pulled out a bag with the centerpieces inside and sat it on the ground; then she retrieved a beautiful wreath she'd created as a housewarming gift for the couple.

The eighteen-inch wreath was made of preserved oak leaves and gilded holly, decked out with gossamer gold ribbon. She had placed pointed canella berries, faux hops, and freeze-dried roses with red ribbon all over the wreath. She thought it would look nice on the front door.

A brisk breeze caressed her face as she looked around the neighborhood. Though it was incomplete, the large homes that had already been built had impressive modern designs and immaculately manicured lawns.

She closed the hatch and picked up her bag and the wreath before making her way up the brick driveway. She noticed a black Lincoln with Massachusetts plates and figured the car belonged to Marc.

Unloading the bag on the top step of the porch, she pressed the gold circle on the side of the huge oak door. She could hear the chimes from outside.

Destiny opened the door, wearing a stunning gray pant-suit.

Rose smiled as she picked up her bag and greeted her cousin. "You look good, girl," she said as she walked inside and past her.

"So do you," Destiny said.

Rose immediately glanced up at the chandelier hanging from the cathedral ceiling above her head.

"Dez, I can't get over how big this place is," she said as she glanced around.

She handed the wreath to Destiny.

Destiny lifted the round floral wreath. "This is beautiful. You didn't have to do this, Rosie, really."

Rose kissed her cousin on the cheek. "I know, but with the holiday right around the corner, I thought it would be perfect."

Destiny pulled Rose to her. "You are so special, Rosie," she said as she squeezed her tightly. Stepping away, she said, "Let me take your coat."

Rose shrugged out of her black suede swing coat. "Was that Marc's car in the driveway?"

"Yes," Destiny said with enthusiasm. "He's in the kitchen."

Rose raised a brow as she handed her the heavy garment. "Really? I didn't know he cooked."

Destiny maneuvered the wreath with one hand and took the coat with the other. She walked to the coat closet a few feet away. "Come with me," she said. "I want to find Nick, so he can hang the wreath." She closed the closet door and turned to walk away, with Rose following her.

As they approached the kitchen, Rose spotted Marc standing in front of the counter, talking to a gray-haired man dressed in a white outfit and a big hat. She noticed the way Marc's black slacks caressed his behind. Suddenly, she felt warm. The sight caused Rose to pull at the cowl of her sweater.

With further glances, she noticed the way his charcoal sweater clung to him. He had his sleeves pushed up slightly, revealing his bulging biceps.

Destiny stopped unexpectedly, causing Rose to walk into the back of her.

"Sorry, girl. I guess my mind was somewhere else," Rose said, looking sheepishly at her cousin.

Destiny smacked her lips and gave her a knowing look. "Umm, hmm, sure it was. Anyway, I was just getting ready to say that all the furniture came in time." She turned around and continued to the kitchen area.

Rose hadn't really been paying attention. Her mind was on Marc, so she hadn't noticed the rooms had furniture in them.

Marc heard Rose's voice before he saw her enter the kitchen. It had been two weeks since he'd last seen her, but to him, it felt longer. Every day he tried to control his thoughts about her, but his mind wouldn't let him. As the days passed, he couldn't help but think about the lovely, curvaceous, brown-eyed woman.

Right now his eyes absorbed the beauty only she could exude. He didn't realize Henry was speaking to him until he cleared his throat.

Marc looked over at the older gentleman. "I'm sorry, Henry, did you say something?"

"Would you like me to prepare the trays now?" he asked again.

"Yes, please," Marc said as he picked up a white linen towel and wiped his hands.

He could never forget Rose's lovely smile, the dazzling sparkle in her eyes, and the single, deep dimple in her right cheek.

"If you'll excuse me, I'll be right back," he said, dropping the towel on the counter before walking away. Tonight would be the perfect opportunity to get to know Rose better, he thought as he approached the women.

With each powerful step, Rose watched Marc walk toward her like a sleek panther. The diamond in his ear twinkled with every movement. His hair was trimmed to perfection again, which told her he took pride in his looks. The closer he came, the more her heart rate increased. Marc stopped directly in front of her.

"Rose, it's good to see you again." He motioned to hug her.

The action surprised Rose, but she wanted to exchange his greeting. She placed her bag on the floor.

Marc drew her to his chest, and she could feel his heartbeat. She immediately thought that maybe it wasn't such a good idea to hug him after all, as his warm flesh caused heat to course through her body. He felt too good, and the embrace reminded her of the night they danced together.

Rose moved out of his embrace, and Marc caught her hand. She met the bold gaze of his dark eyes.

"It's good to see you again, too," she said, watching his eyes twinkle. "How's Jonathan feeling these days?"

Marc didn't respond right away. As he took a step closer, his nostrils flared slightly as he inhaled her fragrance. He assessed her from her hair, which was styled around her face, to her dazzling brown eyes, to her glistening lips.

Destiny cleared her throat. "I'm sorry to interrupt, but I need to go and find my husband." She turned to Rose. "I'll see you a little later." She walked away.

Rose watched Destiny until she was out of sight before re-alizing that Marc still hadn't released her hand. She glanced up at him.

Marc smiled but still didn't let go. "You were asking me a question."

Rose gently pulled her hand from his. "I asked about your brother."

"Jonathan's good. He should be here later." He reached down to pick up her bag. "May I take your bag for you?"

"Thanks, but it's not necessary. These are the centerpieces for the dinner table," she responded, picking up the bag her-self and placing it in the nearest empty chair. "It really smells good in here, Marc. I didn't know you cooked," she added, walking over to the counter where the hors d'oeuvres had been placed on silver trays.

Marc came over and stood close behind her. "There are a lot of things you don't know about me," he whispered. "Maybe I'll just have to enlighten you a little later."

A slight shiver ran down Rose's spine from his lips graz-ing her ear. She shook her head and turned around, smiling as she watched him wink at her.

"I hope you brought your appetite," he said, walking over to the six-burner cooktop.

Rose placed her hands on her ample hips, which made his eyes sparkle. "Are you saying that because I'm a big girl?" she asked, tapping the pointed toe of her shoe on the floor.

Marc went to her and gently took her right hand, putting it to his lips. "No, I didn't mean anything negative. In fact, I like what I see very much, Ms. Hart." He stepped back, lifting her hand, turning her around so he could get a better look at her up close.

Rose gave him a dimpled smile as she pulled her hand

away. "I just bet you do, Mr. Damon." She chuckled, then thought to herself, if he wanted to flirt, she'd flirt right back. "Listen, I'll let you get back to work." She moved over to the table to pick up her bag.

"Rose," Marc called out to her.

She turned around. "Yes?"

"Don't forget we're going to talk later."

"I won't," she said softly before turning to walk away. When she got halfway to the threshold of the door to the dining room, he called her again.

"Rose."

She quickly glanced back over her shoulder, turning back to him. "Why is it every time I try to leave, you stop me?"

Marc hunched his broad shoulders and walked over to her. "Maybe I don't want you to leave me," he said in a husky tone of voice.

Rose looked past him at the older gentleman, wondering if he'd heard Marc's comment. He seemed to be engrossed in his work.

Rose looked back at Marc. "I don't want to get in the way." He was so close, she had to take a quick breath.

Marc gave her a pleading look.

Rose tried to ignore it but only got lost in his eyes. "Okay, I'll come back as soon as I'm finished in the dining room. I want to place the centerpieces on the table."

"That's better," Marc said, stepping back slightly.

Rose tried to shrug away the excitement floating in her stomach as he continued to stare at her. She should have been used to his endless flirting, but there was something in his eyes that made her feel anxious.

"The house is lovely," she commented, trying to ease some of the tension she felt. "Nicholas has great taste."

"Excellent taste runs in the family," Marc said as he walked closer to her.

The nearness of him made Rose even more giddy. "I'll be back." She quickly walked away but turned back around just as fast in case he was about to call her name again. All she saw was his dark eyes watching her.

"That man, that man," she said to herself as she made her way to the dining room.

Rose didn't have to do anything except place the rich floral ensemble on the table. She had chosen hues of burgundy and gold silk flowers, and when she placed the centerpieces on the table, they exuded warmth and intimacy on top of the gold appliqué–accented, deep cinnamon overlay of the table linen. The room was so beautiful. She leaned against the back of one of the high chairs placed under the contemporary dining table, which seated eight.

Clear chargers and amber-tinted goblets at each place setting made the table look so elegant. There were several tall, ivory-colored block candles, which Rose assumed would be lit right before the guests sat down to dine.

Everything was perfect for Destiny's first gathering in her new home, and Rose's evening wasn't half bad, either, she thought to herself.

"Why are you in here alone?"

Rose turned to find Destiny standing in the doorway. She moved away from the table.

"Just thinking."

Destiny walked over to her. "The flowers are so beautiful."

"Everything is lovely, Dez," Rose responded. "The table décor just screams elegant. I don't know why you wanted me to give you decorating tips. You've done a great job."

"Come on. Let's go up to the media room. Vanessa and Desire are here," Destiny said. Destiny was excited to have all her bridesmaids together once again.

Rose looked toward the kitchen. "I promised Marc I'd come back and help him out."

Destiny took a step back. "Well, excuse me, girlfriend." She turned to walk away.

Rose caught her hand before she could get away. "Wait. If Marc doesn't need me, I'll be right up." She patted her cousin's hand.

"Don't hurt yourself, girl," Destiny said as she walked away.

Rose went down the short hallway toward the kitchen. Marc was distributing the prepared trays to the servers when she walked in.

"Need help with anything?" she asked from behind him.

A wide smile grew on Marc's face as he turned to face her. "Yes, as a matter of fact, I do." He held out his elbow.

Rose looked down at his outstretched arm.

"You can agree to be my companion for the evening."

Rose rolled her eyes. She'd decided earlier to flirt shamelessly with him tonight. It couldn't hurt anything, so she continued to challenge his Billy Dee Williams–type gestures.

"What if I already have a companion for the evening?" she asked.

Marc watched Rose's tinted lips as she spoke. He immediately licked his own. "If that were true, you wouldn't be in here with me."

"Is that a fact?" she said, trying not to crack a smile, but she couldn't help herself.

Marc gave her a smirk before turning to check the tray of one of the three servers, Tanya, before she left the room.

After Tanya disappeared down the hall, Marc turned his attention back to Rose.

"Ms. Hart, you haven't answered my question," he said as his dark eyes roamed her body.

After a few moments of her hesitation, he held out his arm once again.

Rose glanced down at his outstretched arm and then into his eyes, which always made her want to squirm.

She looped her arm through his right arm and smiled.

He covered her hand and said, "You won't be disappointed. I promise you."

As they walked from the kitchen to the stairs that led to the second floor of the home, Rose studied the side angle of his rich features.

She tried to remind herself not to read anything into his actions and to just live in the moment. However, she didn't dismiss their excellent chemistry or the fact that she smiled a lot when she was with him.

The media room had carved molding and indirect lighting. Even though Rose had viewed the home earlier in the week, she was still impressed with this room, especially now that it was filled with people. The room actually reminded her of a mini movie theater.

Rose noticed that almost the entire wedding party had arrived except her sister Ivy. She'd meant to ask Destiny if Ivy had made an appearance. Nine times out of ten Ivy simply did not show up.

Rose continued to roam the room, and her eyes clashed with Destiny, who was raising her champagne glass toward Rose.

"Would you like a glass of champagne?" Marc asked.

"No," Rose responded.

"You don't drink?" Marc wanted to know.

Rose nodded. "I do on occasion, but not tonight."

Marc looked for an available server. "Would you like a glass of the nonalcoholic champagne?"

"That would be fine, thank you," Rose said.

Marc walked over to the server, leaving her alone.

Rose tried not to watch him, so she scanned the room a second time. She spotted Jonathan coming in her direction.

He hugged her. "It's great to see you again, Rose."

"You, too," Rose said, moving out of his embrace.

She assessed him. She noticed that he was shorter than Marc, but that they both had the same smooth, rich chocolate coloring. "You look so much better than you did a couple of weeks ago."

Jonathan patted his stomach. "I'm back to my old self, thank you," he said, smiling.

Rose was about to respond when Marc came back to join them. She felt a little uneasy from the intense look in his eyes when she looked at him.

"What's up?" Jonathan said to his brother.

Marc handed Rose a slim crystal flute, then acknowledged Jonathan. "You were the first person she asked about," he said.

Jonathan chuckled. "I have that effect on women."

"Yeah, in your dreams," Marc said sarcastically.

They all smiled.

Rose leaned forward. "Do I detect a little hateration, Mr. Damon?" she asked Marc.

"Not at all. I'm very confident in my abilities, and I get the woman I want," Marc said with certainty.

Jonathan raised his glass. "I guess that makes two of us then."

"All right now," Rose said, raising her glass as well.

"Rose, have you tried the hors d'oeuvres?" Jonathan asked. "I hate to say it because I'm afraid my brother's head will swell, but your friend here is an excellent chef."

"I'm sure he is," Rose responded.

Marc moved closer to her. "Maybe I can give you a private taste test," he suggested.

Rose looked up at him and didn't know what to say. Marc's comments were getting harder for her to respond to.

They all stood silently for a couple of seconds. Marc and Rose were in a hypnotic trance as they gazed into each other's eyes.

Jonathan cleared his throat. "I'm going to talk to Nick before they get started." He walked away, leaving them alone.

Marc captured Rose's attention, but she spoke before he did. "I better go over and speak to some of the others; I don't want to appear antisocial."

Marc watched as Rose walked away. He noticed the sway in her hips and wondered what it would be like to be lost between them.

At that moment, Nicholas announced they were ready to begin.

Marc decided to go and check things in the kitchen.

Rose watched Marc leave the room, and she couldn't help but think of how attracted she was to him. She could hear the small voice inside her whispering to be cautious.

The lights were dimmed, and Rose quickly took a seat in the second row of the sixteen-seat mini theater.

She watched as the video projection screen descended from the ceiling. Immediately, the musical intro to Natalie Cole's "Our Love" resounded in the room. Soon after, Destiny's and Nicholas's baby photos appeared on the screen.

There were ahs from the ladies and laughs from the guys.

"Don't hate," Nicholas yelled from the front.

With the musical background of all their favorite songs from back in the day to Alicia Keys and Kenny G, the video went through a collage of photos of the couple from child-hood to engagement.

Finally, clips of the bridal party getting ready for the ceremony appeared. A photograph of Rose and her Aunt Elizabeth adjusting Destiny's dress and veil made tears well up in Rose's eyes.

Rose smiled when she saw Nicholas wrap his arms around Destiny, then wiped the tears from her eyes.

Destiny turned around and looked at Rose. Both women had tears falling down their cheeks. Rose reached forward and gently squeezed her cousin's shoulder.

They had been through a lot together over the years. From heartbreak to victory, they had always been there for each other. Sometimes, Destiny was the only person who understood Rose's feelings.

Rose continued to watch the couple. Destiny snuggled as close as she could to Nicholas as they watched their first dance.

Rose immediately sensed Marc's presence when he reentered the room. She looked over toward the door as he came near. She knew he would want to sit next to her, so she got up and moved down one seat so she wouldn't disturb others.

Marc did exactly what she thought he would. "Thanks for saving me a seat," he leaned over and whispered.

The combination of the dimmed lighting, his cologne, and the whisper of his breath against her cheek made Rose squirm in her chair.

As soon as Rose looked up at the screen, her mouth dropped open in amazement. There on the screen was a close-up of her and Marc dancing. She had had no idea at the time that the camera had gotten so close to them.

"My, my, my," she heard Destiny say.

Rose slowly looked up and saw that Destiny had turned in

her seat. Quickly, Rose glanced at Marc, who was also staring at her.

He leaned over to her. "Are you alright?"

"Yes, I'm fine," Rose said, raising her head and looking straight at the screen.

They were in a passionate embrace. She knew Marc was still looking at her; she could feel it.

The credits rolled, and Rose thought the video was definitely a testament of Nicholas and Destiny's love for each other. More importantly, what she saw on the screen was exactly what her heart had felt that Saturday evening when she was in the arms of Marc Damon—infatuation, fascination, excitement, and magic. The only question now that stuck in her head was what in the world was she going to do about it?

Chapter 5

As everyone else headed into the dining room, Marc went into the kitchen to make sure Henry and his two helpers were prepared to serve the meal.

Flipping the lever on the faucet to wash his hands, Marc was haunted by the image of himself and Rose dancing on the big screen.

He remembered the amazing feeling of holding her in his arms, causing him to get lost in the moment. As he sat next to her this evening in the media room with the lights down low, the scent of her perfume had made him want to hold her close again.

"Marc," he heard Jonathan call from behind.

Marc quickly looked over his shoulder as he pressed the lever to turn off the water. "Yeah?"

Jonathan approached him. "Man, that was quick."

Marc looked at his brother. "What was quick?"

A slight grin grew on Jonathan's face. He moved in closer so the others busying themselves in the kitchen couldn't hear them. "The way you seduced her. This is the fastest I've ever seen you go after a woman."

Marc stared silently at his brother at first; then he spoke. "Don't come in here and give me a speech, Jonathan. If you have a point, get to it because I'm busy," he said, picking up a dry cloth.

Marc moved away from the sink, with Jonathan following behind him. He picked up a soup ladle and checked the consistency of the creamy mushroom soup he'd prepared earlier.

Jonathan touched his shoulder. "Look, I didn't come in here to give you a lecture. You'd have to be blind not to see the chemistry between the two of you. If it hadn't been captured on film, and I hadn't seen it for myself this evening, I wouldn't have believed it."

Marc picked up one of the small ceramic bowls Henry had placed on a tray and began to fill it with the hot soup.

"So what are you trying to say?" Marc asked, continuing his task. "And don't tell me she's not my type."

"No, I just wanted to remind you that you're not in Boston."

Marc interrupted him. "Don't you think I know how to handle myself?"

"I'm just saying don't get in over your head. And when you get bored and want to get out in a hurry, you'll hurt Rose in the process."

Marc filled the last bowl on the serving tray and motioned for the server named Thomas, who had just entered the kitchen, to retrieve it.

After the young man picked up the tray and walked from the room, Marc turned in Jonathan's direction.

"The thought of hurting Rose never crossed my mind. Anyway, like you told me I'm a grown man." He picked up the cloth to wipe his hands. "I'm going to take things as they come, but I'm not going to miss this opportunity to get to know her."

Jonathan waved his hand. "That's cool and all, but just remember how you felt when you found out Andrea betrayed you when you're working your magic on Rose."

Marc stared into eyes reminiscent of his own. "Li'l bruh, you aren't by chance interested in Rose yourself?" Marc asked with a raised brow. "You seem very concerned about her feelings."

Jonathan walked away, then quickly turned around and purposefully moved back to where his brother stood. "Not in the way you think," he said through gritted teeth. "I like her, yes. She's got a warm and caring nature." Jonathan's eyes became glazed. "She reminds me of Mama," he added, his voice lowered to a whisper.

Marc slapped him playfully on the back. "Well, that's not what comes to my mind when I think about the gorgeous, curvaceous, and lush Ms. Hart. But a brotha had to ask."

At that moment Thomas returned with two bowls still on the tray. Henry came in right behind him.

"Marc, there were two people who didn't want soup; they preferred just the salad," Henry explained.

"That's fine, Henry. Thanks a lot," Marc said.

"Why don't you go and have a seat with the other guests," Henry said, looking around. "I think we can handle things in here."

Marc appreciated the older man's gesture. Henry was an old friend of his Uncle Isaiah. He had owned a restaurant in town before he retired. Nowadays he still catered some events for friends and had volunteered to help Marc out this evening.

"Thanks, Henry." Marc gave him a strong pat on the back before he and Jonathan walked out of the kitchen.

As they walked down the hallway leading to the dining room, they could hear laughter coming from the room. Jonathan looked at Marc. "Don't forget what I said."

Marc nodded. "I hear you."

As soon as Marc entered the dining room, he noticed everyone had been paired off. Nicholas sat at the head of the table, and Destiny at the other end. Richard, another groomsman, and Desire were together, which left empty seats next to Vanessa and Rose.

There was no need for either brother to say anything to the other. It was already understood who would sit where.

Marc's eyes went to Rose. She was having a conversation with Vanessa, showing the deep dimple in her right cheek, when he came to take his seat.

Rose smiled, leaning over to him. "Everything ready?"

"Yes," Marc said, looking down at the small bowl in front of him, then over at her untouched soup. "Were you waiting for me?" he asked.

Rose smiled in response. She picked up her soup spoon, dipping it into the potage. She placed it in her mouth. "Hmmm," she said as her eyes fluttered, savoring the distinct taste.

"So, what do you think?" Marc asked, watching her features change.

Rose opened her eyes and turned to him. "Excellent."

"Where is that beautiful sister of yours, Rose?" Jonathan asked, placing his napkin in his lap.

Rose dabbed the corners of her mouth with the linen napkin in her lap. "Which one?"

"How many sisters do you have?" Richard asked.

"Three," Rose responded.

Jonathan took a sip of his white wine. "I'm talking about

the one you call Vee. I was sick at the wedding, but I wasn't blind." He smiled.

Rose gave Destiny a questioning look. "You did invite her?"

"Yeah," Destiny replied. "I invited her, but she said she already had plans for this evening." Destiny waved her hand. "Rosie, you know how Vee is."

Rose dropped her head slightly. "Yes, I do," she said and stirred her soup slowly.

Marc noticed the sudden change in Rose's demeanor. He bent to the side and whispered in her ear. "Are you okay?"

Rose gazed into the eyes that mesmerized her every time she looked into them. She lowered her gaze to his moist lips and then looked into his eyes again. They both stared at each other as if they were the only two people in the room before Rose spoke.

"I'm good." She gave Marc a smile that didn't quite reach her eyes. She didn't want to tell him that she was worried about her sister.

The servers brought in the entrée.

Rose's eyes dropped to the plate in front of her. Its presentation was beautiful. There was baked salmon roulade, julienne carrots, asparagus, and potato galette with tomato beurre blanc sauce. "Wow," she said.

Marc observed everyone at the table. "I hope you enjoy your meal."

Rose sampled the salmon. "It's wonderful, Marc. The salmon is so light."

Marc beamed with pride. "I have a lot of other dishes I would love to prepare for you," he whispered.

Rose moved closer to him. She had to be careful with all the closeness and whispering they were sharing. It was making her feel warm inside.

"Why are you always trying to feed me? We haven't finished this meal yet," she said, giving him a dimpled smile.

"I just want to show you my skills," he replied seriously.

Rose blushed.

Marc could tell by her reaction that he had succeeded in making her speechless.

"I have an idea," Destiny announced. "The Majestic Gents are hosting the World's Largest Steppers Set, and I think we should all go."

"But, I don't know how to step," Vanessa said quietly.

"It's just the new bop," Richard responded. "Don't you know how to bop, Vanessa?"

"No, but I want to learn."

"Stepping really has evolved," Marc spoke up.

Everyone gave him their full attention.

"Back in the 1930s, Cab Calloway called it the jitterbug; in the East they called it swing dancing. Now I've heard people say that stepping is ten percent technique and ninety percent style."

"That's right because the steps are very simple, Vanessa," Rose said. "There's a lot of places you could take classes. I know the YWCA offers them."

"Yeah, and don't forget the Dating Game on Eighty-ninth and Stony Island offers them, too," Destiny said.

Jonathan lifted up his wineglass. "Let's go stepping, y'all."

Everyone laughed.

"Once I get all the information, I'll contact everyone," Destiny said, taking a sip from her glass.

After everyone had dined sufficiently, they got up from the table.

Tanya brought in a large plastic tub and handed it to Marc so he could clear the table.

Rose got up from her chair. "Why don't I help you?" she said, lifting a crystal goblet.

"Thanks, but I have Henry, Thomas, and Tanya. Between the four of us, we can have everything cleaned up in no time."

"Are you sure?" she asked, continuing to gather the goblets.

Marc looked up at her and smiled. "You can keep me company."

Rose remembered him asking her to be his companion for the evening. She decided to help him, anyway. She picked up the goblets she'd gathered.

Marc tried to stop her. "Really, Rose, you don't have to help out."

"It's okay. The more help you get, the faster your staff can get out of here and you can relax."

"I am relaxed. You're by my side," Marc said as he handed the filled tub to Henry.

Rose blushed again. She leaned over the table. "You are something else. I don't even know how to respond to you."

Marc walked around the table to get closer to her. "Then don't," he said softly.

Rose felt the now familiar churning in her belly. "See what I mean." She gave him a nervous smile.

For the next twenty minutes, Rose assisted Marc, while the servers loaded the dishwasher and worked to put Destiny's beautiful kitchen back in order.

Marc wrote a check to Henry and made sure the servers were on their way. He headed back to the kitchen and found Rose standing in front of the sink. He stood in the doorway, and for the umpteenth time that evening, he studied her, this time from behind.

Finally, he walked toward her at a slow pace.

* * *

As Rose waited for Marc's return, she looked around the now immaculately clean kitchen. The mellow green walls played off the red tones of the natural brick paved floor. The graceful arched cathedral cabinet doors, with handles that had decorative fluted trim and a pewter finish, gave the kitchen a contemporary feel.

The sleek profile of the stainless steel appliances provided a stylish contrast in texture and worked very well. The double sinks with the polished chrome faucets provided continuity with the rest of the contemporary kitchen.

Rose didn't know why her senses were so keen when it came to Marc. She knew the moment Marc had reentered the room. She quickly turned and found him a few feet away from her.

"Everything alright?" she asked, giving him a genuine smile.

"Couldn't be better," he said huskily as he continued to approach her.

Rose watched the gleam in his eye; then her eyes roamed to the wide expanse of his chest. It seemed as if his muscles had grown since she last saw him a couple of minutes ago.

Her eyes widened as she watched him walk purpose-fully toward her. She didn't know what would happen next.

She tried to pull herself together quickly, so he wouldn't notice the effect he had on her. She had to keep the nervousness in her stomach from ending up in her throat, making her voice crack when she spoke.

The tension in the room grew thicker with every step closer Marc came to her. She immediately looked down at the floor in an attempt to calm herself, inhaled a quick deep breath, then looked back at him. His eyes had never left her.

"What is your problem?" she finally asked him in a teasing manner.

Marc took one step forward, putting them almost toe-to-toe with one another. He reached out his hand to touch her face with his fingertips. "You really are very beautiful."

Rose stepped to the side. "Are you just now realizing that?" she said jokingly, trying to cover up her nervousness. She attempted to walk around him, but he caught her hand.

She looked down at the muscled arm attached to the hand that clung to her chocolate skin. She lifted her head, meeting his bold gaze.

"No, I'm serious. You are so beautiful to me," he said, palming her face.

Rose had had enough of the games for tonight. She wanted to stop this before she started to believe his lies.

Pulling her hand away, she placed it on the left side of his wide chest. She could feel the heat radiating from him, prompting her to step closer. She knew she shouldn't do that; it would only encourage him to continue with the game, and she didn't want to play anymore. Her feelings were becoming too real.

"Look, Marc, I appreciate you trying to be nice to me, but we both know you aren't really interested. It was great while it lasted, but you don't have to pretend anymore." She was relieved to get the words out of her mouth. Now things could go back to the way they were before she knew anything about Marc Damon.

Marc gently picked up her hand, intertwining his fingers with hers. His gaze traveled from the top of her dark brown hair to her dazzling brown eyes and stayed there. "I'm not pretending."

Rose's eyes grew larger. Speechless, nervous, and aroused by the gesture, she knew that she had to get away from him. She motioned to move away.

"Wait," he said, his voice taking on the husky, seductive tone it had earlier.

They stood silently in front of the sink.

"Hey, what's taking—" Destiny stopped when she saw them standing together.

Marc turned to find that Destiny had entered the kitchen. He didn't release Rose's hand. He held it behind his back, and Rose stared down at their still attached fingers.

"What's up, Dez?" he asked.

Destiny studied the couple. "I just came to see what was taking you two so long. Did I interrupt something?"

"Thank you," Rose said to herself. Her cousin had just given her an excuse to leave. She didn't think she could take much more of his honesty.

As she was about to move away, Marc spoke up. "We'll be down in just a minute. We were discussing something."

Destiny looked at Rose. "I see," she said.

Rose felt she had to say something. "We'll be down in a minute, Dez," Rose said, with a slight shake in her voice. *Dang, I blew that one*, she then thought to herself.

Destiny didn't respond. She walked away, but not before Rose could see the smirk on her face.

Marc turned back to Rose. He lifted her chin with his thumb and forefinger. Glaring into her eyes, he said, "Don't you have something to say?"

Rose rolled her eyes slightly and tried to move away again.

Marc took one step to the side to stop her. "I would like for us to get to know each other. Nothing serious. Just two people who are attracted to each other having a good time." He lifted her chin once again. "What do you say, Ms. Hart?"

Rose couldn't deny she was interested. The problem was she was very interested. But she did tell herself there was nothing wrong with having fun, and she surely didn't want to end up like Ivy…mad at the world. Getting hurt again wasn't an option for her, either.

Finally, she shook her head in agreement. "Okay, we can go out sometimes. I think it will be fun." She wanted to believe the words coming out of her mouth. Hopefully, when everything was over, she would not mess up and fall in love with Marc Damon.

Chapter 6

Rose and Marc left the kitchen and walked down to the game room, where the men were playing pool. Rose took the empty chair next to Destiny at the bar.

When Destiny nudged her on the arm, Rose knew she had a smart remark about what she had seen in the kitchen, so Rose stopped her before she could even begin. "I don't want to hear it," she said.

Rose watched her cousin's eyes dance in her head.

Destiny sat up straight on the stool. "Cool, I'll keep my thoughts to myself," she said, narrowing her eyes at Rose.

Rose elbowed her. "You're a liar; you've never kept your thoughts to yourself...ever."

They both laughed, and Rose looked up and right into Marc's eyes. He smiled easily at her as he prepared to hit the white cue ball with his pool stick.

"I didn't know you were dating Marc, Rose," Vanessa said.

"We're just friends," Rose said, glancing at Marc, and then waited for Destiny to respond.

"Why don't we pair off," Destiny suggested, getting off the stool.

"Yeah, baby, I think that's a great idea," Nicholas said as he turned on the old jukebox he'd purchased with all of his and Destiny's favorite music inside.

Destiny walked over to her husband and hugged him from behind. "Jonathan and Vanessa can go against me and my baby, Rose and Marc can play whoever wins, and then Desire and Richard can play," she suggested.

Rose sat for a few seconds, giving her cousin the "I'm going to kill you" look.

Vanessa and Desire came over to her. "Come on, Rosie. I'm sure it can't be as hard as it looks," Vanessa said. "All you have to do is hit the ball in the hole."

The men started laughing, and Rose shook her head.

Vanessa looked around the room. "Is that another sport?" the dark-eyed beauty asked.

Rose knew that playing pool wasn't hard, but being with Marc was another thing. She followed the other women over to the pool table.

The hair on the nape of her neck prickled. She didn't need to turn around to know that Marc was standing directly behind her.

"Don't worry. I'll coach you along," he whispered quietly in her ear.

Rose leaned back. "I've watched my father and uncle play before."

The other two teams watched carefully as Destiny and her husband beat Jonathan and Vanessa. Rose noticed how helpless Vanessa seemed around Jonathan, but, hey, who could blame her.

When it was her and Marc's turn, Rose couldn't concentrate. She really didn't know how to hold the pool stick, and when Marc tried to show her, she could feel the heat from his body, and all her thoughts of pool vanished and were replaced with hot bodies sprawled across the pool table.

She tried to hit the cue ball and almost scuffed the green carpeted surface with her stick. At that point she knew it was time for her to go.

Destiny and Nicholas won the game, and Rose told them she was ready to leave.

"Why don't I walk you out?" Destiny offered.

"No, you go ahead and play the next game. I'll walk Rose to her car," Marc said.

Rose didn't protest. She said her good-byes to the others and headed for the stairs.

They walked to the closet in the foyer. Rose pulled her coat out, and Marc took it from her.

"Let me help you," he said, holding it open so she could slip her arms into the sleeves.

"Thanks," she whispered as she felt his strong hands gently squeezing her suede-covered shoulders.

"You feel so good," he said huskily.

Rose wanted to turn to face him, but she didn't because of the lust, passion, and fire she knew she would see in his eyes.

This was happening too quickly. Someone had to have some sense about the situation. She hadn't quite grasped the fact he was really interested in her, anyway.

Slinging her Coach purse on her right shoulder, she pushed her hand down in her coat pocket to retrieve her keys.

Marc opened the front door to allow her to exit first.

Rose pulled the collar of her suede swing coat together once they stepped into the brisk night air.

Marc pulled her closer to his side. "It's a bit chilly out here tonight."

The breeze felt good on Rose's skin. It helped her cool

down the smoldering heat he radiated. It had been a long time since she had had that kind of attention from a man.

"So, when do you want to get together?" Marc asked.

"Why don't you call me," Rose said as they approached her SUV.

"No problem," Marc responded, opening the door for her. Rose climbed into the SUV.

"I had a good time this evening. It's too bad I was working for most of it, but it was good seeing you," Marc said.

"I had fun," she smiled, placing her key in the ignition.

Marc closed the door.

Rose started the motor and waited for him to step back before she drove away. She glanced in her rearview mirror and saw him standing at the curb. She knew that after this evening, her life would never be the same because of the presence of Marc Damon.

Rose pulled into her driveway and parked her SUV in front of the garage door. As she entered the darkened house, the sinking feeling of loneliness suddenly came over her. Before she could stop it, tears began to roll down her cheeks.

The harsh words of her ex-boyfriend Dwight came to her like an Amtrak Superliner. "Fat girls are good to play with but not to marry." *Was that what Marc was doing, playing?* she thought to herself.

Rose made her way through the house to her dressing room so she could get ready for bed. After slipping off her clothes, she went over to the freestanding mirror and stared at her reflection.

Even though her body was in balanced proportions, she was thick. Her breasts were large but firm. At five foot ten, two hundred and twenty pounds, she was much taller and larger than her siblings.

She turned to the side to examine her profile at that angle. Although she didn't have three stomachs, the one she had wasn't completely flat. She always took care of her skin, but she ran her hands across her large thighs and wondered how soft they might feel to a man's touch.

Suddenly, the silliness of her critical self-assessment came to her; she sighed and grabbed her red silk robe from the bed and walked across the hall to the bathroom.

She cleansed her face and walked back into her dressing room to hang up her clothes.

Rose opened her dresser drawer and pulled out a slinky, red chiffon chemise with a draped cowl neckline and slits up the side. She loved beautiful lingerie, even if she was the only person to see herself in it. Buying sexy things like that was always a pick-me-up for her.

Dropping her robe on the bed, she slipped the chemise over her head and went to her bedroom. She looked around the delicately decorated red room. She was happy with her accomplishments but had to admit to herself that she was tired of being in the big house alone.

She couldn't help but think about Marc and the words he'd said to her tonight. She wanted to believe he was sincere, but the last time she had believed in someone, her life ended up in turmoil.

Pulling back the duvet, she slipped under the covers. At that moment, Rose made herself a promise not to give Marc the opportunity to hurt her like Dwight did.

Monday morning, Marc and Jonathan were scheduled for another walk-through at Magic Moments. Rob was supposed to meet them there at nine o'clock.

As Marc pulled into the parking lot, a crew was installing

the marquee. Jonathan had already arrived, so Marc got out of his late-model Lincoln and walked inside.

He walked into the business office. "Good morning," he said, removing his black wool trench coat.

Rob got up from his seat and offered Marc his hand. Marc accepted, then waited for his brother, who was looking at some papers on his desk.

Jonathan glanced at his watch, then at Marc. "We're ready to get started." Standing, he walked around his desk and over to the door.

Marc and Rob followed behind him.

"Rob, I hope we've made progress on the kitchen," Marc said as they walked down the corridor.

"I think you'll both be pleased," Rob responded confidently.

As they walked through the building, Marc felt good about how things were taking shape. The chandeliers were being installed in two of the ballrooms. Carpet was being laid in the others.

Marc still worried about the kitchen. He wasn't confident that Rob and his crew were going to complete the job in a timely manner. For him, the kitchen was the most important part of the facility, outside of the whole overall look. If the food served there was not exquisite, the business would never get off the ground.

As they entered the kitchen, the brothers discovered that the walls had been completed, the cabinets had been installed, and the wiring for appliances had been finished. It was much better than the last time, but they still had a ways to go, which Marc didn't like.

"Rob, I thought I'd see more progress than this," Marc said sternly.

"The flooring was on back order and hasn't come in yet.

The appliances can be delivered and installed in a week after the flooring."

Marc looked at the tall, balding man curiously. "No more excuses, Mason; I want this finished in two weeks. If the flooring isn't here in a week, I'm going to take matters into my own hands." He walked swiftly from the room and back to his office.

Several minutes later, Jonathan opened the office door, walked in, and closed it behind him.

Marc leaned forward, placing his elbows on the desk. "I don't like this. If we're going to open in the next eight weeks, I want that kitchen completed, so I can figure out the other things we need."

Jonathan leaned forward. "I hear ya, bruh. I think we'll make it. Have you finished your menu?"

Marc sifted through the papers on his desk and pulled out a green folder. "Yes, here it is," he said, handing it to his brother.

"Good, I wanted to take this to the printer so we can have the brochures, business cards, letterhead, menus, and the contracts printed. I also have several interviews set up this afternoon for the receptionist position."

"I'm proud of you, li'l bruh. You really are handling your business," Marc said with a smile.

"You still haven't hired anyone for the sous-chef and catering manager position."

"I think I'm going to talk to Henry about it. He wouldn't have to be here every day, but I think he'd be an excellent catering manager," Marc suggested.

"He would be an excellent asset," Jonathan said, rising to his feet. "Well, I need to check on a few more things before heading off to the printer, so I'll catch you later," he said, walking to the door.

Jonathan opened the door before turning back to his brother. "I would like to contact Hearts and Flowers to help us with the grand opening. We can talk to them about their vision of what we should do."

A smile grew on Marc's face. "You are brilliant. I'll call Rose right now. She could help us with the floral décor."

Jonathan opened the door wider. "Cool. I'll see you later on," he said, leaving the room, closing the door behind him.

Marc opened his bottom desk drawer and pulled out the telephone directory. As he thumbed through the yellow pages, he looked up the number of Hearts and Flowers. The half-page ad read "Hearts and Flowers…where wedding dreams that last a lifetime begin.…"

He wore a silly grin on his face as he dialed the number in anticipation of speaking with the sassy Rose Hart. Marc thought that Jonathan's idea of the Hart sisters working with them was a little more than genius.

He strummed his fingers on the desk as he waited for someone to pick up the phone.

"Hearts and Flowers, Gwen speaking. How can I help you?" Marc heard a high-pitched voice say.

"Yes, good morning. I would like to speak to Rose Hart, please."

"May I tell Ms. Hart who's calling?"

"Yes, Marc Damon."

"Mr. Damon, please hold while I connect you."

Sultry ballads played as Marc waited patiently until he heard Rose's soothing voice come through the phone.

"Hi, Marc, how are you?" Rose asked, trying to keep the surprise out of her voice. She didn't think he'd call her so soon. She hadn't given him her number.

The sound of her voice stroked him. "I'm doing great, beautiful. How's it going with you?"

"Oh, busy as usual," she said casually.

"Well, I was wondering if you'd have dinner with me this evening," Marc asked.

"I'm sorry, Marc, but I've got so much to do here. I'm actually going to work late."

"What about lunch then?" He hoped she'd agree.

"I'm working through lunch. Why don't I call you by the end of the week, and we can get a bite then." Her tone was apologetic.

Marc had a spark of an idea, but he didn't want to divulge it to her. "Okay, let me give you my number, and I'll talk to you later."

Marc recited his number to her. He also wondered how she was going to react when he showed up at her shop with lunch.

"I'll talk to you soon," she said, drawing a circle around the number he'd just given to her.

After Marc placed the receiver on the cradle, he scribbled the address of her shop down, got up, and grabbed his coat on the way out of the building. He was going to prepare a lunch for Rose that she couldn't refuse.

Chapter 7

Marc drove through the white wrought-iron gates that led to the beautiful Georgian-styled mansion where Rose worked. He noticed the running fountain in the front of the circular driveway and the meticulously manicured lawn.

He pulled into a parking spot in the spacious lot, got out of the car, and retrieved the small wicker basket he'd found in Jonathan's pantry. He'd stopped by a local deli before going to the apartment to prepare a picnic.

Marc was impressed by the total look of the mansion as he made his way from the parking lot to the main entrance.

The oak double doors of the mansion had oval frosted glass with a large heart etched on one side and a bouquet of flowers on the other. A white wooden plaque with HEARTS AND FLOWERS spelled out in navy block letters was situated above the doorbell. He pressed the circular white button of the intercom.

"Hearts and Flowers, how can we help you?" said a soft voice through the speaker.

He pressed the button so he could speak. "Marc Damon here to see Rose Hart."

He pulled the gold handle when he heard the buzzing sound unlocking the door.

When Marc stepped inside the foyer, he couldn't believe how elegantly the place was decorated. The crystal chandelier hanging from the ceiling added to the royal look of the place.

He took note of the foyer's white marble flooring, which had the navy-blue-and-gold company crest of Hearts and Flowers in the top two corners and the monogram *H & F* in the bottom corners.

He continued down the hall until he came upon a large mahogany desk to his right with a petite, young woman sitting behind it.

Her intense stare amused Marc. She didn't greet him; she just stared.

"Hi, I'm Marc."

The young woman batted her eyes as if she was trying to pull herself together. "Mr. Damon, Rose will be with you in just a minute," the young woman said quickly, going back to the magazine that was open on her desk.

Marc continued to look around as he waited for Rose. There were more chandeliers, fluted columns, wall coverings, and rich-looking draperies. The mansion even had a *Gone With The Wind*–style staircase with a balcony.

He was admiring a painting on the wall when Rose approached.

"Marc, what are you doing here?" she said, surprised at his presence in her establishment.

He turned around, and his eyes soaked in her beauty. There she stood in front of him, wearing what looked like a company uniform. The white, cotton, button-down shirt with navy-blue-

and-gold embroidery gently hugged her lush breasts. She wore navy slacks and black boots with a side buckle. Her sleek sable hair was swept up. She was so beautiful.

Not wanting him to know how excited she was to see him, Rose tried to keep her eyes blank as she met his intense gaze. She had to admit to herself that his persistence should be commended.

His thin mustache curved upward.

She smiled. "You didn't answer me, Marc. What are you doing here?" Her eyes dropped to the wicker basket he held. "What's this?" She pointed.

"Since you were too busy to go out, I thought I'd bring lunch to you."

Rose gave him a dimpled smile this time. "That was so sweet of you. Come with me." Rose walked toward the corridor leading to her flower shop.

Marc watched the sway of her hips as he followed her. There were eighteenth-century Sheraton chairs and Louis the Fifteenth side tables situated along the hallway.

They came upon a long panel of see-through glass.

"This door leads to Ivy's office. Also the invitation and accessories viewing rooms are back there," Rose said as she continued to her shop.

They came to another door with a long panel of glass. The Hearts and Flowers crest, along with the words FLORAL STUDIO, was etched on the door.

"Rose, you all have done well. How did you find the building?" Marc asked as he stepped through the threshold of the door to the receiving area of her flower shop.

The small area was neat, with its sofa and two antique armchairs covered in red and gold damask. A large floral tapestry hung from the wall above the sofa. The coffee table had a spread of magazines devoted to everything from wedding flowers to gardening.

"Thank you. My uncle died and left the estate to me and my sisters," Rose said, continuing to walk through the receiving area. "We all love some aspect of a wedding and had been talking about opening a business for about two years. So when we inherited this place, Ivy thought it would be a great place to open a full-service wedding facility."

"It was certainly a brilliant idea," Marc said, following her.

They stepped into a much larger room, which Marc guessed was the showroom area.

He stopped to check it out. There were two wall units filled with flowers located on either side of the door. Bouquets of many sizes and an array of colors were beautifully displayed on the glass shelves.

Another display had been set up like an altar. It was beautiful, with three white, staggered columns with floral arrangements sitting on top. Lighted tulle connected the columns together, with two brass candelabras standing nearby.

"Rose, your creativity is unbelievable," he said, lifting one of the floral bouquets from the shelf.

"Thanks," Rose said, walking over to the wall unit he stood in front of.

He lifted another bouquet from the shelf. "Do you have photos of your work? You know, to show people if they ask," he asked, fingering the pearls and beads hanging from the flowers.

"Of course. I've been taking pictures as long as I can remember," Rose answered, touching the satin flower basket on the shelf next to her.

Marc placed the bouquet back on the shelf and then glanced

around the room. It was also decorated elegantly and had its own sitting area, but with a bigger, much sturdier worktable. There was also a huge, finely carved and gilded gold mirror on the wall.

"I really am impressed, baby," he said as he went to stand next to her.

Marc had to be careful when he got close to Rose because all he wanted to do was touch, hold, and caress her. And he didn't want to scare her away before he had the chance.

Rose turned to walk away. "Let me show you my workroom, and then we can go into my office to have lunch."

Marc tried to be careful and watch where his footsteps led him instead of concentrating on Rose's backside.

The workroom was a spacious one, with display coolers that had roses, lilies, and orchids of many shades. Any-thing a person might need when doing floral arranging lay on the shelves of the wooden wall unit in the room.

"So, this is where all the magic happens?" he asked her.

"Yes. I spend many hours in this room."

"It's so quiet back here. Don't you get lonely?" Marc said, eyeing a supply shelf.

"No, I listen to music while I work. Makes the time go by faster, and I seem to design better."

"I like listening to music as well when I'm cooking." He smiled. "See, we have a lot in common."

Rose gave him a smile in return. "Okay, now the tour is over. Let's go into my office. We do have a kitchen, but it's on the other side of the building. I think we'll be more comfortable in my office."

She didn't want her family to get the wrong impression, and if she took him into the kitchen to have their picnic, someone would surely make comments.

Rose had a spacious carpeted area in her office. "Why don't we set up here?" she suggested.

Marc opened one end of the picnic basket and pulled out a tablecloth, spreading it on the floor.

He dropped to his knees, then helped her down. "Thanks for taking time out to share this meal with me," he said before he kissed her hand.

Rose felt a tickle from his thin mustache. "You gave me no other choice."

"I didn't want you working so hard without any nourishment."

Rose laughed. "I would have eaten eventually."

"This may be true, but not with me."

Marc got up and went over to the CD player that sat on a shelf, looked for the power button, and turned it on.

Going back to his place on the tablecloth, he removed two paper plates, a container of potato salad, and two bags of Lay's plain potato chips from the basket.

Rose picked up one of the small bags of chips. "I love Lay's potato chips." She tore the bag open and popped a chip into her mouth.

"I didn't know what kind of sandwich you preferred, so I brought both tuna and chicken salad on a croissant for you," he said.

"Tuna's fine. Did you bring some eating utensils? If not, I have some," Rose said, touched by his gesture.

Marc pulled out prepackaged utensils and handed a set to her. "I brought strawberry-flavored bottled water," he said, pulling it out next.

Rose unwrapped her sandwich. "This is so nice, Marc. It feels good to take a break for a minute."

"Well, I hope you like the company, too," he said with a smile.

Rose reached over and placed her hand on top of his. "Of course, I like the company. I let you come in here, didn't I?" she said, laughing.

Marc chuckled. "That's true."

He took a bite of his sandwich. "Now, tell me how you got into the floral business. Why not do something else?"

Rose picked up the potato salad and spooned some onto her plate. "Well, when I was a little girl, I used to help my Aunt Daisy in her garden every summer. She told me that flowers can change a person's mood. They are lovely, delicate, and smell wonderful. Once I started working with her, I fell in love with them."

"I could tell you were very passionate about them when I saw what you did for Nicholas's wedding and the dinner party."

Rose felt her cheeks redden. "I can't see myself doing anything else."

"Did your Aunt Daisy give you the name Rose?"

Rose smiled at the mention of her dear Aunt Daisy. "As a matter of fact, she named all four of us. Ivy, Lili, Violet, and me."

"Your mother must have really trusted her sister to allow her to name all of you after flowers," Marc said.

Rose laughed. "Yeah, my father said that if they'd had a boy, my Aunt Daisy probably would have named him Thorn or Branch." She continued to laugh. "My mother said she couldn't bare the thought of calling her child a tree, so they stopped after my baby sister, Lili, just in case they did have a boy."

Marc's eyes twinkled as he watched Rose's features. He scooted closer to her and palmed the side of her face. "You are so beautiful when you smile."

Rose placed her hand on top of his without saying a word.

Marc studied her. With both hands now touching her face, he moved closer until their lips touched slightly. Her full, bronze-tinted, supple lips were warm and inviting.

Rose felt her resistance melting under his intense gaze and the warmth of his lips so close to hers.

He deepened the kiss, but only for a brief moment, then pulled back and noticed her eyes were still closed.

As her eyes fluttered open, Marc came into view. It wasn't her imagination; she'd just shared a kiss with him.

Marc stood and walked over to the CD player and turned it up. The beautiful acoustic sound of India Arie singing about someone being a beautiful surprise filled the room. The song said everything he'd been thinking since the day he'd met Rose Hart.

After kissing her, he hoped he hadn't been too quick in his actions, but he couldn't waste another day without experiencing the feel of his lips on hers.

He turned to her. "Rose, I'm sorry if I was too forward. I couldn't help myself, but I don't want you to think—"

Before he could complete his sentence, Rose was standing in front of him, with her finger over his full lips.

"It's okay, Marc. There was no harm done. I'm glad you did," she said, then paused briefly. "I wanted it just as much as you did," she admitted, giving him a nervous smile.

Marc stepped closer, aligning their bodies, his mouth hovering close to hers. He wrapped his arms around her, and she rested her head on his chest. They held each other like the other was the most precious thing in the world.

Rose lifted her head, and her eyes widened as she saw the smoldering passion lying in the dark pools of his eyes.

"Now what?" she asked softly.

Marc gazed down at her. "We'll take everything one step at a time. Nothing will happen that you don't want to happen. I promise you." He kissed her on the forehead.

For a few more minutes they stayed in each other's arms.

"Would you like a tour of the rest of the facility?" Rose asked.

"Sure. Why don't we finish what's left of our lunch first," Marc said, looking down at the spread of food on the floor.

They went back to the tablecloth and picked up where they had left off.

"Can I see you on Friday?"

"Sure," Rose said.

As soon as she tucked her legs to the side, she heard the chime go off in the front room, signaling someone had walked into the shop. Rose got back up to investigate.

Ivy was standing just inside the door, along with Dianna Hawkins and her two daughters, when Rose walked into the receiving area.

Ivy stepped forward. "Rose, I'd like you to meet Dianna Hawkins and her daughters, Cassaundra and Phoebe."

Rose approached the older woman first. Dianna Hawkins was a tall, light brown–skinned, statuesque woman wearing an expertly tailored dark green pantsuit with a big jeweled broach on the left lapel. Rose could tell the woman liked designer clothing and accessories because she was covered from head to toe with them. Even her handbag was a famous label.

Rose extended her hand. "Pleased to meet you, Mrs. Hawkins."

"Pleasure," Dianna said, giving Rose a slight handshake, barely touching her palm.

Rose approached the other two women. "Which one of you is the lucky bride?" she asked, giving them her famous dimpled smile.

"It sure isn't me. Not yet anyway," the taller one said, reaching her hand out to Rose. "I'm Phoebe."

"I figured as much." Rose accepted the offered hand.

Phoebe was just as tall as her mother, with a smooth, slender face and very slim figure.

Marc stepped from the back room. "Rose, I've got to get back."

Phoebe quickly came forward. "Marc Damon?" she inquired, walking toward him.

Marc looked at the cocoa-colored beauty. He'd recognized her right away and wished he hadn't come out. Anytime Phoebe Hawkins was present, it spelled trouble with a capital *T*. "Phoebe Hawkins?"

Phoebe hugged him. "I thought that was you. I haven't seen you since… I know it's been a while."

Not long enough, Marc thought to himself, trying to keep the pleasant smile on his face.

Ivy stared inquisitively at them, then at Rose.

Rose stood by and watched the exchange between them and wondered how they knew each other.

"Phoebe, honey, you know this man?" Dianna asked, walking over to her daughter.

Phoebe waved her perfectly manicured hand at her mother. "Sure, I know Marc," she said, throwing her hand on his chest. Phoebe looked up at him as she lightly rubbed his chest. "Still looking good, I see," she said, giving him a wink.

Marc moved away from her before she could stroke his chest again. He greeted Dianna and Cassaundra and met the scowl Ivy wore on her face. "It was nice to meet you. Now if you ladies will excuse me," he said and walked out of the room.

Rose watched him retreat, then turned around and looked right into Phoebe's curious eyes.

Dianna walked around the room, looking at the floral displays. "Rose, we would like to speak to you concerning the décor for Cassaundra's wedding," she said.

Rose glanced at the petite, young woman standing next to her mother. Cassaundra Hawkins was just as beautiful as her sister but in a subtle sort of way. She wasn't as tall, and by her quietness, Rose suspected she was not as confident. She hadn't said anything since they'd walked in.

Rose understood all too well how it felt to have an overbearing sibling. And from the exhibit Phoebe Hawkins just gave, Cassaundra didn't have a thing on her.

Cassaundra's quietness could also mean her mother was definitely in control of the wedding.

"I can schedule some time on next Thursday to meet with you," Rose said.

"What's wrong with right now?" Phoebe all but yelled, interrupting her mother before she could respond. "We'll be spending a considerable amount of money here."

Rose could tell Phoebe was used to getting her way, but today that would change. Rose wasn't quick to draw conclusions about not liking someone, but she knew she wasn't going to like working with Phoebe Hawkins.

Rose looked directly at her and spoke slowly. "Apparently, you misunderstood me. I'm not available until next Thursday."

She glanced at Ivy to make sure she wasn't going to contradict what she'd just told their customers. Ivy didn't say a word.

"Thursday will be fine," said Cassaundra. She gave Rose a sympathetic smile.

"Great," Rose said, walking to the back to retrieve her appointment book. Flipping it open to Thursday's date, she glanced at the page. "How about ten o'clock? You'll be my first appointment. I'll block off two hours."

"Sounds good to me," Cassaundra said, this time with a little more enthusiasm, giving Rose a genuine smile.

"Well, ladies, why don't we finish our tour?" Ivy suggested, extending her hand toward the door.

Cassaundra approached Rose. "Thanks for your time, Ms. Hart."

Rose shook the young woman's hand vigorously. "You are very welcome, and congratulations on your engagement."

"We've got some other stops to make, so let's go, darlings," Dianna said to her daughters.

Phoebe sauntered over to Rose. They both gave each other polite smiles.

Rose figured Phoebe's was fake.

"Would you be a dear and tell Marc good-bye for me?" Phoebe asked, pulling her leather gloves from her designer bag.

At first, Rose stared at her like she had lost her mind. She pulled herself together. "Marc doesn't work here, sweetie, so he doesn't have a secretary. But you could tell him yourself," Rose said politely, snapping her appointment book shut. "Have a good afternoon, ladies," she said, dismissing Phoebe Hawkins from her presence.

Phoebe frowned and stared for several seconds before turning and walking away.

After the Hawkins women were out of the room, Ivy gave Rose an unpleasant stare before she followed them.

Rose didn't care. She wasn't going to allow Ivy to steal her joy or Phoebe Hawkins to ruin her lunch with Marc.

Marc came from the back room with the picnic basket in his hand. "I've got to get back to work, baby, but I wanted to thank you for a wonderful lunch," he said before quickly kissing her lips.

"Phoebe told me to tell you good-bye," Rose said, wondering how he would respond.

"Umph," Marc said.

Rose was surprised at his nonchalant response. He acted as if she'd just said, "it's cold outside." "Thanks for coming by," Rose said, grabbing his hand, squeezing it firmly.

"Don't forget about Friday," he said, kissing her one last time before walking to the door.

"I'm looking forward to it," she said as she watched him walk out of the room.

Rose stood in the middle of the floor, with the taste of him still on her lips. She realized she'd stepped over that imaginary line she'd drawn between them to the point of no return. Now she had to let the whole scenario play out, no matter what.

"Rosie, girl, what have you gotten yourself into?" she said to herself as she walked back to her workroom to finish her tasks.

Later in the afternoon, Rose was cleaning up her work area when Ivy walked into the room.

"I just got off the phone with Jonathan Damon."

Rose stopped sweeping the floor. Her eyes immediately filled with panic. "Did something happen to Marc?"

"No," Ivy said, moving closer to her younger sister. "He called to ask if we would help with the grand opening of Magic Moments."

"Really?" Rose exhaled immediately, relieved.

Ivy looked puzzled. "Marc didn't tell you about it?"

"No, he didn't mention it." Rose went back to sweeping up the stems and debris from the floor.

"Well, why was he here earlier?" Ivy asked.

"He brought lunch in for me," Rose said, leaning against the broom.

"You shouldn't be entertaining men in here, Rose. This is a business establishment," Ivy spat out.

"We were just having lunch," Rose said, her volume increasing. She was about to explain but decided against it.

Rose began to push the broom with a little more vigor. Ivy was making her angry. "I'm not going to waste my breath trying to explain anything to you," Rose said sternly.

"I still say—" Ivy began before Rose cut her off.

"It's none of your business, anyway, Vee." Rose walked away.

"None of my business?" Ivy yelled, walking behind her. "We are running a business, Rosie, not the Love Connection."

Neither one of them saw their mother enter the room.

"Look, both of us are over three times seven, and you're not my mother." Rose spun around and spotted Louvenia standing in the doorway, stopping her words before she could form them.

"She sure isn't your mother, but I am," Louvenia interrupted, walking farther into the room.

She stared at both her daughters. "What is going on in here? I can hear you clear down the hall."

Neither young woman responded to her question.

Louvenia looked curiously at them. "Let me remind you two that you are sisters. You will always be sisters, no matter what happens in this life."

Rose stared at her mother, then at Ivy, who had her nose turned up.

"Why don't you invite Marc to dinner? I would love for you to introduce him to me," Louvenia said to Rose.

Rose looked puzzled.

"There's no need to give me that 'Mom, what are you talking about' look. I saw him as he was leaving the building." Louvenia gave her a bright smile.

Rose looked at Ivy, who still stood there with a deep frown on her face, then back at her mother. "I'll do just that."

"Good," Louvenia said before turning to Ivy. "You need to stop it." She pointed her finger in Ivy's face before she walked to the door. "I'll talk to you two later. I'm going upstairs to hem Bridgette Williams's wedding gown." She walked out, leaving Ivy and Rose alone once again.

They stood staring at each other. Rose broke the silence.

"Vee, why did you all of a sudden agree to work on a grand opening? I thought we were going to concentrate only on weddings," Rose said, not wanting to go back to the previous conversation.

"I think it's a sound business decision. It could build a partnership between us for future celebrations at Magic Moments," Ivy explained, walking to the door. "I've scheduled to meet with them at their establishment on Wednesday morning at ten," Ivy said as she walked out of the room.

Rose shook her head as she watched her stuck-up sister leave. The incident between them wasn't going to deter her from savoring her blossoming relationship with Marc.

Chapter 8

Two days later, Rose and Ivy drove over to Magic Moments for their meeting with the Damon brothers. Rose thought the facility was eye-catching on the outside, with the name of the company spelled out on the white building in gold.

Ivy pulled her navy blue BMW into the massive parking area.

"Wow, Vee, they really fixed up this old building," Rose commented, opening her car door.

"I wondered why it wasn't being used. It had so much potential," Ivy responded as she picked up her purse from the floor of the backseat. "I just hope they know what they're doing."

Rose rolled her eyes. Only Ivy would think of something like that to say.

They walked to the front of the white brick building, where there was a portico for limousine drop-offs and pickups. Rose pulled the handle on the glass door. She stepped inside, onto a wide, black floor mat with MAGIC MOMENTS written in gold cursive lettering. Underneath it was an Italian marble floor.

She waited for Ivy, who was checking out the place as if she were an inspector. They continued straight ahead until they reached the champagne- and taupe-colored oval lobby. It was surrounded by a striking winding staircase on each side. Rose immediately thought of several ways she could decorate the beautiful oak rails.

Her eyes traveled upward to the large chandelier. It looked like it had over a hundred crystals throughout.

"Vee, a huge floral centerpiece on a round glass table-top would look lovely right here." Rose pointed to the empty space.

"You could even decorate the stairs to make it look more dramatic," Ivy said.

"I was just thinking the same thing a minute ago."

They found a gold floor sign nearby with arrows pointing in the direction of the business office; restrooms; and the four ballrooms, the Embassy, Royal, Grand, and Chateau.

Rose pointed in the direction of the business office.

As they started to the left, Rose saw Marc coming toward them. She got that giddy feeling she always had when she saw him.

When he approached, Marc grabbed her hands and pulled her to him for a brief kiss. "Good to see you, baby," he said, looking into her eyes.

Rose's heartbeat accelerated. He always made her heart race. "This is a beautiful place, Marc. You and Jonathan should be proud of yourselves," Rose commented as she glanced at the traditional furniture placed throughout the hallway.

Marc turned and placed his arm around Rose's waist. "Thank you. It's still not completed. I'll show you around after the meeting."

He turned to see Ivy walking behind them and stopped, still holding Rose to his side. "Good morning, Ivy," he said with a smile.

"Good morning, Marc," she said dryly.

Marc gave her a smirk and squeezed Rose tighter to him. "Jonathan's in the conference room," he said as he led them down the hall.

Marc took them down a long corridor, then around the corner. He opened a door. Inside, Jonathan was sitting at a long black lacquer table, writing notes in a book.

Jonathan rose to his feet and smiled. "Ladies," he said and reached for Rose, hugging her to him. "Great to see you both again," he continued, attempting the same gesture with Ivy. She stepped back quickly.

"Please, have a seat," Jonathan said, pulling out Ivy's chair while Marc did the same for Rose.

The men took their seats as well, and Jonathan began sifting through his notes.

Ivy pulled out her PDA. She looked between the brothers. "Tell us, gentlemen, what can Hearts and Flowers do to help you with your grand opening?" she asked.

Jonathan laced his fingers together. "Well, first of all, we would like this meeting to be informal. We're practically family, and we don't want you two to feel pressured or uncomfortable."

The statement was too little too late because Rose had been uncomfortable ever since Marc had kissed her in the hall. Showing affection in public was something new to her.

"That's fine," Ivy said, situating herself erectly in her chair.

"Great," Jonathan said, going back to his notes. "We want the grand opening to be an elaborate affair, and we want to have it in six weeks."

Ivy shook her head in disagreement. "I thought I heard Marc say you're not quite finished with the renovation."

Marc nodded. "Yes, we're still working on the kitchen. I'd say it should be completed in two weeks."

"You can't pull off a spectacular event in four weeks," Ivy said. "There are too many tasks to be completed if you want it to be a success."

Rose sat up straight in her chair. "I think they can if we help them," she said to her sister.

Jonathan sat silently, with his fingers together and resting against his lips. Lowering them, he said, "That's why we called you two beautiful ladies over. We know we can't do it, but we figured you guys could since you're the best in the business."

"Don't stroke me, Mr. Damon. That's a lot of man hours, and we would have to monitor the completion of the kitchen to gauge when we can move forward."

"I realize that, Ms. Hart, but I would like you to help put the plan in place. We will follow your instructions to the letter."

Rose looked back and forth between Ivy and Jonathan. From the look on Ivy's face, she knew Jonathan was in for trouble. She glanced up at Marc, who was standing.

"While you two come up with the plan, I'm going to take Rose around to take a look at the place." He walked around the table and reached for Rose's hand. "Come on, baby."

After Marc closed the door behind them, he pulled Rose into his arms. "I really missed you," he said, his voice tinged with desire.

Rose smiled. "Marc, we just saw each other on Monday."

He gently touched her loose curls. "I know, but it seems like a decade ago." He leaned to kiss her, but Rose stopped him.

"You are such a flirt. Do you talk to women this way all the time?"

"What way, baby?" He lifted her hand, placing a kiss on her knuckles.

"See what I mean? Most men don't kiss a woman's knuckles. Only the suave and debonair guys do that stuff."

A twinkle appeared in Marc's eyes, and the hair above his lip moved upward. "Well, I could kiss you somewhere else, but we'd have to be alone for that."

Rose gently hit his shoulder. "You are something else. Let's take that tour before you say something that gets you in trouble."

They walked hand in hand back toward the lobby area of the facility. Marc took her into the ballrooms. The high ceilings in each projected a sense of openness and added comfort, as did the brass chandeliers, the marble bar areas, and the hardwood parquet floor, which stretched the length of the dance floor.

In one of the ballrooms, Marc twirled Rose around the empty space, then drew her close. He began to sway to the beat of the music in his head.

"You feel so good, Rose," he whispered, moving even closer to her.

Rose shivered as his warm flesh touched her ear. She had no desire to move away from the fire that had ignited between them so quickly.

She ran her hands across the wide expanse of the back of his shoulders. The smoldering look in his eyes when she looked into them made her nipples harden. Its intensity was almost too much, and Rose took one tiny step toward him, resting her head on his shoulder.

For several minutes they swayed to the quietness of the room, until Marc released her.

Grabbing her hand, he said, "Let's see the rest of the place before I lose control of myself."

Rose followed him to the staircase inside the Royal Ballroom, where he allowed her to walk in front of him up to the Bridal Suite.

Rose walked around the spacious area. "Marc, this is really elegant," she said, looking at the beautiful paintings and sconces on the antique-looking walls.

"It also has a private bath," Marc said, walking over to the door that led to it.

"So the bride and groom could actually be announced and come out of the door we just came in?" Rose asked.

"Yes, but this is the only ballroom that has stairs on the inside of the room as well as the outside."

"I really like the place, but I want to see the kitchen." Rose began to walk toward the door.

Marc stopped her. "It's too dusty in there right now, baby. Have you gotten any ideas about the floral décor?"

"There's so much we could do with a place like this. Let me think about it, and I'll tell you what I come up with."

"I trust you, baby. I know whatever you do will be fantastic." Marc reached out and palmed the side of her face. He moved toward her inch by inch until their lips were mere inches apart. "I don't know what you've done to me, Rose Hart, but I'm hooked."

Rose searched his eyes. "I think you already have an admirer."

Marc pulled back, looking at her curiously. "What are you talking about, baby?"

"Phoebe Hawkins."

Marc dropped his hands and began to walk away. "I knew Phoebe when I lived in Boston. I used to date a friend of hers, but that's the extent of it." He promised himself not to think about, much less discuss, the conniving ways of Phoebe Hawkins.

"Umm hmm," Rose said slowly.

"No, really, and I never dated Phoebe." He lifted her hand, pulling her close to him again. "I've got everything I need right here."

Rose looked into his eyes and saw the sincerity in them. She couldn't deny the fact that she was interested in him as well.

"Hmm," he said before kissing the tip of her nose. "So, can we drop the Phoebe subject and talk about us?" He rested his forehead against hers.

Rose slowly nodded in agreement; then she thought to herself that everything she'd done to protect herself from getting hurt again didn't seem important now. All she wanted was Marc.

He captured her lips, this time in a soulful kiss filled not only with passion, but promise. It made Rose's stomach flip-flop with excitement.

She relaxed her body against his, and Marc slipped his tongue in her mouth, caressing it seductively. The thoroughness of his tongue undid her. He made her lose herself in the kiss.

The next time, he went a little deeper, intensifying the kiss to the point where she had to stop to catch her breath.

As many women as he'd had in his arms over the years, none of them had ever touched his heart the way Rose did. Her voice stroked him, her body called to him, and the kiss they'd just shared hypnotized him.

"Marc, I think we should get back. I'm sure Ivy is looking for me."

"Sure, baby, but can I see you tonight?"

"Marc, I usually don't get this serious with a man so fast."

Rose wanted to explain herself. She didn't want things to go too fast but loved the attention he gave her.

Marc gently squeezed her to his side. "Baby, don't worry. Remember I told you nothing will happen that you don't want to happen."

That's what I'm afraid of, Rose thought to herself. At the rate they were going, she would let a lot of things happen that maybe shouldn't, but oh well.

They walked out of the ballroom and headed back to the conference room.

Ivy glanced at her gold bezel watch when Rose entered the room.

"Have you guys come up with a game plan?" Rose asked with enthusiasm.

Ivy looked up at her. "Took you long enough."

Rose picked up her purse from the chair and pulled out a piece of paper and a pen. She scribbled her home telephone number on it and gave it to Marc.

"Call me this evening," she said to him.

He took the paper and placed it in the front pocket of his black slacks. "I'll talk to you soon," he said, kissing her briefly on the lips.

"Rose, we need to get back. I have several afternoon appointments," Ivy said, leaving her chair. She reached over the table and held out her hand. "Jonathan, we'll talk in a couple of days."

Jonathan rose to his feet and took her hand, drawing it to his mouth. "Thanks for all your wonderful ideas," he said. But just as he was about to place a kiss on her knuckles, she quickly pulled her hand back.

As Ivy walked past Marc to the door, she gave him a dry good-bye.

Rose looked at the two men and hunched her shoulders. She didn't understand why Ivy acted the way she did, but it was definitely time to find out.

Pulling the door behind her, she caught up with her sister, who had already made it halfway down the hall.

"Vee, wait for me, please," Rose said, walking swiftly and trying to catch her breath at the same time. "You know I can't walk as fast as you, so wait."

Ivy stopped in a huff when she got to the lobby.

As they walked to the car, both women were silent until they were seated inside.

"Vee, why did you treat Jonathan the way you did? He was only trying to be nice," Rose said, pulling the seat belt across her and securing it.

"What are you talking about, Rosie? I was very cordial to him," Ivy said, pulling out of the parking lot.

"Every time he went to touch you, you'd flinch or jerk your hand away. You did the same thing to Marc at Destiny's wedding reception."

"It's all in your mind, Rosie," Ivy said, pressing the silver knob of the radio.

"You were just plain rude." Rose turned and stared at her sister. "And don't ignore me, Vee. Why didn't you come to Destiny's dinner party?"

"I was busy." Ivy glanced in Rose's direction. "Now just because you want to fall all over yourself for Marc and Jonathan Damon doesn't mean I have to do the same. I'm not falling for their bull. Men like them don't mean any woman any good."

Ivy turned up the volume on the radio. It now blared the sounds of Luther Vandross singing about a woman being on his mind.

Rose turned the radio back down. "How can you say that? You don't know anything about them and wouldn't give them a chance to get to know you." Rose rolled her eyes and then hit the window ledge with her elbow before she blew out a big breath, leaning her head against her palm.

When they were little, she and Ivy argued a lot. Rose had promised herself she wouldn't allow her sister's know-it-all attitude to influence her. She took a deep breath before she said anything else to Ivy.

Rose glanced at her sister from the corner of her eye. "Vee, did you hear a word I just said to you?"

"I heard you, Rosie, but like you said the other day, we're both grown, so I'll mind my business as soon as you mind yours." Ivy snapped her head in Rose's direction.

They both were silent; then Ivy reached over and patted Rose's arm. "Rosie, don't get your hopes up too high with Marc."

Rose rolled her eyes at Ivy. She wanted to hit her. Ivy always brought gloom with her, so Rose didn't say anything else. She just shook her head in distaste. She had chosen that method because if she'd opened her mouth, they would probably have gotten into an accident.

Chapter 9

Ivy wore Rose out so much with her shenanigans that Rose had barely finished the sample bouquets she was supposed to have ready. She had made up her mind to come in an hour early in the morning to complete them before her client came to view them.

By the end of the day, she was tired, but she did, however, want to clean up her work area, so she could go home and relax.

"Rosie." She heard her baby sister call out to her.

"Lili, I'm back here," she yelled.

Her sister Lili was small and petite like their mother, with skin the color of a walnut like their father. She was really a free spirit. She didn't have a problem telling you exactly what was on her mind. She wanted to live her life her way, by her own rules, and anybody who didn't like it, well, that was too bad. She'd even had red streaks put in her hair in spite of their mother's disapproval.

Rose watched the door, waiting for her to walk in.

"What did you do to the Ice Queen?" Lili asked, smiling.

Rose laughed because Lili had given Ivy the nickname. She

always said if a man wanted to get next to Ivy, he'd have to defrost her first. Rose smiled at the memory.

Lili wore their signature Hearts and Flowers embroidered white shirt, but she had added the letter *L* to the left side. She liked to wear monogrammed shirts or a pin with her initials.

Rose threw her right hand in the air. "I'm not thinking about Vee. Who cares about her being mad."

Lili's eyes widened. "What happened between you two, girl, and don't leave out the juicy parts." She chuckled as she took a seat at the worktable.

Rose told her about the meeting they had had over at Magic Moments and about Ivy's behavior.

Lili stood up. "See, I told you. Vee ain't ever going to get a man. She's going to be an old maid."

Rose shook her head. "But she doesn't have to be. She's beautiful, smart, and very business savvy."

"Girl, a man wants something warm to cuddle up next to in bed at night, not a day planner," Lili said as she wrapped her arms around herself, swaying from left to right.

"I thought you had a cake to prepare for this weekend?" Rose said, laughing, just as the telephone rang.

"I do."

Rose walked over to the wall phone and picked it up. She hoped it wasn't Ivy wanting to tell her off. She didn't feel like getting indignant with her.

She picked up the receiver. "Rose Hart speaking."

"Hey, baby,"

"Marc?" Rose smiled, then saw the animated look on her sister's face.

"Have you heard of Shaker Village?"

"Yes, as a matter fact, Ivy bought a condo there last year. Why?"

"I wanted to go over and check it out. Would you like to come with me?"

"What time are you going over there?" Rose asked, watching Lili inch closer and closer to her, trying to hear her conversation.

"Not until Friday at four o'clock. The business office closes at five," he said.

"I can meet you over there. What section are you going to see?"

"I don't know, so meet me in the business office."

"Okay."

"I'll see you soon," Marc said.

Rose waited for Marc to disconnect the call before she hung the receiver in the cradle.

Lili was right in her face. "Uh, it looks like you left something out of the story you told me earlier." She stared at Rose.

"What?" Rose asked, looking at her curiously.

"You are a trip. I'm talking about Marc. Since when did you two become an item?"

Rose held up her hand to stop Lili. "We're getting to know each other," she said, smiling.

"Umph."

"Lili, don't run with what you think is going on between me and Marc, okay?" Rose pleaded. "You'll be way off base." Rose could tell by the gleam in her little sister's eyes that she was going to go blab what she thought she knew to her family. Lili loved to do that.

"I'm not running anywhere." Lili leaned closer to Rose. "Does Mama know you're seeing him? Girl, 'cause if she does, she'll have you married to him before the sun goes down."

Both women laughed.

"She told me to invite him for dinner on Sunday."

"Bad career move, sis. You know Mama just might have Aunt Liz, Aunt Willa Mae, and Uncle Jack over for dinner. Then they're going to give the man the third degree. You shouldn't do that, girl." Lili shook her head.

"Stop it, Lili," Rose said, playfully hitting her sister's arm. "Everything will be okay because I'm going to keep Louvenia in check," Rose said with assurance.

"Yeah, right. Louvenia is a hot mess, and we both know it. Remember she wants one of us to get married, and since you're the one with man potential, my sister, it looks like it's going to be *Y O U*." Lili pointed at Rose. "I'll check you later. Don't forget to be careful 'cause the Ice Queen is on the rampage."

Lili walked out the door, leaving Rose to think about what she'd said about their mother. Louvenia Hart could be a force to be reckoned with when she wanted something. Rose hoped she wasn't making a mistake by inviting Marc to dinner at her mother's. She got ready to go home and get some rest. She hoped to avoid seeing Ivy on her way out.

On Friday, Rose met Marc at the condominium complex. Shaker Village was a fairly new condominium community on the east side of Taylor. The condos were exquisite contemporary living spaces in a quiet neighborhood.

The leasing manager showed them three different floor plans that were available. Marc decided on the last one they were shown. It had two bedrooms, a master bath, an office, a dining room, and a huge eat-in kitchen.

"Ivy lives in section B on the other side," Rose said and pointed in the general direction as they were leaving the condo.

Marc pretended to wipe his forehead. "Thought you were going to tell me she lives next door."

Rose grinned, playfully hitting his arm. "Stop that," she said as they walked back to the leasing office. "It didn't take you long to choose a condo. You really didn't need me here."

Marc grasped her hand. "Yes, I did," he said, squeezing it. He wanted her to be with him.

Inside the office, he looked at the digital clock on the wall. "Why don't we grab a bite to eat? We'd planned to go out tonight, anyway."

"Sure. Where do you want to go?" Rose asked.

"I would invite you back to the apartment, but I don't know what Jonathan's plans are for the evening."

"That's not a problem; we can go some place around here," Rose said. "Let's go to Bennigan's. It's pretty fast," she continued.

"I'm not in a hurry, baby. I want to spend as much time as I can with you," Marc said. "Let's leave your SUV here in the lot and take my car," he suggested.

They beat the weekend crowd at Bennigan's. They sat at a table and looked over the menu, then ordered their food and drinks.

Rose pulled out a small card. "This is for you," she said, handing it to him.

Marc's eyes sparkled as he accepted it. "Gifts already? I must be doing something right."

He tore it open and found a note written on her personalized stationery. It had a faint floral scent to it. Placing the paper close to his nose, he inhaled before flipping it open.

As he read the note, he glanced up at her, causing Rose's cheeks to redden.

Rose had told him how the simple gesture of bringing her lunch had touched her deeply. She'd never forget it.

Closing the card, he reached across the table and waited for her to respond.

Rose looked down at his hand stretched across the table toward her. She'd meant every word she'd written. Slowly, she stretched out her right hand, and as soon as the tips of her fingers touched his, he picked up her hand, lacing her fingers with his.

"You believe I'd do anything for you, baby, don't you?" he said huskily.

"So when did you decide to be a chef?" Rose asked, changing the subject.

She gently removed her hand from his.

"When I was thirteen."

"That's pretty young. Were you burning up your mom's kitchen?" Rose chuckled as the waitress placed their drinks on the table.

"Before my mom got sick, she taught me and Jonathan how to cook. I guess I was about eleven and he was nine. She started us with easy things, you know." He stopped and took a sip of the Sprite from his straw. "She didn't want us to have to depend on someone else for things we could do for ourselves."

"Smart mama. To teach boys how to be independent is fantastic." Rose sipped on her iced tea with lemon.

Marc sighed. "Yeah, she was."

Rose slid her hand over and caught his fingers.

Marc looked up at her. "She died when I was thirteen."

Rose laced her fingers with his. "Oh, Marc, I'm so sorry."

"Don't be. She was a great woman."

"What happened to her, if you don't mind me asking?"

"She had breast cancer. At first, it looked like she was going to be okay, but after she came home from the hospital, I just knew things would never be the same."

Rose pulled her hand back. She could see the sadness in his eyes.

Marc picked up the card she'd given him and placed it in the inside pocket of his jacket. He was the first to speak after they sat silently for several moments. "My mother's sister Rachel and her husband, Isaiah, raised us."

"Where was your father?" Rose asked.

"My father died eight months after my mother at his job. They say he died of a heart attack, but I think his heart was broken."

"Wow, that's a lot for two teenage boys to handle."

"Yes, but Aunt Rachel always told me that I handled myself like a little man."

"I think your mother prepared you in her own way," Rose said, picking up her glass.

"Yes, I agree, and that's why all of our children, be they boys or girls, will learn how to cook," he said casually.

The waitress came just as Rose was about to choke on her tea. The young woman patted Rose on the back vigorously.

"Ma'am, are you okay? I'll get you some water." She rushed off.

Marc quickly got to his feet and was by her side, hunkered down beside her.

"Rose, baby, are you okay?" he asked, then looked up to see the waitress bringing Rose a glass of ice water.

Rose cleared her throat and picked up the glass. Taking small sips, she kept trying to clear her passageway. Finally, she shook her head yes.

"I'm fine," she said as Marc made circular motions on her back.

"Are you sure?"

"Yes." She leaned down and kissed him.

Marc went back to his seat.

"See, there you go again, Marc," Rose said, now that she'd caught her breath and cleared her throat.

"Did you hear yourself a few minutes ago?"

"Which part?" he asked, looking down at the plate the waitress placed in front of him. When she walked away, he leaned forward. "I should have made us dinner," he said, picking up his fork and knife and cutting into his steak.

"Don't try to change the subject," she said.

"Oh, you're talking about the part when I said all of our children will learn to cook."

"Precisely." Rose nodded her head.

"They'll be beautiful children, too," he said easily, continuing to eat his food.

"Stop saying things you don't mean, Marc. You might say such things around the wrong person one day and regret that the words ever came from your lips."

"I can repeat anything I say, baby. I say what I mean and mean what I say."

She sat staring at him, not even sampling the grilled chicken she'd ordered. "Would you like to come to my parents' house for dinner Sunday afternoon?"

Marc beamed. "Oh, so now I'm meeting the family."

"It's only dinner, Marc." She giggled.

"I'd be glad to come."

"Bring Jonathan, too," Rose suggested as she sprinkled pepper on her broccoli. She looked up and spotted Phoebe Hawkins coming toward them.

Rose hoped Phoebe hadn't seen them, but once she saw the beaming smile on the slender woman's face, she knew Phoebe's destination was their table.

"Your friend is coming our way," Rose whispered right before Phoebe approached the table.

"Good evening." Phoebe beamed, looking only at Marc.

Marc looked up briefly from his meal and muttered a hello, then went back to his dinner.

Phoebe stood next to the table for several moments before she turned and spoke to Rose.

"Ms. Hart," she said to Rose, her eyes still on Marc.

"How are you this evening, Phoebe?" Rose responded.

"Great," Phoebe said as she continued to stare at Marc, who wasn't paying her any attention.

Rose noticed that this was the second time that Marc had withdrawn when Phoebe was around. Now she was really puzzled by his reaction to the beautiful woman. She suspected they had a history.

"Marc, I heard you and your brother have gone into business together. Congratulations," Phoebe said.

"Thanks," Marc responded. He hoped she didn't think he was going to ask her to join them. The only place he wanted to invite her to he'd never say aloud.

"Well, I guess I'll let you get back to your meal," Phoebe finally said after she saw Marc didn't wish to engage in conversation with her.

"It was good seeing you, Phoebe," Rose said, watching the disappointment on her face as she walked away.

Phoebe didn't say another word. She walked over to her waitress, who was still waiting for her to take her seat.

Rose stared at Marc, who had become quiet.

"Marc," Rose called out to him.

Marc looked at her. "Yes, baby?" he whispered.

"What is going on with you and Phoebe? Every time she comes around, you treat her like the plague," Rose said.

Marc reached for her hand. "Baby, it's a long story."

"But I thought you two never dated." Rose was confused as to why he didn't want to explain things to her.

Marc squeezed her hand. "I told you the truth, baby. I wouldn't lie to you about something like that." He had put the past behind him and didn't want to dredge it up.

Rose looked at him curiously. She decided to leave the subject alone for now. She remembered something her Aunt Daisy told her once about catching more flies with honey than with vinegar. She'd find out what Phoebe Hawkins's real story was soon enough.

From where the waitress had seated her, Phoebe had a good view of Marc and Rose.

She opened her designer tote bag and pulled out the morning's paper. She hadn't had time to read it. She turned to her horoscope. It read, *You will have a second chance at love today. Grab hold of it, and you will get your heart's desire.*

Phoebe smiled, looking up from the paper and over at Marc. She never thought she'd get another opportunity to pursue him. After running into him the other day, she figured it was a sign that she could make things right between them.

But after he treated her coldly, she felt she needed to approach this situation another way.

"Time to put plan B into action," she said to herself. Phoebe always got what she wanted, and her horoscope had never failed her.

Phoebe stared across the room at Marc, with a wicked smile on her face. "Ready or not, Marc Damon, here I come," she whispered.

Chapter 10

Marc and Rose finished their meal, and the waitress came with the check. Marc pulled several bills out of his wallet.

They headed to the car. Marc opened Rose's door and allowed her to slip into the passenger seat before going around to the driver's side.

Rose turned slightly in her seat. "I need to warn you that my family isn't like the Huxtables. They are a trip, so get ready."

Marc squeezed her hand. "Baby, everybody's family has a few oddballs in it," he said, glancing back at the road.

"Ivy's going to be there, too, and you've already experienced her, so just a word of caution."

"Rose, your sister doesn't bother me. She just needs somebody to rock her world."

Rose laughed.

Marc's face grew serious. "No joke. Aren't you much happier now that I'm in your life?"

Rose's face reddened. "You and I just started seeing each other. I've never acted like my sister, Marc."

"That's exactly my point." Marc reached over to squeeze her hand.

"The right brotha just hasn't come along and swept Ivy off her feet. I'm already taken, and she's not my type, anyway."

Rose looked at him curiously. "Oh, and I am?"

"If you'd asked me that question this time last year, I would have said no. But from the moment I laid eyes on you, there was no turning back. I can't even tell you the one thing in particular that attracted me to you. All I know is I want to get to know the real you."

Marc pulled into the parking lot of the condominium complex and killed the motor.

He removed his seat belt and turned slightly sideways. "I want to get to know the Rose Hart that only the reflection in the mirror is privy to."

Rose was speechless. She didn't know if she was ready to reveal herself like that to another person. Confusion hit her because she didn't know if she wanted to take the gamble and maybe lose.

"You don't have to say anything right now. I want to be with you, and nothing will stop me. I know you're feeling me, too. I can feel it in here," he said, pointing to his chest.

Marc opened his car door and then turned back to her. "I'm going to follow you home."

"You don't have to do that, Marc," Rose said, pulling the handle of the car door.

Marc had made it around to her side by the time the door opened wide.

He reached for her hand to assist her.

Rose went to her car and climbed in.

Marc stood inside her open car door. "I don't want you to take anything I've said tonight lightly, Rose. I meant every single word."

Rose patted his face. She was so touched by him. She didn't want to believe that it was happening to her, that a handsome man was interested in her. She was afraid she'd wake up and find out it was only a dream. But she was touching the man she was starting to fall in love with. His honesty only added to her attraction to him.

Marc gave her a gentle kiss before shutting the car door.

Rose started her car and drove away. As she looked through her rearview mirror, she saw him following behind her. She realized then, it was really too late to back out or give excuses. She was falling in love with Marc Damon.

All the way home, Rose glanced into her rearview mirror to see if Marc was still following her. Sure enough, he was right there. That thought made her smile. The only other man that really cared about her safety was her father.

Rose pulled her car up to the back of her house and got out. Marc had parked behind her and was getting out of his vehicle by the time she'd walked to it.

"This is me," she smiled, nodding toward the house behind them.

"I'll wait until you're inside before I leave," Marc said.

Rose wanted to ask him to come inside, but she didn't want him to get the impression that she was inviting him to her bed. As that thought quickly entered her mind, she wondered if that was really what she wanted…to share a bed with him.

She glanced at her watch. "Would you like to come inside?" she said quickly, before she changed her mind. "It's still early."

A wide grin grew on Marc's face. "Sure. Lead the way."

Rose walked around the back of his car to the side door that led to the kitchen.

Marc took the keys from her and unlocked the door. He stepped back in order for Rose to enter the house first.

Rose flicked the light switch near the door and walked up several steps to the hall leading to the kitchen. She sat her purse down in a chair and took off her coat.

"Marc, would you like something to drink?" she asked, walking into the kitchen.

"No, I'm good. Why don't you show me the house?" he said, looking around the room.

"Okay. Would you like for me to take your jacket?"

Marc shrugged off his lightweight black leather coat and handed it to her.

"Come with me," Rose said, taking it from him. She walked through the hallway to the coat closet.

"Let's start down here." She pointed to her right.

Teak bookcases and African abstract art in shadow boxes lined the hallway leading to the living room.

The regal-looking room was decorated with a sophisticated gold damask sofa with a feather pattern and distinctive gold, scrolled arms and a camel back. There were four decorative pillows plumped on it. The wing chair was made of solid hardwood and had a black finish and a gold damask, trellis leaf pattern.

The wrought-iron cocktail table featured alternating scrolls and medallions with an aged gold finish. On top of the table stood three stylish gold resin candlesticks with a red marble finish and decorative gold acanthus feet. They held three ruby red pillar candles.

There was a seventeenth-century French savonnerie carpet lying on the floor not too far from the Victorian-style beveled glass screen in front of the fireplace.

"You could help me decorate my place," Marc commented as he followed her to the next room.

Her dining area was just off the living room. A beaded chandelier with an antique gold finish and five lights hung above an antique dining table that seated six. A hutch was nestled in a corner, giving the room a very formal feel.

"Baby, you didn't answer me about helping me decorate my new place," Marc said.

"Whatever you need me to do, just let me know."

Marc raised his brow. "Anything?"

Rose looked over her shoulder. "You know what I mean, Marc." She continued down the hall, and they ended up back in the eat-in kitchen. "You sure you wouldn't like something to drink?" she asked.

"Am I making you nervous, Rose?" Marc whispered from behind her.

He had come so close, she could feel his breath on the back of her neck.

In an attempt to cool down from the heat that had begun to rage through her, Rose opened the refrigerator door. "What made you ask me that?" she said without looking at him.

"Show me the rest of the house?" he suggested.

Marc knew Rose was afraid to take him to the second floor of the home. Because if he was having the same effect on Rose as she was having on him, their relationship would change drastically tonight. For him, it had already changed.

Rose bent to glance at the contents in her refrigerator. She pulled out a bottle of water. "Let's go into the den," she suggested, closing the refrigerator door.

Her action just proved Marc right. He smiled and followed Rose into a spacious room decorated in a more relaxed and nontraditional tone. There was a large, fabric-covered pit styled set, a big-screen television, and an entertainment center. In the corner was a tall wooden curio cabinet with all types of salt and pepper shakers inside.

Marc walked over to the curio cabinet. "You collect salt and pepper shakers. I've never seen a collection this extensive before." He opened the door and picked up a matching set.

Rose had salt and pepper shakers made of everything from wood to fine crystal.

"I've been collecting them since I was a teenager. I like to get the odd ones," she said, picking up a pair in the shape of a small cabbage. "Like these, which I got when I went to visit my cousin in Detroit one summer." Rose picked up another set. "I bought these when I went to California to a floral show."

Marc picked up the pair on the end. "This one looks pretty special." They were in the shape of ceramic roses.

Rose replaced the items she held in her hand at the same time as Marc did.

Their hands touched. Their eyes met and held.

"Baby, there is no need for us to deny what we both know is there," Marc stated after a brief pause.

Rose closed the door to the curio cabinet and moved away, and Marc came behind her. Placing his hands around her waist, he buried his face in her neck, holding her tight.

"There's nothing to be ashamed of, Rose," he whispered. "It's a natural reaction when two people are physically attracted to each other. It is even more powerful when they are emotionally connected."

Slowly, he turned Rose around and lifted her chin so he could look into her eyes. "I know what I feel for you is real. I want to explore a deeper relationship with you. What I don't want is to make you feel obligated to make love to me. I want you to feel the same as I do when our bodies connect."

Tears were brimming in Rose's eyes as she watched the intense passion in Marc's. He was serious, and she wanted to share the pleasure she knew he could give to her, but she was also frightened that he would be disappointed.

Standing in front of her was a man she wanted more than she'd ever thought she could want another person.

Rose took one tiny step forward. Her lips trembled. "I want it too," she began, but Marc covered her mouth with his, arresting her words.

She responded to his kiss with passionate fervor. His lips drove out a depth of feeling and emotion she never knew she had.

Marc slowly led her over to the sofa. He sat and pulled her onto his lap. He rained kisses on her forehead and then behind her ear.

Finally, he planted a wet kiss on her soft lips, then retreated, only to come back again with the same vigor and intensity as before.

"Marc," Rose called in a whisper. Her hands explored his hard chest through his button-down shirt. She wanted to be loved by him.

"Hmm," Marc said in an almost incoherent voice. He rubbed the palm of his hand across the front of her blue pullover shirt.

Her nipples hardened, and sensations rushed through her. Using the pad of his thumb, he slowly ran his hand across the protruding points in her shirt.

Rose began to squirm on his lap as she felt his manhood come alive.

Marc placed his hand at the hem of her shirt, and she automatically lifted her arms, allowing him to remove it.

"You are so beautiful," Marc said in a raspy tone.

His eyes beheld the lacy peach bra. Her rounded breasts pressed against the demicup. He held the outer curve of them both, causing Rose to push against them.

Marc pulled Rose closer, and he buried his face between her breasts, moving his hands around to the back to free them.

As Rose shrugged out of the bra, Marc assisted her by sliding the lacy material down her arms, dropping it on the floor. Switching their positions on the sofa, he laid Rose against one of the large pillows so he could get better access to her.

He lifted her legs and pulled off her shoes, kissing her ankles and continuing upward.

Rose didn't have a single sensible thought. She was in a sexual haze. She didn't want to think; she just wanted to feel. She'd avoided this intense pleasure for so long, and tonight she wanted to savor as much as she could.

Rose felt Marc's hands on her exposed breasts.

She reached for his belt buckle, trying to unfasten it, but Marc stopped her.

"I don't want to take this moment for granted. The first time we make love, I want to take my time and love you like you deserve to be," he said huskily.

He looked down at the evidence of his erection. "If we continue, there will be no turning back. I don't want you to think this is a booty-call, because it's not."

Rose watched the tender look Marc gave her as he spoke. Her own eyes were expressive and quick. She pulled him on top of her and kissed him passionately.

Marc retreated first. "Baby, I don't think we're ready yet," he said, lifting himself up from the sofa.

Marc rose to his feet. "If I stay, I'll be here til morning." He picked up her undergarment from the floor and handed it to her.

Suddenly, Rose felt ashamed.

Marc palmed her face. "Baby, you never disappoint me. When the time is right, we will share something magical and wonderful." He kissed her again.

Rose put her clothes back on, and Marc sat beside her once again. He pulled her into his arms, and she lay against his chest, without either of them saying a word.

"I like the way this feels," he said, kissing the top of her dark brown hair.

Rose sighed. "Me, too," she said, circling his nipples through his shirt with her finger.

"I'd better go before we start all over again, and I can't stop," he said.

Rose walked with him to the coat closet and removed his leather coat.

She handed it to him and watched as he slipped into it.

Marc stretched out his arms. "Come here, baby."

Rose went into his arms, and he held her securely.

"We have more between us than a lot of people who've been together for years," Marc whispered. "We have an emotional connection, and whenever we do make love, it will only be an expression of what's already there."

The tears that welled in her eyes began to spill down her cheeks.

Marc wiped them away. "Sometimes this whole thing scares me, so that's why I want to take my time. So I won't scare you. I want us to share this experience step-by-step together. Do you understand?"

Rose could only shake her head because she didn't want to open her mouth. She didn't think anything would come out.

Marc kissed her forehead. "I'll call you later."

Rose walked him to the door.

"Go on and lock up," he said, waiting for her to close the door and engage the locks.

Marc went to his car, placed the key in the ignition, and sat there. The sexual chemistry between them was explosive. Even now he felt desire swirling so deep, he had to calm himself before he could start his automobile.

He had expressed to Rose more than he'd planned. After her submissiveness, he couldn't help himself. He felt her return his kiss with reckless abandon. He now knew her feelings matched his in that way.

He looked up at the light shining in a second-floor window. From the silhouette he saw there, he knew Rose was watching him.

Backing out of the driveway, he glanced back at the house. He promised himself he would get the opportunity to show Rose just how much he loved her. *Did I just say love?* he thought to himself as he drove away from 1542 Hendricks Street and possibly the greatest love of his life.

Rose watched Marc drive away until she couldn't see his red taillights anymore. Tonight had been a turning point for them and a new discovery for her. She had never imagined becoming so emotionally involved with someone so quickly, but that's what happened to her.

She went to the bathroom to free her face of her makeup and quickly jumped in the shower. After drying herself off with a thirsty mauve-colored towel, she wrapped it around her body and headed to her dressing room.

Instead of picking up the gown she always wore at night, she chose to put on one of her new outfits. She opened the top drawer of her dresser and pulled out a long white nightgown with deep splits on both sides. Marc had already made her feel feminine, but she wanted that feeling to last a little longer.

She slipped on the skimpy fabric, noticing how her large, rounded breasts fit neatly in the sockets of the gown. She wondered what Marc would think of it. Before her mind could conjure up a bad thought, she caught herself.

His words of promise came back to her, and with a smile on her face, she turned out the light, went across the hall, and went to bed.

Marc had a serious attitude on Saturday morning, after Jonathan told him they had to go to Magic Moments because Rob had a problem.

Marc had prepared breakfast and was about to sit down.

"Why didn't you say something to me yesterday?" he asked his brother.

"Rob didn't two way me until eleven o'clock last night, and I didn't feel like hearing your mouth," Jonathan replied, taking a bite of his French toast.

Marc wagged his finger. "I told you Rob wasn't going to be able to get the job done. You were the one who said the man was good. The only thing I can see he's good for is getting on my nerves."

"Man, we don't know why he wants to talk to us. Let's hurry, so we can get going," Jonathan said, sipping from his black ceramic coffee cup. He eyed his brother. "Did you find a condo?"

Marc cut a piece of his omelet. "Oh yeah, I did. It's a two-bedroom in Shaker Village. The kitchen is huge."

Jonathan's facial expression froze.

Marc glanced up at him. "What's the matter?"

Jonathan dropped his head. "I guess I had kind of gotten used to you being here with me. We hadn't lived together since before you went off to school."

"Yeah, I guess you're right, but I think it's for the best. I would never want to continue to invade your space as I've been doing these last couple of months," Marc said, giving his brother a pat on the back.

Jonathan got up from the table and tossed his paper plate in the trash. "So how's things going with Rose?"

Marc followed suit. "I think I love her," he said plainly.

Jonathan was astonished. "You love her," he repeated.

Marc met his brother's stare. He immediately wished he hadn't said anything.

"Jonathan, don't make me regret telling you."

"Have you told her?" Jonathan asked.

"Not yet, but I will." Marc placed his cup in the sink, along with the utensils he'd used to prepare their breakfast.

Jonathan came over to stand next to his brother. "You're serious, aren't you?"

Marc shook his head as he squeezed a dollop of dish detergent into the hot water in the sink.

Jonathan didn't respond. He stood there for a minute.

"Why are you standing there like a statue?" Marc asked. "Why don't you move out of the way or say something, please?"

"Am I going to have a sister-in-law in the very near future?"

Marc shrugged the question away. He didn't want to think marriage even though he knew he was ready to settle down. But the last woman he'd thought was Ms. Right had turned out to be Ms. Totally Wrong For Him. He didn't want to rush things even though he knew Rose cared for him as well.

Instead of answering the question, he gave his brother one of his own. "So how are you and Ivy coming along with the grand opening?"

"We've gotten the invitations out, and it seems we're right on schedule," Jonathan said as he picked up a coffee cup from the dish rack and place it in the cabinet above his head. "Hey, once she warms up to you, she's not so bad to work with," he said, placing the utensils in the drawer next to him.

Marc unstopped the sink. "I'm glad you're getting along so well with her." He turned away from Jonathan and grinned.

After drying his hands with a clean dishcloth, he hung it up on the towel rack. "Let's get out of here," he said, walking away from the sink. "I'm telling you now that if Rob says something ridiculous, I'm going to send him packing," he said over his shoulder as he walked out of the kitchen.

When Marc and Jonathan pulled into the parking lot of Magic Moments, Rob hadn't yet arrived, and Marc was not happy.

"Where the hell is he?" Marc yelled over the hood of his car to his brother, who sat in his Lexus with the window down.

Jonathan glanced at his watch. "Let's give him a couple of minutes, Marc. It's just nine o'clock."

As soon as Jonathan rolled his window up, Rob pulled up in his pickup truck. He jumped out quickly.

"Man, you better be glad you showed when you did because you've already got two strikes against you. We all know what three will get you," Marc said, motioning with his hand like an umpire in a baseball game.

"Sorry, I'm late. I had some family business to attend to this morning," Rob said, walking toward the building.

"What's so urgent that you had to see us this early?" Jonathan asked, unlocking the door to the facility.

"Follow me," Rob said after Jonathan disengaged the alarm system.

Marc held his questions until he saw what Rob had to show them.

"We stayed last night until after I communicated with you,

Jonathan," Rob said as they walked down the right corridor of the building.

They continued until they reached the kitchen area. Rob hit the switch, and the room was flooded with light.

"Marc, I know you feel the kitchen is the heart of any facility that serves food, so I hope we've done this one justice."

Marc walked slowly around the extraordinary kitchen. He rubbed his feet back and forth on the nonslip surface of the new floor and smiled. Most people would say its only a place to cook, but every chef should be comfortable in his own kitchen. The planning and efficiency of the design were crucial.

"Great job, Rob, and to think I was ready to pulverize you if you had showed us an unfinished kitchen." Marc gave Rob a smack on the back, jerking the scrawny man forward.

"Now, we can set up appointments with suppliers and the health inspector to come in," Jonathan said.

Marc checked the preparation, cooking, and storage areas and all the service equipment. He even went into the walk-in freezer. Everything seemed to be in place. "We shouldn't have any problems passing inspection," he said, slamming the freezer door. Rubbing his hands together vigorously, he said with a grin, "It's time to rock and roll."

Chapter 11

Rose got up early to set up for a wedding at First Church in Gary, the next town. She drove the company van and asked Destiny to assist her in completing her task.

"Why don't we go stepping tonight?" Destiny suggested. "Vanessa told me she's been going to step class."

"Fine with me, but where are we going to go?" Rose asked, looking in the passenger mirror before changing lanes. "If we're going to the Fifty-Yard Line, I just hope David Crenshaw doesn't show up."

Destiny teased Rose. "You know you love how David steps 'cause that's your boy." She grinned. "With his flashy suits," she added and burst into laughter.

Rose couldn't help but laugh herself. "I think he's a nice guy, but for some reason the man gets on my last nerve. And the only stepping he does is on my toes." Rose laughed at the memory.

Rose parked the van in front of the historical church and got out. Walking to the church's double doors, she pulled on a door handle and discovered the doors were locked. She rang the bell and waited for someone to come.

A tall, dark, gray-haired man in green corduroys and a plaid shirt opened the door for her.

"Good morning. I'm looking for Mr. Ed Brown," Rose said.

"I'm Brother Brown." The deep baritone voice of the older man surprised Rose.

Rose extended her hand to him. "Hi, Mr. Brown. I'm Rose Hart. I'm the decorator for the Spencer-Douglas wedding here this afternoon."

Mr. Brown held the door open and looked out. "Okay, pull around back. You have better access to the elevator from there."

"Sure, thanks." Rose walked back to the van.

"I'll prop the door open for you," he shouted.

Destiny looked puzzled. "Don't tell me this is the wrong place."

Rose started the engine and put the van in drive. "No, I've got to pull around back, closer to the elevator door. Girl, that's a blessing. We won't have to carry those candelabras and things up the stairs."

Rose whipped the van around and headed for the empty parking lot at the back of the church.

"How did you get this job, and why isn't Ivy coordinating the wedding?" Destiny asked.

"Erika wanted her aunt to coordinate the day so she met with Ivy every month and took notes." Rose spotted Mr. Brown at the far end of the building.

"Do you think that's going to work?"

"Girl, who knows. People do what they want. We provide the service." Rose pulled into the closest spot to the door and got out of the van.

Rose opened the back door of the van, removed a large box with her supplies inside, and handed it to Destiny, who stood on the other side.

"Do you girls need any help?" yelled Mr. Brown from the doorway.

"No, thanks, Mr. Brown. I think we can handle it," Rose yelled back as she pulled the brass candelabras out.

They walked inside, loading the elevator with as much of their equipment as space allowed so they wouldn't have to make more trips to the van than necessary.

First Church of Gary was the oldest church in the town. Many politicians and dignitaries attended the historic house of worship. It was a gray brick building with beautiful stained-glass windows and a huge steeple on top. The sanctuary had recently been remodeled. Rose could tell the place had been well taken care of during its hundred years.

"What a beautiful place to get married," Rose commented as she set up the columns for the floral arrangements down front.

She and Destiny worked diligently at decorating the church to look like the Garden of Eden, as requested by the bride, even though it was fall.

"This fruit looks so good, it's making me hungry," Destiny said as she handed some extra grapes to Rose to go into the pew decorations.

Rose laughed. "I hope she likes this," she said as she stood at the end of the middle aisle, checking out the décor from the back.

"Have you seen Marc lately?" Destiny asked.

"Last night I went with him to Shaker Village to see a condo," Rose said.

Destiny smiled with her eyes. "Really?"

"Yes, then we went to Bennigan's for dinner, and he followed me home."

Destiny put down the box she had in her hands. "And…" She waited for Rose to finish.

Rose looked at her curiously. "And what?"

"Rose Marie Hart, I know there is more than you're telling me," Destiny said with her hands on her hips.

Rose stared at her cousin for a minute, then glanced at her watch. She sighed. "Help me get this stuff back in the van, and I'll tell you on the way to the next stop."

Destiny came over to her and leaned in close. "Is it juicy?"

"Hurry up, Dez; it's already after one o'clock. We've been here over two hours already," Rose said.

The two women finished packing their things, and Rose took one last look at the garden scene before they left. She hoped Erika had a magical day. On her way out the door, she saw Mr. Brown, and they said their good-byes.

Rose climbed inside the van and attached her seat belt. As she was about to turn the key in the ignition, she heard Destiny clear her throat.

Rose glanced in her direction.

"So are you going to tell me, or am I going to have to guess?" Destiny asked.

Rose smiled wickedly as she started the van. "Let me think about it," she said with a grin, putting the gear in reverse and backing out of the parking space.

Rose knew Destiny hated when she was quiet, especially when she thought Rose had something to tell her. After a while Destiny broke the silence.

"I hate when you do me like that, Rosie," Destiny huffed.

Rose laughed, tickled by her cousin's third-grade antics. "Dez, you are such a baby sometimes when you can't get your way."

Rose turned down Broad Street and headed to An Affair to Remember so they could set up for the reception.

Rose sighed. "I'm really digging him, cuz. I don't really know how to put the way I'm starting to feel about him into words. He's so different from anyone else I've ever met before."

Rose glanced at Destiny's face, which now beamed. Taking her right hand off the steering wheel, she lifted it like a stop sign. "Wait. Now before you start naming our children, I must tell you that I'm feeling things for him that I haven't felt in a long time, but I also feel I should take things slow." She was relieved she had finally said that to someone else besides the mirror in her dressing room.

Destiny stared at Rose. "A man like Marc doesn't grow on trees. The man is fine, a businessman, and he can cook. And did I mention he's fine?"

"Yes, you did." Rose grinned.

Destiny laughed but immediately changed her facial expression to serious. "Rosie, you're a strong woman, and I know in the past you've had some hurts that you never thought you would get over, but you did. Why not give Marc a chance? Take the next step, because it's obvious he's into you."

"I want to so badly, Dez, it's just—" Rose stopped her sentence in the middle, so Destiny finished it for her.

"It's just that you're afraid your dream will turn into a nightmare, and that your prince is really a frog." She touched her cousin's arm.

Rose shook her head in agreement, then whispered, "Yes. And I thought about the way Dwight treated me. He didn't have to say all those mean things to me if he wanted out of the relationship. He could have just said he wanted out."

"But you'll never know if Marc is the one if you don't take a chance. Girl, roll that dice and see what you come up with," Destiny said.

Pulling into the parking lot of An Affair to Remember, Rose parked the van. "I know you're right," she said, unbuckling her seat belt.

"Why don't you invite Marc to go stepping with us tonight?" Destiny suggested.

"He may already have plans for the evening," Rose said quickly.

"Do you have his cell number? We can call him. If not, I can have Nick call him."

"Not on me."

"I'll call Nick. Let's get this done, so we can get back," Destiny said, pulling out her cell phone.

Rose went into the facility and straight to the room she'd be decorating. The bride's colors were teal and gold. The room was very quaint, but elegant.

The tables had already been dressed and set. She noticed Lili had already been there and had set up the wedding cake. All Rose needed to do was place the centerpieces and drape the sweetheart table, where the bride and groom would sit.

"This is a pretty place," Destiny commented as she entered the room. "It doesn't look as good as mine did though," she snickered.

Rose put her finger to her mouth. "Be quiet, girl. Somebody might hear you."

"I talked to Nick, and he called Marc about tonight. Marc told Jonathan at work, so he's game, too. Vanessa, Richard, and Desire will be there, too."

Rose smiled. "Which Fifty-Yard Line are we going to? The new one in Harvey is bigger than the one on Seventy-fifth Street." She immediately thought about what she would wear.

"The one on Seventy-fifth Street probably," Destiny said.

"Help me with the centerpieces, Dez," Rose said as she pulled one of the glass vases from the padded box.

They got busy and completed their task in thirty-five minutes.

They went back to the van and headed back to Hearts and Flowers.

"Thanks for helping me out this morning. It would have taken me forever. I'd still be at the church."

"No problem. I'm surprised Vee hasn't called to check on your progress."

"She hasn't said very much since that blowup the other day."

"Does Aunt Luv know about Marc?" Destiny asked.

"Yes, she saw him leaving the estate the other day, then caught Vee and me arguing about him."

Destiny's eyes got big. "What was he doing there?"

"Bringing me lunch."

Destiny's cell phone rang before she could comment. "Hello?" She looked over at Rose, then handed her the phone. "It's for you."

Rose frowned. "Who would be calling me on your cell phone?" She placed the phone up to her ear. "Hello?"

"Rose, it's Marc."

"Marc?"

"I called Nick, and he gave me Destiny's cell number. I don't know why I didn't get yours before, but anyway. I wanted to know if it would be okay for us to go to the club together tonight."

"Uh, um, sure," Rose said, then glanced at Destiny.

"Great. I'll pick you up at about eight."

"I'll see you tonight," Rose said before handing the phone back to her cousin. "I didn't hang it up, so…"

Destiny pressed the button to end the call. "Rosie, remember what I said about taking a chance on him. Maybe tonight you will feel like you can go further with the relationship," Destiny said.

"We'll see," Rose murmured as she made a right turn onto Bridlewood Lane. She hoped her life didn't go up in a puff of smoke.

Chapter 12

Rose had just placed a ruby stud in her right earlobe when she heard the doorbell. She rushed to the full-length mirror to check her outfit before sprinting to the door.

"Hi, I'm almost ready," she said quickly, moving behind the door to allow Marc to enter her home.

Marc walked in and kissed her quickly on the lips. "You look great," he said as his eyes roamed her lush curves.

Rose smiled. "Thank you very much," she said cheerfully. "Let me get my coat," she added, moving away from the door. "Have you ever been to the Fifty-Yard Line?"

"Not since I've been back."

"Do you want me to drive then?" Rose asked, walking in front of him.

"No, I remember where it is," he said, leaning against the closed door. He studied her for a few moments. "Come here," he said, beckoning her with his forefinger.

Rose walked over to him.

Wrapping his arms around her, he pulled her close. "I didn't get to greet you properly when I came in." His head descended, and his warm lips were demanding and persuasive on hers.

Rose had to catch a quick breath when his hands went to her round bottom and squeezed gently.

Marc continued to hold her close. He then laid his forehead against hers. "I don't know what it is, but I just can't keep my hands off you," he said in a low voice.

"I don't want you to, either," she whispered in return.

"Well, we don't have to meet the others," he suggested slyly. "We could spend the evening here, alone, if you'd like," Marc said, his tone hushed.

Rose looked up at him. This was the opening she needed to take that next step. "Okay," she whispered softly.

Marc lifted her chin. "Baby, are you sure this is what you want?"

Rose nodded. "Very sure," she said, moving out of his embrace. She took off her coat and held her hand out for his.

Marc shrugged out of his leather bomber jacket and gave it to her. He waited for her to take the next step.

Rose placed both coats on hangers and hung them in the closet. After she shut the closet door, she held out her right hand, waiting for him to grasp it. "I never showed you the second floor."

Marc watched the sway of her hips as she led him up the stairs.

Midway, Marc stopped. "Baby, we don't have to do this if you don't want to." He didn't want to make her feel as if he was pushing her to do something she didn't want to do.

Rose didn't answer; she just kept climbing, pulling him along with her.

The first door on the right was the guest room. Decorated

in pale yellow, the mid-size room was filled with heavy, dark cherry furniture.

They walked into her dressing room. Then they went into her bathroom.

"Wow, you have a huge tub," Marc commented as they entered the bathroom. A vision of them together naked and wet came to mind.

"Yes, I love it in here, and every chance I get, I like to take long baths," Rose said, standing over the tall claw-foot tub.

"I can tell by all the candles you have in here. You could start a small forest fire," Marc joked.

"I'm always very careful," she said as she made her way to the door. She hesitated in the hallway before pointing to the end. "M-my bedroom is down the hall." She began walking in that direction.

Once they got to the threshold of the door, her palms began to sweat.

She had never invited a man into her bedroom. The one and only time she'd made love with her ex-boyfriend, they were at his apartment. She was relieved at that fact, since it turned out to be the worst experience of her life. She had a feeling this time would be different.

Marc waited patiently for Rose to take the first step into the bedroom, even though he wanted to sweep her off her feet and carry her over the threshold.

Marc followed closely behind her, trying to read her body language to determine what to do next. The last thing he wanted to do was scare her. He could tell by the slight fidgeting of her hands that she was nervous.

All done up in red, her bedroom had a romantic atmosphere. The brass bed had scroll and arch designs in the headboard, and the footboard dipped down, forming a contrast with the square posts of the four-poster bed, which had an autumn leaf finish. The lamps on the nightstands had beautiful red lace doillies covering them.

In the corner of the room, she had a custom-made chaise lounge covered in red and gold jacquard.

Marc decided to take a seat there. "Baby, come over here," he said, patting the empty space next to him. As soon as Rose came over to him, he pulled her hand into his lap. "Listen, you don't have to prove anything to me. If you're not ready, it's okay, really." He picked her hand up and placed his lips against her knuckles.

"No, I'm ready," she said, pulling her hand from his grasp and standing up. "Give me a couple of minutes, and I'll be right back." She walked to the door. "Make yourself comfortable," she said before disappearing.

Marc wondered what she was up to but decided to allow her to do what felt good to her. He walked over to the opened armoire, where he found a CD changer on the top shelf. He pressed the power button, and the room was flooded with Marvin Gaye crooning about getting it on.

"Now that's what I'm talking 'bout," he said aloud, nodding his head, smiling.

As he swayed to the beat of the music, he didn't realize that Rose had reentered the room until the smell of her sweet perfume wafted through the air.

He turned in her direction, and their eyes locked in a battle of wills, each trying to see if the other would back down first.

Rose couldn't stand the penetrating stare Marc gave her, so she looked away.

Marc's jaw dropped slightly. He couldn't believe the voluptuous beauty was standing just out of his reach in a red, sheer peignoir set.

She's serious, he thought to himself just as Marvin Gaye said, "Oh wanna get it on, I wanna get it on."

At first Marc didn't move, and then he found himself reaching for her.

"Baby, you're gonna kill a brotha with outfits like this." He turned her around so he could get a better look at her. The long slits on the sides of the gown exposed her hips.

"Come here," he said, leading her back over to the chaise lounge. He thought it would be the safest place for them right now because if they sat on the bed, he'd be deep inside her in no time flat.

No, tonight he wanted to take his time and brand his style of loving on her memory forever.

He pulled her down on his lap, then ran his fingers through her loose curls, causing her to drop her head back, exposing her long neck. He began placing kisses along her nape before capturing her lips. Her arms went around his neck.

Rose boldly slipped her tongue into the hot recesses of his mouth.

Marc's response was swift and immediate. He permitted her to have her way with his mouth, and as she did so, his own sexual desire increased.

He groaned as he felt his manhood harden. Breaking the kiss, he pulled her so close that her breasts were surrounding his face.

He was more than ready to take her to ecstasy, but he wanted to make sure she was ready.

Marc pulled down one of the thin straps on her gown, revealing her left breast. He lightly pinched her protruding nipple, and a moan slipped from her lips, causing him to launch a full-fledged assault on the chocolate tip with his mouth.

Peeling the other strap down, he filled his hands with her

right breast. Now that she was bare, Marc was burning up inside and wanted relief.

Moving Rose beside him on the chaise lounge, he knelt before her. With his eyes fixed, he lifted the hem of the gown slowly. She stood to assist him in removing the flimsy garment. She didn't think about the Rose she saw in the mirror every morning, or the person she thought she should be. Her only thought was of the man in front of her and how he would make love to her until she was as limp as a wet dishrag.

Soon, Rose stood in front of Marc, completely naked. The glow from the table lamp gave Marc just enough light to see all her glorious features. He sat back on his haunches, staring at her body. Finally, he looked up at her. "This is the last time I'm going to ask if you're sure, baby," he said, gently rubbing her thighs.

Rose was getting weaker by the minute. "Marc, make love to me," she barely said.

Marc pulled her body close to him, providing support for her weakening legs as he rained kisses on her thighs.

Rose's eyes fluttered shut. She had no idea what was happening to her, she was in such a sensuous place. The next thing she felt was her back hitting the comforter on her bed. Finally, she opened her eyes just as Marc removed his shirt.

She allowed her eyes to absorb the sight of him. He was truly a magnificent male specimen. Her eyes roamed his broad shoulders, chest, and flat stomach.

Marc retrieved his wallet from his back pocket and pulled out a small foil packet. He quickly tossed it on the bedside table before unbuckling his pants, pushing them to the floor.

Rose's eyes widened and her heartbeat accelerated as she waited for him to remove the rest of his clothing. There was a thin line of dark curly hair that ran from the top of his navel and disappeared into his underwear.

His dark chocolate skin looked so rich, she licked her lips, wanting to get up and touch him.

In one swift movement, Marc removed his underwear.

Rose allowed her gaze to drink in the sight of him, naked and proud. She wanted to continue to explore more of him with her eyes by checking out his thighs, but they kept going back to his protruding sex. Hot shivers ran down her spine as he approached the bed.

Marc climbed onto the bed and lifted her leg. He kissed the inside of her ankles and moved higher. He lowered her leg and slid next to her giving her a tongue-thrusting kiss. Rose was unraveling before his eyes.

He went to her right breast and laved the tip before suckling, applying more pressure. He gave the twin the same motion.

Marc continued to place kisses on her hot flesh. His large hands caressed her outer thighs as he slowly parted her legs and settled between them. He kissed her belly and continued to move lower.

A deep moan slipped from her lips as his tongue made brief contact with her clitoris with slow and deliberate circles.

Rose thought she had lost her mind. Her head thrashed back and forth while she grasped the bed covers. She had never experienced anything like this before. She was anxious now, and the sooner he was deep inside her, the better.

Marc continued taking his time assaulting her slick, wet heat, causing her body to lift from the bed.

Rose automatically maneuvered herself so she could spread her legs wider, giving him greater access to her. Suddenly, she could feel the spasms grab her from deep inside. She had never felt them before, but she was aware of what was happening to her.

Marc was also aware of what was happening and decided

not to penetrate her. He wanted this moment to be for her. "Let go, baby," he said huskily. "Let it happen. I'm right here with you," he whispered as he moved next to her and held her close.

Kissing her still closed eyelids, then her cheeks, nose, then her lips, he continued to whisper sweet thoughts to her as she pulled herself together after the powerful climax.

Rose finally opened her eyes.

"Are you okay, baby?" Marc asked, placing a light kiss on her lips.

Rose looked down at her nakedness, suddenly wanting to pull the covers over her, but they were lying on top of them. She tried to pull the covers on the side, but Marc reached over her, stopping her.

"I love every beautiful inch of you, Rose Hart," he said, moving back to his side.

Rose turned on her side to face him, and he pulled her close. She kissed him. "I love you, too, Marc."

Marc knew they had a strong bond, but hearing her say the words affected him more than he could have ever imagined.

He kissed her again. "I wanted to be so deep inside you, I almost couldn't stand it, but I also wanted the moment to be just for you. I know I'll have another opportunity to make love to you."

Rose felt around on the nightstand next to the bed and picked up the remote control to her CD player. As she pressed the volume button, the soulful sound of Freddie Jackson calling his lover filled the room.

"Let's get under the covers," Marc whispered in her ear.

Rose smiled. "I have a better idea. Why don't we take a long hot soak?"

Marc's mustache curved upward. "My kind of woman."

Rose got up from the bed. After picking up her robe from

the floor and slipping it on, she padded barefoot down the hall to the bathroom.

Twisting the handles on the old-fashioned tub, she filled it with hot and cold water. She liked to take hot baths, but with Marc in the tub with her, she figured they'd have plenty of heat, so she didn't want it too hot.

She stood in front of her pedestal sink, pushing her tousled shoulder-length hair away from her face, staring at the person looking back at her. This was not the same Rose Hart she woke up as this morning. This person was the new her, a woman who had finally found love.

Her next thought was whether love would keep her or end like the *Shrek 2* movie, with the prince turning into a frog.

Soon after the tub had filled halfway, Marc came in, wearing only his shorts. He watched Rose as she crouched on her knees, running her hand through the water.

"You ready for me, baby?" he asked, bending over and massaging her shoulders.

Rose turned slightly and looked up. "Yes." She got to her feet and went over to pick up her white-handled candlelighter. She lit all the candles in the bathroom. "Now for some mood music," she said as she turned on the CD player on the shelf in the corner.

"What do you listen to when you're in here? Nature sounds, waterfalls, or jazz?" Marc wanted to know.

"It depends on how I'm feeling when I come in here. Sometimes I'll listen to Miles Davis, Sarah Vaughan, Nancy Wilson, and the like, and then there are other times when I listen to my Body and Soul collection, the smooth old-school R & B. I have one in the CD player in the bedroom." She picked up a stack of CDs from the top shelf.

Sifting through them, she decided that for this special occasion, she would play the *Night Moods* compilation CD with The Isley Brothers singing about a special voyage to ecstasy.

Rose turned out the overhead lights and looked around at the flicker of the candlelight. She untied her robe.

Marc came to her. "Let me help you with that." He gently pushed the robe open and off her shoulders, watching it tumble to the floor.

Rose waited for him to remove his shorts and then allowed Marc to assist her in getting in the large tub before he sat behind her.

Rose pulled the long rack on which she kept her spoofs, sponges, and body washes toward her. She squirmed a bit, trying to get comfortable, but didn't know how long she would be able to sit with his erection sticking her at the top of her behind.

Marc reached around her and picked up a sponge and dipped it in the water. Moving Rose's hair aside, he squeezed the excess on her back.

As the soothing water relaxed her, she closed her eyes and felt him gently rub her back with the wet sponge in circular motions.

"How does that feel?" he asked, replacing the sponge on her back with his lips.

"Hmmm," Rose moaned with her eyes closed. "You've done so much for me already. Why don't I rub your back?"

"You're going to repay me, sweetie, with interest, too. Don't worry. Enjoy this because your turn is coming," Marc said in a sexy voice as he began to caress her breasts with the sponge.

Rose could only laugh at the way he'd said it; then she relaxed against him as he continued to lightly brush her nipples with the sponge.

Marc rested his head on the back of the tub. "Why didn't you go all the way with me, Marc?" she asked carefully, hoping she hadn't just spoiled the mood.

Marc kissed the back of her head. "Baby, I told you. I wanted that moment to be yours."

"You are so sweet, Marc."

"I know this," he said jokingly. "But remember what I said about payback."

Rose smiled and closed her eyes, and they both were quiet, relaxing together in the intimate atmosphere with the candlelight and with Earth, Wind & Fire talking about not being able to hide love.

After a while the water started to cool.

Marc caressed her breast. "Are you ready to get out? The water's getting cold."

Rose pulled herself forward to allow him to climb out first.

Marc picked up a bath sheet and wrapped it around himself before assisting her from the tub. Picking up another towel, he held it opened as she got out. He wrapped it around her and walked from the room.

"I'll be there in a minute," she said, closing the door behind him.

Rose unstopped the tub to release the water, turned off the CD player, and began to straighten the bathroom. She felt alive for the first time in her life…really alive. The moment he took her in his arms, there were no inhibitions about her weight, no doubts or concerns. Marc also showed his unselfishness in a big way.

As she threw warm water on her face to wash away the residue from the cleansing solution she'd just used, she realized the evening wasn't a dream. Marc wasn't a figment of her imagination, and what they shared was real. The beginning of a big smile grew on her face. She pointed to herself in the mirror. "You go, girl," she said before she flicked off the light on her way out.

Marc had gone down to the powder room on the main floor to finish drying off. He could tell Rose wanted some time alone. He understood perfectly; he himself had replayed the sensuous dance between himself and Rose over and over again in his mind. The casual caress of her soft hands on his skin and her hot, voluptuous body next to his were more than just a sexual act.

Who did he think he was kidding? He couldn't continue to fool himself; he had allowed his heart to be stolen. Usually it was the other way around, and he'd have to talk himself out of a relationship when a young woman had fallen for him.

And since moving back to Taylor, he'd only had a couple of dates, and those women had tried to cling, which was something he definitely wanted to avoid.

He had made a promise to himself a long time ago that he would never ever give another woman his heart so she could rip it to shreds. It was so easy to let his guard down around Rose because she was caring and considerate and a great listener. "And that body," he said to the mirror.

Tonight had intensified his thoughts about her, and now he wanted her for his own. He also knew he would have to prove to Rose he was serious and was ready for the challenge. He wrapped the bath sheet back around his waist. *Watch out, Rose Hart, 'cause here I come,* he thought to himself as he climbed the stairs to her bedroom.

Standing in the threshold   , Marc watched Rose get comfortable underneath   .

"Hey, baby," he said, walking into the room.

"Hey," she said, smiling, her dimple prominent.

He pulled back the covers as she patted the empty space next to her.

Marc dropped his bath sheet and slid under the covers and snuggled against her warm body. He planted a wet kiss on her lips. "I've fallen in love with you," he whispered before kissing her passionately. Breaking the kiss, he gently pushed her hair back off her face and then cupped it with his hand. "What am I going to do with you now?"

Rose tried not to let the surprise she felt show on her face. "What do you want to do?" she whispered.

Marc lay back on his own pillow, looking at the ceiling first before turning back to her. "Let me show you," he said as he reached over and turned off the lamp next to the bed.

Chapter 13

The shrill ringing of the telephone woke Rose out of her sleep.

"Hello?" she said groggily.

"Where are you?" the caller asked.

"Evidently, I'm at home. Duh."

"Why didn't you call me earlier to tell me that Marc didn't come by to pick you up?" Destiny was confused because Rose was so calm about the situation. She hoped Marc hadn't crushed Rose's feelings.

Rose looked at the antique clock on her night table. It was eleven-thirty.

"Well, it's a little late to be asking why I didn't show up, don't you think?" Rose responded.

Destiny smacked her lips. "I just can't believe he didn't pick you up like he said he would."

Rose hated when Destiny went off on a tangent; she didn't know how to shut up. Rose knew she'd have to tell her cousin the truth.

She looked over at Marc, who seemed to be sleeping

soundly. She didn't want to wake him, so she turned her back to him and whispered, "Yes, he did come by to pick me up, Dez, so bring it down a notch."

There was a pregnant pause before Destiny spoke.

"Is he there now?" Destiny whispered, trying to match the volume of her voice with Rose's.

"Yes."

Destiny yelled into the phone. "You go, girl. Why didn't you just say you were getting your freak on? I'll talk to you later," she said, immediately disconnecting the call.

A wide smile appeared on Rose's face as she clicked the off button on her cordless phone.

"Destiny trying to find out your whereabouts, huh?"

Rose's head turned in his direction. "Did I wake you?"

"No, I wasn't asleep," Marc said, turning on his side. "What bad names did Destiny call me?"

Rose chuckled. "She thought you stood me up."

"Did she just realize now that you were missing?" he said, laughing.

"Who knows. I'll talk to her later." Rose slid closer to Marc and began to rub his chest.

"Do you still want me to come to your parents' house tomorrow for dinner?" he asked.

"Of course, I do. Unless you don't want to come."

"Baby, you know what happened tonight changes our relationship drastically."

"I know," Rose said, her voice trailing off.

Marc lifted her chin. "You're not worried, are you?"

She shook her head no.

"That's my girl," he said, holding her chin with his thumb and forefinger.

"Let's get some sleep," she suggested.

Marc's left brow lifted. "I can think of something else we could do." He pulled her close yet again.

Rose was nervous about dinner. Marc didn't leave her house until the sun came up this morning, and now he and Jonathan were late. Her mother hated when people were late for Sunday dinner.

As she stood in front of the bay window in her parents' living room, Rose looked out, trying to spot Marc and Jonathan when they drove up.

Rose had noticed her mother's strange behavior the moment she'd walked into the house this afternoon. Louvenia had a silly grin on her face and had been humming a song Rose didn't recognize as she prepared to put dinner on the table.

Louvenia went all out for dinner, adding several other dishes to the regular Sunday meal. She always liked a big meal presentation when they had guests. Since launching her "marry my daughter please" campaign, she'd gotten worse.

Rose kept checking her watch and wondered what could be keeping Marc. As soon as she lifted her head to look out one last time before she called him on his cell phone, he pulled up to the curb in front of the house.

She walked swiftly down the three stairs from the living room to the foyer, rushing to the front door, but her mother beat her to it.

"I've got it," Louvenia yelled, turning the handle on the dark cherry wood door. She stepped back when the two tall gentlemen entered the foyer.

"I thought we were going to have to eat leftovers for a week," she said, closing the door behind them.

Rose walked around her mother to Marc.

Marc pulled her to him. "Hey, baby," he said, giving her a peck on the lips.

Rose didn't allow her lips to linger on his because she knew her mother was making a mental note of it. She retreated, then hugged Jonathan. She turned to her mother. "Mama, this is Marc and Jonathan Damon.

"Pleased to meet you, Mrs. Hart," Jonathan said.

Louvenia pointed her forefinger at him. "I don't remember seeing you at the wedding," she said, her eyes assessing Jonathan. She quickly thought he could be a nice catch for one of her other daughters.

By her mother's expression, Rose knew she already had plans for Jonathan.

Louvenia then went to Marc. "Now, you I do remember." She held her dainty hand out for him to take.

Marc bent to kiss her knuckles. "Pleased to meet you, Mrs. Hart." He knew that if he were trying to score points with Louvenia, he had just hit a home run. The petite, dark brown-skinned woman was just as beautiful as her daughters. Now he knew where Rose got her beautiful brown eyes.

Louvenia blushed. She turned to her daughter and then smiled. "Rosie, I really like these two. Hang up their coats for me, honey, and take them into the family room where your father is. Dinner should be ready shortly." Louvenia turned and walked away.

"Thanks for inviting us, Rose," Jonathan said, handing her his trench coat. "Is your sister Ivy here?" he asked.

"Not yet, but she'll show up before dinner is served," Rose responded, accepting his coat, then Marc's. She walked to the closet not too far from the front door and placed them inside.

They walked down the hall and stepped down into the family room. The huge space had a fireplace on one side, built-in bookcases, a wet bar, and sliding doors that led to the patio. The whole room was filled with photos. They adorned the walls, the coffee table, and the end tables, and there were even several tall, three-panel mahogany room dividers with three photos in a row on each. The room dividers held one glamour shot of each of the Hart children and several others of the whole family together.

"You guys really like a lot of pictures, Rose," Marc commented as he looked at the vintage black-and-whites as well as the color portraits.

"Remember, my dad is a photographer, so every time he thought there was a Kodak moment, he'd pick up his camera. He even kept one in the glove compartment of his car." Rose laughed.

Andrew Hart was sitting in a chair, sorting photos on the coffee table in front of him. He looked over his reading glasses when he saw them enter the room.

"Daddy, what are you doing? Today is Sunday," Rose commented.

"Well, baby, I had some time to kill, so I thought I'd sort through the photos from the wedding last Saturday." Andrew rose to his feet.

"Daddy, I'd like you to meet Marc and Jonathan Damon. They're Nicholas's cousins," Rose said.

"Good to meet you, fellows," Andrew said, firmly shaking the young men's hands. "Won't you have a seat?" he offered.

Andrew went back to his chair. Marc and Jonathan sat on the sofa on the other side.

"Guys, I'll be right back. I'm going to see if my mom needs any help in the kitchen," Rose said, turning to leave.

"Go on, sweetheart. I'll take good care of them," Andrew joked.

Rose waved her hand at her father and walked out of the room.

"Mr. Hart, might I say you take great photos," Marc said, staring at the black-and-white family photo on the coffee table.

"Well, the camera only takes what it sees," Andrew commented, going back to his task.

"Hi, Daddy," called a husky voice from the doorway.

Andrew looked up to see Ivy standing there. "Hey, baby, why are you so late?" He checked his watch.

"I had a stop to make," she replied, glancing at Marc and Jonathan. She stepped down into the room and walked over to them. "Jonathan, did you get my e-mail?"

"Yes, the one about the special table linen. I did. I need to have Barbara call back the company that supplies the linen. I want to make sure they have the color we talked about."

"Time is running out; we need to get that settled," she said, then turned to leave.

"Hello to you, too, Ivy," Marc said with a smile.

Ivy nodded. "Marc," she threw over her shoulder as she continued out of the room.

Andrew watched the exchange and then shook his head before continuing what he was doing.

Several minutes later, Rose appeared to announce dinner was ready.

As they were about to be seated, Louvenia interrupted everyone. "Has everyone been introduced?"

Rose looked around, then made the proper introductions. They were about to take their seats when Louvenia stopped them again."

"Wait," she said, placing the bread on the table. "Rosie, you sit here, and Marc you sit next to her," she said pointing to the two middle chairs at the dining room table.

Rose looked at her sister Lili, who simply hunched her shoulders.

Marc guessed Louvenia's plan, and he wanted to tell her that she didn't have to try to get them together. He was already in love with Rose. His only task now was to get Rose to believe it.

Louvenia moved to the other side of the table. "Jonathan, you sit here next to Ivy," she said, pulling out his chair.

Ivy gave her mother a strange look but didn't say anything. Her eyes shifted to Rose, who was trying to maintain a blank expression on her face but couldn't seem to hide the smirk she had there.

Louvenia was pleased with the new arrangements. She went back into the kitchen to bring out the lemonade before taking her seat.

After Andrew said grace, everyone was ready to dig in.

Louvenia watched how Rose interacted with Marc, and it brought a smile to her face.

"So, Marc, how long have you been back in Taylor?" she asked, already knowing the answer since her sister Elizabeth had already told her.

"I've been back for about four months now," he replied as he spread butter on his corn bread. "My brother and I are opening a new banquet facility called Magic Moments. It's the old Queens building on Broadway."

"I remember that place. How are things coming along?" she asked.

"Ivy and I are assisting them with the grand opening," Rose said.

Louvenia's eyes widened. "When is this grand opening?" she asked, looking at Ivy, who still hadn't said anything.

"In a couple of weeks," Jonathan offered after Ivy still didn't respond.

"I hope we're invited." Louvenia smiled.

Marc smiled. "Of course, we would love it if you and Mr. Hart could join us."

Andrew Hart pushed his chair back and stood. Lifting the empty plate where the hot corn bread had been, he called out to his wife. "Luv, come with me so we can refill the platters."

Louvenia was watching Rose and Marc so intently, she didn't hear her husband nor did she see him move.

"Luv," Andrew called out to her once again. He tilted his head quickly toward the kitchen and walked away when he finally got her attention.

Louvenia scooted her chair back. "If you'll excuse me," she said, lifting the empty ceramic dish for the collard greens and walking into the kitchen.

"I can see what you're trying to do," Andrew said as soon as she was out of earshot of the others.

Louvenia looked innocently at her husband. "I haven't done anything, Andrew."

"I'm telling you, Luv, don't try to play matchmaker for the girls. You know how they hate it when you do that," Andrew said.

Louvenia's face turned crimson. "I'm doing no such thing, Andrew. I promised the girls I wouldn't meddle," she said, placing the ceramic dish on the table with her left hand and crossing the fingers of her right hand behind her back.

"You can't fool me, Luv. I've been married to you for over thirty-two years, so I know when you're not telling me the truth." Andrew walked closer to her. He lifted her chin, so he could look into her eyes. "Now, I'm not going to let you meddle in Rose's business. Give her some space to figure out if there is something between her and the young man."

Louvenia stood on the tips of her toes, threw her arms around her husband's neck, and gave him a quick peck on the lips. "I would never do anything to hurt Rosie." She kissed him again. "I promise."

Andrew pulled his petite wife against his slender frame. Once their lips touched, he immediately deepened the kiss. Lifting his head, he looked deeply into her eyes again. "You know I'm going to be watching you, Luv," he whispered.

She walked around him. "I know, baby," she said just as he patted her on the behind as she passed him.

Andrew lifted the remainder of the corn bread from the baking pan and headed back to the dining room. At the threshold of the door, he stopped. "Luv," he called out to her.

Louvenia looked up from her task. "Yes, honey?"

"I mean it," he said before a smile appeared on his light brown face. He winked and left the room.

Louvenia refilled the ceramic dish with the collards and looked heavenward, praying for God to forgive her for lying to her husband. She would keep her promise to him and wouldn't interfere in her daughter's love life, but she would give Rose a gentle push in the right direction.

After everyone had dined sufficiently, Jonathan and Ivy left the table, Andrew went into his darkroom, and Lili and Violet assisted their mother with clearing the table.

Rose was pleasantly surprised that her mother hadn't interrogated Marc any further. She knew she had her father to thank for that.

"Mrs. Hart, dinner was delicious. I think I ate too much," Marc said, rubbing his stomach.

Louvenia picked up the last serving dish and handed it to Lili. "You and your brother are welcome here anytime, Marc," she said, giving Rose a big smile before heading back to the kitchen.

Marc pushed his chair back from the table and walked around to where Rose was sitting. "I think she likes me."

Rose stood to her feet. "My mother likes any single man she thinks might be interested in one of her daughters."

They both chuckled.

Marc pulled Rose into his arms. "Baby, I'm sorry to have to rush off, but I want to start moving my things into my new place this afternoon."

"Do you need any help?" Rose asked.

"We're just moving the furniture I have in storage, but I would like for you to come by this week to help me decorate."

Rose smiled. "Not a problem."

Marc released her. "I'll call you later on," he said before placing a light kiss on her lips.

Rose walked in front of him into the hallway. "Let me get your coats."

Marc followed behind her. "I really hate to eat and run, but I wanted to be moved before the grand opening."

Rose stopped and turned toward him. "Marc, don't worry about it. I understand completely. I'm glad everything went well this afternoon."

As they approached the coat closet, Rose saw Ivy handing Jonathan his coat, with what seemed like a genuine smile on her face.

She couldn't believe Ivy was actually being nice. She pretended not to see the exchange between the two, but it did answer one question. Ivy could be kind to a man when she wanted to be. Rose thought for a moment that Ivy might have had a smile on her face because Jonathan was leaving.

Ivy handed Marc his coat as well and moved away from the closet.

Jonathan turned to both the Hart women. "Thanks for dinner; I'm stuffed," he said with his eyes on Ivy.

"Don't forget to call me on Monday about the table linen, just in case we have to change it," Ivy responded before walking away.

Jonathan stood there and watched as she retreated, his eyes glued to Ivy's backside. He shook his head and walked toward the front door.

Rose couldn't help but smile, and when she glanced up at Marc, he gave her a knowing look.

Marc pulled Rose into his arms once again, placing a kiss on her forehead. "I'll call you later," he said before following Jonathan to the door.

Rose walked behind him and then stepped forward to open the door for them.

Marc gave her one final kiss before he and his brother left the house.

Rose closed the door, then leaned against it, thankful for the success of the dinner and the glimpse of the softer side of her sister. *There's hope for her after all*, she thought to herself before heading back to the kitchen to finish helping her sisters.

Chapter 14

Rose had been spending so much time helping Marc with decorating his condo that she didn't have a chance to prepare for her Thursday meeting with Dianna, Cassaundra, and Phoebe Hawkins.

She printed out the customer profile on Cassaundra that Ivy had entered into the computer. It was incomplete.

Rose hoped that Dianna and Phoebe would be on their best behavior, but if the other day was any indication, she needed to be ready for whatever they brought her way.

Rose sat down and began putting some thoughts together in the notes section of Cassaundra's printed profile.

The chime alerted her of their arrival. Rose adjusted the sleeves on her shirt, took a deep breath, plastered a smile on her face, and walked out to greet them.

"Good morning, ladies," Rose said in her cheeriest tone of voice. She relaxed even more when she realized Phoebe wasn't with them. Dealing with one obnoxious Hawkins was better than two.

"Ms. Hart, we don't have a lot of time," Dianna Hawkins

began immediately. "I want you to tell me what you can do to make Cassaundra's wedding spectacular."

Rose held out her hand. "Why don't we go into the showroom and talk about it."

The women followed her to the next room. Dianna and Cassaundra sat on the sofa, while Rose took the armchair across from them.

Rose looked down at the customer profile, then directly at Cassaundra. "Your wedding will take place in the garden of your parents' home?"

Cassaundra glanced at her mother before responding. "That's what Mother wants," she answered dryly.

"The gardens are lovely, and we can make the whole thing an outdoor affair," Dianna added, twisting her mouth to one side. "I want them to get married under a lavish white rose gazebo," Dianna said, completely taking over even though the question had been meant for her daughter.

Cassaundra dropped her head slightly. "But, Mother, I told you that I wanted to go to Jamaica and get married," she said quietly.

Dianna patted her daughter's hand. "Now, dear, what would it look like if the mayor's daughter eloped and didn't have a grand affair for the whole town to see?"

Cassaundra glanced at Rose before quickly moving her hand away and hugging the purse on her lap closer to her body.

Rose could see the tears welling up in the young lady's eyes. She wrote down the information Dianna provided on the printed profile.

"Mrs. Hawkins, I would like to come out to the mansion so I can get a better look at the gardens and the location you would like the gazebo to be placed," Rose said.

"That's fine," Dianna said. "Now, I want all the floral arrangements to be huge," she continued, demonstrating with her hands.

Rose placed her pen on the clipboard. "Well," she said

slowly, "extravagant is nice, but we don't want the floral designs to overshadow the bride or to be so overbearing that they detract from the ambiance of the garden."

Dianna's face turned serious. "I'm telling you what I want, Ms. Hart. I want huge floral arrangements. Spare no expense."

Rose sighed. "Okay, that's no problem, Mrs. Hawkins." Rose looked at Cassaundra once again. She wanted to pull the poor girl into the conversation to get a feel for what she really wanted, but it didn't seem to be going too well.

Rose tried again. "Cassaundra, I don't see your choice of a wedding gown in your profile."

Dianna butted in again. "We haven't quite found the right one."

Rose immediately thought Dianna was the one who hadn't found the gown she wanted her daughter to wear.

"I really need to know the type of gown you're wearing so we can create a bouquet that will not only complement, but will enhance, your overall look for that day."

Rose could tell that Cassaundra Hawkins wasn't going to be permitted to make one decision about her wedding. Dianna Hawkins controlled the whole affair. It made Rose's heart very sad to see such a beautiful young woman planning for the most exciting day of her life and yet looking like she'd lost her closest relative.

"Mrs. Hawkins, what day can I come out to the mansion?"

"Monday, at eleven o'clock, would be fine," Dianna said, looking at her watch. She rose to her feet. "Like I said from the beginning, we don't have a lot of time today. So I guess we'll see you on Monday."

Cassaundra stood with her head bowed.

Rose led them back to the receiving room. She couldn't help but put her hand on the young woman's shoulders, giving her a reassuring squeeze as she passed her.

Cassaundra glanced up at her, and Rose smiled, hoping she

would smile in return. All the young woman gave her was a glimpse of a smile, which faded quickly.

Dianna turned around. "Good day, Ms. Hart," she said before leaving.

"Good day, Mrs. Hawkins, Cassaundra."

Rose watched as Cassaundra followed two steps behind her mother as they walked down the corridor.

Weddings were an exciting business, but Rose had seen her share of unhappy brides and family relationships torn apart because of them. She felt Cassaundra Hawkins's wedding was more for show for her parents than a sacred occasion for her, which made Rose sad.

Every bride wanted their fantasy wedding day; Rose was determined to find out what that fantasy was for Cassaundra and to make sure she gave it to her. When she went to her appointment at the mansion on Monday, she would try a little harder to find out.

Later that evening, Rose went to Marc's to get started on their next project. She'd picked up a small can of paint to make a faux finish for the kitchen walls and some stencils to show him.

Earlier in the week, he'd placed brown leather ottomans in the living room and a Nepalese rug on the floor. The living room was also decorated with vintage Murano glass table lamps on a French fifties lacquer console. A Venetian mirror had been placed above the fireplace mantel.

Rose parked her SUV and collected her supplies before climbing out.

She rang the bell, and Jonathan opened the door for her.

"Hey, I'm glad to see you. Now I can take a break," he said with a smile, taking the bag of supplies from her.

Rose entered the condo. "You guys look like you've been busy," she said, looking around the room.

"I'm in here, baby," she heard Marc say from the other room.

Rose walked into the dining room, which was connected to the living room area, with Jonathan following behind her.

Dressed in blue jeans and a white T-shirt, Marc was on his knees beside the dining room table, replacing a screw in one of the chairs.

Rose walked over to him and bent to give him a kiss.

"How's it going?" she asked, reaching for the bag Jonathan held in his hand.

Marc wiped his brow. "Moving is a lot of work."

Rose looked around the spacious room. "I see you guys have brought in more heavy furniture. Have you emptied your storage unit?"

"Yes, I've taken everything out of it."

Marc stood up. He looked in Rose's bag of supplies. "What did you bring?"

Rose opened it. "I wanted to show you the grape stencils I told you about for the arch over the kitchen. I also brought the brick pattern for the far wall of the kitchen." She looked at him. "Come on, so you can tell me what you think."

They walked into the kitchen. It had vintage pendant lamps suspended above the kitchen island and aluminum bar stools sitting in front of the island.

Rose stepped back until she was right outside the doorway. She pointed upward. "We would use this grapevine stencil up here," she said, pulling the stencil kit from the bag. "It should be easy to use. The instructions are on the back." She flipped the package over. She dug into the bag and pulled out a small spray can. "This is an adhesive to help on curved or challenging surfaces."

"I like the idea," Marc said.

Rose smiled. "Let's get started then."

Jonathan came into the room. "Since you've got company now, I'm leaving," he said to his brother.

"Jonathan, don't leave. I may need your help," Rose said.

Jonathan took a handkerchief out of his back jeans pocket and wiped his forehead. "Oh no, this man has worked me like a slave for the past couple of days. And to top it off, we've been working just as hard at Magic Moments, so I'm just ready to kick up my feet and relax."

Marc waved at his brother. "Let him go, baby," he said to Rose. Then to Jonathan, he said, "I'll see you bright and early in the morning."

Jonathan hugged Rose. "I'm out," he said, turning to walk away.

"Okay, baby, I have one of those sturdy stepladders. Let me go and get it right quick." Marc rushed from the room.

Rose decided to look around the condo a little more. She walked down the hall and thought to herself that they could fill the empty spaces with paintings and decorative pieces once Marc decided the theme for the area.

The first room on the right was an office. Next to it was a room with only a daybed in it, and next to it was the master bedroom.

Rose was surprised when she walked into Marc's bedroom. It was very neat, with a masculine king-sized bed with dark bed linen.

The maple and glass armoire, which was carefully sectioned off, looked like an antique piece. It had several spaces for his shirts, three rows for shoes, and tie racks on the inside doors. She hadn't seen anything quite like that before.

"I see you found the bedroom," Marc said from the doorway.

Rose turned around and smiled. "This cabinet or armoire… I'm not sure what to call it, but it really works well in the room. I love the antique look of it."

Marc walked over to her, pulling her into his arms. "My Aunt Rachel found it for me some years ago. It helps keep me organized, so I made sure I took care of it."

They held each other for several minutes before Marc began to sensuously rub her back while he planted kisses on her neck.

Moans began to slip from her lips, and Rose wanted to stop before she lost her train of thought. She gently pushed him away. "Marc, let's get the stencil up in the kitchen before we forget the real reason I'm here."

"You mean you didn't come over to be my love slave?" He grinned.

Rose hit him playfully on his shoulder. "Let's get back to work."

"We can work on the kitchen later," he whispered. "I think I've found something else I'd rather do instead," he added, pulling her back into his arms.

Marc kissed Rose so deeply, she almost couldn't catch her breath. She attempted again to step out of his embrace. "I'm serious; let's get this done," she said, trying to step away from him. "You won't have time later since the grand opening is coming up."

This time she succeeded in getting out of the bedroom and down the hall to the kitchen.

Marc picked up the stepladder and followed her.

For the next hour and a half, the couple worked diligently at applying the grapevine stencil to the arch of the kitchen.

Marc assisted Rose in stepping down from the ladder. They both took three steps backwards in order to get a better view of their handiwork.

Marc pulled Rose to him. "Baby, it looks great." He kissed her temple.

"It sure does," she commented. "Do you want to tackle the wall tonight, too?" she asked.

"No, now I think we need a little downtime. I've been working since I came in." Marc walked back into the kitchen. "Are you hungry?"

"Yes, I could use a little something."

"Why don't we clean up our mess? And after we wash up, I can whip us up something quick."

"Sounds good," Rose said as she picked up the paper and other supplies she'd used, placing them in the trash can.

She walked down the hall to the bathroom and washed her hands thoroughly. She smiled as she looked at her reflection in the mirror above the white pedestal sink. She had gotten further in her relationship with Marc than with any other man since her breakup with Dwight.

Marc made her feel things she'd only heard about from Destiny or read about in a romance novel. After the other night, she was sure she could probably write a steamy love scene similar to those of her favorite authors.

She snapped a piece of paper towel from the dispenser and wiped her hands as she left the bathroom. When she got back to the kitchen, she saw Marc slicing red peppers and onions. Chicken breasts cut into strips were sizzling in a black wok on the stove.

"I thought I'd whip up some chicken stir-fry," Marc said.

"Is there anything I can do to help?" she asked.

"I haven't had time to unpack the dishes, so we'll have to use paper plates. You can pull a couple out of the cabinet for me," Marc commented as he added the vegetables to the wok. "It should be but several more minutes. I'm using minute rice so we should be dining shortly."

Rose went over to the cupboard and pulled out the paper plates and two cups. "Do you have anything in the fridge to drink?" she asked.

"There's some iced tea Jonathan made earlier and beer, but that's about it. I'd be careful with the tea if I were you. Jonathan likes a lot of sugar in his iced tea." Marc chuckled.

Rose pulled out the half-empty pitcher of iced tea and brought it over to the island countertop.

"Well, everything's ready. Bring over the plates," Marc said to her. Marc filled both their plates. "Let's go into the living room and sit," he suggested.

Rose followed him with the pitcher of tea, eating utensils, and two cups filled with ice.

They both took a seat on the floor near the sofa.

At first they both sat quietly eating their dinner. After a long moment of silence, Marc got up.

"I think we need some music. The mood in here is somber, and I can't have that if I plan on making love to you tonight in my new place."

Rose couldn't believe he'd made that statement. "You sound very sure of yourself, Mr. Damon." Rose couldn't help but grin.

Marc went over to the entertainment center, which hadn't been properly positioned but was plugged in, and turned it on.

"You know we've got to christen the place, baby. Where do you want to start?"

"Marc, we haven't even finished eating yet," Rose said.

Marc came back and took his seat again. "I know, but I wanted to give you something to think about while we're doing so." He winked at her. "Rosie, you know I want your sweetness. It's my weakness, or hadn't you heard?"

"Listen at you. Now you sound like a Barry White record."

Marc moved his plate away and scooted his body toward her. He took her plate from her and placed it next to his.

He cupped her face and placed a kiss on her forehead, then her nose, and finally her lips.

Marc deepened the kiss, pulling her on top of him as he leaned against the sofa.

Her breasts were pressed solidly against his chest, and the feel of his long fingers caressing her back and even farther, until he reached the tail of her shirt, heightened her senses.

Marc slipped his hand underneath so he could touch her flesh. In slow circular motions, he caressed her back.

"Marc, please," Rose whispered, her skin on fire.

"I know, baby," he responded, continuing to use the same technique, only more intensely.

"Come with me," he said in a husky tone of voice.

Rose got up, and Marc followed suit.

Catching her by the hand, he led her down the hall. "Do you trust me, baby?" he asked.

Rose looked into the recesses of his dark eyes and knew right away, she trusted him with her life. She nodded before speaking. "Yes."

Marc walked to the doorway leading to his bedroom.

"What do you have in mind?" she asked, leaning against his shoulder.

"I'll lead and you follow." His husky tone had grown rough.

Rose followed Marc into the bedroom, and an aching desire began to swell within her as thoughts of their last encounter swept through her mind.

Marc turned around to her after he stopped in front of the bed and lowered his mouth to hers. He groaned against her parted lips, slipping his tongue between them.

Breaking the kiss, he placed his hand on the top button of her shirt. From the glow of light radiating from the master bath, he could see her dark brown face. "May I?" he asked.

Rose didn't try to speak; she only nodded her answer.

Marc methodically unbuttoned her shirt. He palmed her large, round breasts through the blue lacy bra she wore before reaching behind her and unhooking it.

"Marc," she whispered before her head fell back as she savored his hands on her body. He had become like a drug to Rose: the more she tasted him, the more she wanted him.

"Yes, baby," Marc answered, sliding the bra forward down her arms and letting it drop to the floor.

"I'm all sweaty. Don't," she said, her body starting to tingle all over.

Marc ignored her comment and got down on his knees. He rubbed her stomach right before Rose tried to cover herself there with her hands. He removed her hands and gave her an opened mouth kiss on her belly as he loosened her navy blue belt and unbuttoned her slacks.

Rose could barely stand.

Marc stood and kissed her passionately.

Rose broke the kiss. "Marc, I don't think I'm going to be able to stand this."

"Don't worry, sweetie." He kissed her on the forehead before stepping back, then eased her onto the bed.

Marc pulled at the cuff of her slacks; Rose lifted her buttocks so he could slide them off. Dropping them to the floor, he traveled up her shapely legs until he eyed her blue lacy underpants through her pantyhose.

Rose felt herself sinking back into the sexual haze she experienced anytime she was intimate with Marc.

"You are so beautiful, inside and out," he said in a husky voice, cupping her sex.

Rose exhaled a sensual moan that reflected the sensations that crept through her insides.

Marc let out a deep and heated moan as he grabbed the top of the hose and lace.

Rose stayed his hand and pulled herself up. She positioned herself on her knees on the bed and pulled at the hem of his T-shirt.

Marc raised his arms. Rose lifted the garment over his head and off his body. The white material hit the floor next to her bra.

Next, Rose unbuckled his belt. The evidence of his erection caused her to slowly unzip his jeans.

Rose looked into his eyes, and she pushed at the top of his jeans.

"You know it's payback time," he said, smiling, pushing his pants all the way down and stepping out of them.

"Yes, I know," she said, watching the bulge between his thighs.

As Marc eyed her, his body became even hotter. He reached out to her. "Come here, baby. I just need to touch you."

Rose scooted to the end of the bed on her knees and reached up to put her arms around him.

Marc lifted her from the bed like she weighed ten pounds.

"Marc, I'm too heavy for you to be lifting," Rose said, burying her face in his neck.

"You're not heavy, baby. I like the way you feel in my arms," Marc said, repositioning her on the bed, then joining her.

He kissed her deeply before slipping his tongue in her mouth. He retreated quickly. "Give me your tongue, baby," he said huskily.

Rose did as she was asked.

Marc moved his hand down her silky, dark chocolate brown skin until he reached the top of her pantyhose. This time he was successful at removing them, along with her underwear, from her body.

Sensations rushed through her when his fingers found the wet, slick pearl of her femininity.

Rose decided to be bold, and she reached inside his underwear. As soon as she held his stiffening manhood in her hands, her heartbeat increased. It was long, lean, and muscular. She ran her fingers along his shaft, gently stroking its head.

Marc let out a deep moan, and his breathing grew heavier. He had to stop her before he spilled his seed before they got started.

Turning her on her side, he kissed her again. He gently pinched her pointy chocolate peaks and then replaced his fingers with his mouth. He suckled gently, circling over and over with his tongue, gently biting her protruding nipples.

Rose cried out in ecstasy; her body was throbbing. She rubbed her feminine heat against him, hearing his groan once again before he turned over to the nightstand.

Marc opened the drawer and pulled out a condom. Lifting his buttocks, he removed his underwear, sending it sailing.

He watched Rose's facial expression as he opened and secured the condom, and then gently spread Rose's legs. Their eyes never left each other.

Marc positioned himself on his knees between her legs and held his upper body weight with his elbows. He rubbed her hair back from her forehead, looking into her eyes. Their faces were mere inches apart. "I love you, Rose," he said, lowering his body as the tip of his throbbing sex came in contact with her wet heat.

Rose began to inhale quickly at the intrusion, but Marc placed a breath-snatching kiss on her lips as he eased his manhood into her lush body.

To help her accept the length of him, he tried to keep still until he felt she could handle more. He began to move slowly until he felt her responding to his rhythm.

Once they were in sync, Marc placed his hands underneath her buttocks and lifted her body to meet his thrusts as he caressed her bottom.

The intense lovemaking had Rose out of her mind. She could feel the love they shared in every stroke.

He began to whisper to her, telling her how much he loved her body, about her sweetness and beauty.

Rose realized the words were sincere as he kissed her face, the corners of her eyes, her nose, temples, and ears, making passionate love to her.

Pretty soon incomprehensible cries of pleasure came from them both as they spiraled to ecstasy.

Rose lay in Marc's arms afterward. He continued to kiss her face and temples.

"Are you okay, baby?" he asked, kissing the top of her hair.

Rose nodded. She felt better than okay, but she couldn't put her feelings into words.

"I hope I didn't hurt you," he said with concern.

Rose lifted her head so she could look into his eyes. "No, you were very gentle, and I feel wonderful."

Marc planted a quick kiss on her lips. "Good, I'm glad." He pulled her to him and hugged her.

As he watched Rose's eyes flutter, he got up from the bed and picked her up. Quickly, he pulled the covers back, then position her on the cool sheets. He climbed into bed, pulling her in his arms, and they both went to sleep.

Chapter 15

Monday morning, Rose asked Ivy to come along with her to the mayor's mansion.

On the ride over, Ivy was exceptionally quiet, which was okay with Rose because the last time they rode together she'd wanted to strangle her. In this case, silence was definitely golden.

As they announced their arrival, Ivy pulled into the estate and parked her BMW in the driveway behind a green Porsche.

They got out of the car and walked to the door, reaching it just as Phoebe Hawkins opened it. "Ladies," she said with a smile, moving behind the door until they entered the foyer.

Phoebe had had no idea that Rose was stopping by today, but it was an excellent opportunity for her to put her plan in motion.

Rose frowned a bit at Phoebe's cheerful attitude. She wondered whether the person at the door was the same one she met the other day.

Walking into the foyer, Rose looked around the beautifully decorated mansion.

Ivy followed, standing next to her while they waited for instructions from Phoebe.

Phoebe closed the door behind them. "My mother's on a phone call, but I can take you to her," she said cheerfully.

She walked around them. "Follow me," she said, turning to the right, down a hallway.

Phoebe looked slightly over her shoulder. "Did Cassaundra know you guys were coming this morning?" she asked.

"Yes, she did," Rose responded. "We were supposed to talk about the floral décor as well as see where she would like to have the ceremony."

Phoebe hunched her shoulders. "Well, I'm sorry, but she's not here at the moment. But maybe my mother can tell you ladies when she's going to return," she said, trying to sound apologetic.

Phoebe led them into the room where Dianna, sitting at a desk, was speaking on the telephone. They stood in the doorway for quite some time before Dianna acknowledged their presence.

"Why don't you ladies have a seat. My mother should be with you shortly," Phoebe said as she invited them to sit across from her on the sofa.

Rose couldn't believe her ears. Phoebe was actually being cordial. Maybe she had been having a bad day the first time they'd met.

While they waited for Dianna to complete her phone call, Rose surveyed the room. She really didn't know what to call the huge, overly decorated room. There was so much furniture and so many things, what her Aunt Daisy used to call whatnots, lying around, the room look crowded.

Seeing the home décor, though, did make it clear to Rose that Dianna Hawkins liked everything gaudy.

Dianna finally finished her phone call. She rose from her chair and walked over to them. "Ladies, good morning," she said in a formal tone of voice.

Rose and Ivy stood. Rose offered her hand first. "Mrs. Hawkins, how are you this morning?" she asked.

"I'm doing fantastic, Ms. Hart," Dianna responded, giving Rose a slight handshake before running her fingers through her overprocessed hair.

"I was hoping to speak to Cassaundra today about some ideas I have for her bouquet, but Phoebe just informed me she's not here," Rose said, with a tinge of concern in her voice.

"She had a hair appointment, so I told her I'd handle everything for her. And call me Dianna, dear," Dianna said casually as she shook Ivy's hand also.

Rose looked at her sister, who had on a straight face.

Dianna walked over to the double doors that led to the garden area as if Cassaundra's absence was of no importance.

"Follow me, ladies," Dianna said just as the butler came in, interrupting her next sentence.

"Ms. Hawkins, I'm sorry to interrupt you, madam," he said.

"Yes," she said to the short older man.

"I wanted to let Ms. Phoebe know her gentleman friend is waiting for her in the foyer," he said, then turned and walked away.

Rose watched Phoebe's expression carefully. She seemed to be glowing at the announcement.

Phoebe walked over to her mother. "Lance and I are going out for lunch. I should be back before dinnertime, or I'll call you." She kissed her mother on the cheek.

Dianna smiled. "Okay, sweetie, have a good time."

Phoebe walked toward the door. "Rose and Ivy, it was good to see you two again. Who knows, you might be working with me soon." She smiled. "I hope Cassie comes back before you leave." She walked out of the room.

Dianna Hawkins opened the double doors that led to the garden area in the back of the mansion.

Ivy walked out behind Dianna first and looked around the area, where, as they had discussed, the wedding ceremony would be held.

There was a lion wall fountain with a hammered copper background on the patio portion. Several round ceramic planters were situated by the entryway, but because it was fall, the flowers had all died.

"This is very spacious, Dianna," Ivy commented, glancing over her shoulder at Rose.

Rose stood outside the doors, scanning the garden area. It was a large space and could easily be transformed into whatever Dianna wanted, but it would only be large enough for a floral arch, some other floral decorations, and a handful of guests.

Rose walked over to where her sister and Dianna were standing. "Mrs. Hawkins, approximately how many guests will be witnessing the ceremony?"

Dianna shrugged. "I'm not sure, dear, but at least four hundred. Why?"

Rose shook her head. "Four hundred people will not fit in this space." She walked farther out on the grounds, with Dianna and Ivy following her.

Rose pulled a black pen from her purse. On the back of her folder, she drew a quick sketch. "Now if we use the widest part of the lawn, we could make the layout like an orchestra pit. It could work," Rose suggested, showing them her sketch.

Dianna moved her head from side to side in disagreement. "No, that's not what I want. I want Cassaundra to get married in the garden area."

Ivy spoke up. "Mrs. Hawkins, what my sister is trying to say is Cassaundra can marry in the garden, but it can't accommodate your décor and the guests, too," she said, hoping she could get through to her.

Dianna frowned. "I heard what she said, Ms. Hart. I'm telling you that I want Cassaundra to marry in the garden, period."

Ivy placed her hand on her sister's back and led her farther out in the yard, out of earshot of Dianna.

"It doesn't look like she's going to give up on this. Let's try something else." She looked back at Dianna, who was staring at them as if she could hear every word they said.

Rose had started to get frustrated. She knew exactly what her customer was requesting, but there was no way the idea would work correctly.

"Vee, the woman can't have it both ways. The space is too small." Rose turned and pointed. "We've done enough of these for you to know better."

"I know, Rosie, but she doesn't understand that. She wants what she wants, so we'd better think of something to pacify her," Ivy responded, looking the other way at the rest of the grounds. She walked back over to Dianna.

"Mrs. Hawkins, Cassaundra is planning to get married next April, correct?"

"Yes, that's what we've planned," Dianna responded curtly.

"I was thinking that maybe we could construct a 100-by-130-foot tent for the four hundred or so guests to be seated comfortably," Ivy began before Dianna interrupted her.

"What does a tent have to do with my daughter getting married in the garden?" Dianna replied.

Ivy released a sigh as quietly as she could before she began again. "Cassaundra could get married inside the tent. We could create a garden inside the tent," Ivy suggested, looking over at her sister. "We could do that, right, Rose?" She looked to her sister to agree.

Rose smiled, imagining Ivy's vision in her own mind. "We sure could. We could have six-foot cone and square topiaries with lights running through them placed in different areas of the tent. And a floral arch and anything else you'd like. The guests would already be seated at their table for the reception. And we wouldn't need four hundred extra chairs for the ceremony."

Dianna had a blank look on her face for several minutes. She placed her hand over her mouth as if she was in deep thought.

Rose hoped the finicky woman wasn't about to blow a gasket.

Finally, Dianna spoke. "What about my flower gazebo and the huge floral arrangements?" she asked.

"We can still do everything on a grand scale; we could use orchids, lilies, peonies, roses, and lush foliage. We'll just have everything inside the tent and not out here in this area," Rose explained carefully.

"What about the table decorations? I wanted to have tall floral displays with long candles coming from them," Diana said, moving her hands to demonstrate the height she wanted.

"We can still arrange for the table to be exactly the same way you planned. The only difference would be the couple would get married inside the tent," Rose said again. She didn't know exactly what Dianna Hawkins was trying to prove to the masses, but Rose knew she wanted to get a plan down.

Rose and her sister waited several more minutes for the woman to say something, and when she didn't, Rose asked a question of her own. "Would you like to talk it over with Cassaundra first before you agree to our suggestion?" she asked.

Dianna shook her head. "Oh, no, that's not necessary. Cassie will go along with whatever I say. We don't have to worry about her," she said with assurance.

Rose couldn't believe her ears. You would have thought Dianna Hawkins was the bride, and not her twenty-four-year-old daughter.

Rose concentrated on the vision she had for the idea Ivy had set before her. She always wanted to do the best job she could no matter how much she disagreed with her customers' choices or the manner in which they conducted their business.

Rose scribbled notes in the folder; then she looked up, right into her sister's eyes. She noticed Ivy's head sway slightly from left to right. Rose knew then that her sister felt the same way she did. *April can't come fast enough,* she thought to herself.

Dianna headed back inside the house. Rose and Ivy followed her. For the next hour and a half, they brainstormed in more detail their new concept for Cassaundra Hawkins's April wedding.

Phoebe had gotten halfway down the hall before she could no longer contain the giant smile that continued to grow on her face.

"And the winner for best actress in a drama, Phoebe Hawkins," she whispered, laughing out loud.

Talk about right on time, she thought to herself as she proceeded to the foyer. She was glad Rose Hart was there when Lance arrived. Things were already starting to work in her favor. And even more relieved that her mother didn't ask her who Lance was, since she'd never met him.

When she'd gotten up this morning, she'd started with her daily ritual of drinking decaffeinated coffee while she read her horoscope. This morning it had said she would have a new beginning.

Phoebe understood the horoscope to mean that she would get another chance with Marc.

She'd been reading her horoscope ever since she was a junior in high school. Since that time, she'd believed in palm readings, horoscopes, astrology, and numerology. Phoebe planned her days and nights around them.

She never went anywhere without her gold necklace with her zodiac medallion hanging from it.

As she approached the foyer, she saw the tall, dark-skinned man waiting patiently. She thought to herself, *Lance Cooper will work out very well.*

"Lance?" she asked as she approached him, assessing his well-groomed appearance. He had mocha-colored skin and a close-cropped haircut—every strand lay flat against his head.

Lance extended his hand to her. "Yes, you must be Phoebe," he said, enveloping her hand.

Phoebe looked into his eyes as her hand disappeared in his. She saw a tinge of grey in them.

She had to make sure she thanked her friend Sophie, who owned Absolute Male Escort Service, for hooking her up with Lance. Sophie had told her Lance was her best employee. Phoebe didn't know if he was or not, but one thing she knew, he was very handsome.

Phoebe pushed her arm through his. She looked up at the mountain of a man as she massaged his muscular arm through the fabric of his shirt.

"Oh, yes, we are going to get along very well," she said as she opened the front door and they walked to his waiting black Mustang.

Chapter 16

Rose was so glad when it was time to leave. They had gone over and over Cassaundra's wedding plans with her mother. Every time Rose thought they were making headway, Dianna changed things again.

On the way back to the estate, Rose couldn't help but want to discuss the meeting with Ivy.

"Vee, Dianna Hawkins is something else. She should be ashamed of herself for robbing her daughter of something as special as planning her own wedding. I really feel sorry for Cassaundra," Rose said.

Ivy shook her head in agreement. "I felt the same way. I guess she feels she has the right to do it."

Rose looked out the passenger window at their surroundings as her sister drove. "There should be a way we could talk to Cassaundra alone to find out what she really wants for her day."

"When I get back, I'm going to call Mimi at The Design Group and talk to her about the tent," Ivy said making a mental note.

Rose opened the manila folder lying on her lap. "I think I'm going to do a lot with orchids for this affair. They're fascinating, versatile. The colors are gorgeous, and they're always available," Rose said.

"The baby blue and silver color will look nice in April," Ivy commented as she hit the expressway ramp and headed toward Hearts and Flowers.

"I wonder if Cassaundra even likes baby blue," Rose said, wondering how the young lady really felt.

Ivy glanced over at Rose. "Rosie, you can't worry about this situation. Cassaundra Hawkins is a grown woman, and if she doesn't put her foot down, her mother is going to continue to rule and super rule her event. This is their problem."

"I know you're right; it just upsets me to see this kind of thing happen. Cassaundra might get married again and again, but to me there's something really special about the first time," Rose responded.

Ivy shook her head. "Yes, and you never forget the experience…good or bad." She turned down Bridlewood Lane and headed through the gates to their business.

Ivy pulled into her designated parking space and cut the motor. As she took the key out of the ignition, she turned to Rose. "Rosie, did you notice the difference in Phoebe Hawkins's attitude today?"

"I sure did. Maybe I was wrong about her. At first, I thought she was a spoiled snob," Rose said, picking up her purse from the floor in front of her.

"Umph," Ivy responded, getting out of the car. "Maybe we can talk to her about her mother's behavior," Ivy suggested.

Rose thought for a moment. "That could be a possibility." She got out and slammed the car door.

Rose followed her sister into the building. "Well, I'll talk to you later," Rose said, turning to her left and heading to her shop.

"I'll call you once I've talked to Mimi," Ivy said, walking to her own office.

"Alright," Rose said as she continued to her shop.

She couldn't stop thinking about Cassaundra Hawkins. She hoped the young lady was handling her mother's decisions okay.

Suddenly, Rose thought about her own mother. When the time came for one of them to plan a wedding, would Louvenia act like a drill sergeant in the army?

Rose and her sisters would probably tie their mother to a chair in the attic until all the wedding decisions had been made before they stood for behavior similar to Dianna Hawkins's.

Rose sat at her worktable, pulled out a clean sheet of legal-sized white paper, and began to draw a layout for Cassaundra Hawkins's wedding.

Marc and Jonathan were both nervous as they waited for the health inspector to come and give them the green light on their facility. They had already seen the fire inspector, and now they had one last inspection to go.

Marc tried to think positively about the outcome.

They'd finally hired the staff needed to assist them in running the business smoothly. An older woman named Barbara was hired as booking manager. She would also perform light receptionist duties.

Henry's son Thomas took the job as sous-chef. Henry did agree to help them out whenever he could, and Marc was grateful for the older man's willingness to assist them.

They also hired four dishwashers, two prep cooks, line cooks, and a kitchen manager.

Jonathan thought it would be a good idea to have teenagers

work at the facility as servers. It would occupy their weekends, and they could make some decent money in the process. So they hired thirty-five teens, on a rotating schedule, just in case they had an event in all four of the ballrooms at the same time. They hired six adults to make sure the serving portion of an event went smoothly.

Marc sat at his desk and looked down at a self-assessment form similar to the one the health department used. He had decided to do his own inspection yesterday.

He had started from the outside, as he wanted to get an outsider's impression of the place. Then he had gone into the kitchen and had gone over all the food, hand washing, temperature, and awareness of food types with the kitchen staff.

Marc looked up from his form at his brother, who was standing over at the window.

Jonathan checked his watch once again. "What time were they supposed to arrive again?"

"Health inspectors don't usually have a specific time. They just show up. Come to think of it, when I was in Boston, they came at mealtimes. After the visit today, we should get our health permit; then after that they can show up anytime," Marc responded, noticing his brother's nervousness.

Marc got up from his chair and walked over to him. Slapping Jonathan on the back, he said, "We're going to be fine. I've been through this before. Everything is in place, and we've done our own self-assessment. I think we'll do alright."

Jonathan shook his head. "I sure hope you're right. We've got everything riding on this, and the grand opening is next week."

At that moment, the intercom beeped.

Marc walked around his desk and picked up the phone. "Yes," he spoke into the receiver.

"The health inspector's here," the receptionist said.

"Thank you, Barbara. We'll be right out," Marc said, placing the receiver back on the cradle.

"It's time," he said to Jonathan, then picked up a folder and headed to the door.

Jonathan followed behind him.

They walked together to the front office, which was three doors from where they were.

When they walked into the front office, they found a short, brown-skinned man with wide-rimmed glasses, sitting with a black briefcase in his lap, looking around.

The man looked over his glasses and stood, placing his case on the floor. He reached into his jacket pocket and pulled out his identification.

"Good afternoon, gentlemen," he said, offering his right hand to Marc first. "My name is Inspector Riley from the health department." He handed his ID to Marc and then shook Jonathan's hand.

Marc looked at the badge he'd been given and then handed it to his brother. After careful examination of the photo and information contained on it, Jonathan gave it back to the inspector.

"I'm here to view your establishment," Inspector Riley said.

"If there is anything we can do to help you, just let us know," Marc said, trying to sound as cordial as possible.

The inspector didn't crack a smile. His facial expression was stoic. "You can show me to your kitchen," he said, waiting for them to lead him to it.

Marc thought he would be able to read the inspector's feelings by trying to talk to him, but he couldn't. He didn't know if it was a good sign or not. He'd just have to wait and see.

Marc and Jonathan followed Inspector Riley at a respectful distance for the next hour and a half as he went through everything, from their cutting boards to the temperature of their salad dressing. Inspector Riley took lots of notes and barely said a word.

Soon, the inspector had completed his task without incident, which made Marc and Jonathan breathe a sigh of relief.

When they didn't get any citations, Marc finally relaxed and signed the form the inspector gave to him. He and Jonathan walked Inspector Riley to the door and watched him walk away.

Marc and Jonathan turned to give each other a high five after the inspector was out of sight.

Jonathan looked at his older brother. "Man, did you see my palms sweating?" he said, wringing his hands together.

Marc smiled. "I was cool at first, but when he didn't change his facial expression when I talked to him, it kind of made me nervous," he said as they walked toward the front office.

As they passed the door, Marc did a double take. He thought he saw Phoebe Hawkins. Taking several quick steps backward, he stopped in front of the door. He knew his eyes weren't deceiving him. "I'll catch up with you later, Jonathan," he said.

"Okay. I'm just glad that's over," Jonathan said before continuing to his office.

Marc went back to the front office, with a deep frown on his face. He wondered what had prompted Phoebe to show up at his place of business.

Phoebe stood up on her three-inch heels as soon as she saw Marc walk into the room. "Hi," she said, batting her newly applied, extra-long eyelashes.

Marc stood in front of her. "What can I do for you, Phoebe?" he asked. He couldn't help but notice how her short purple skirt hugged her hips.

"If you've got a minute, I'd like to speak to you," she said innocently.

Marc flicked his wrist to check the time. "I can spare a few minutes. Won't you come with me?" he said, opening the door for her.

Phoebe batted her eyes and walked out of the room first, waiting for him in the hall.

Marc extended his hand in front of him. "My office is this way."

They walked side by side down the hall. Marc opened the door to his office for her and waited for her to enter the room first.

Phoebe took the empty chair in front of the large desk. "Thank you for seeing me on such short notice," she said, watching him watch her as she crossed her legs, causing her short skirt to rise even farther up her thighs.

"It's not a problem. What can I do for you?" Marc asked as he took his seat behind the desk.

Phoebe leaned forward in her chair. "I wanted to straighten out what happened between us."

Marc pulled himself forward and held up his hand. "Phoebe, that's over and done with."

"For me, it's not, Marc. I'm ashamed of what I did to you," she said sadly.

Marc clasped his fingers together. "I'm not angry at you anymore."

Phoebe's face beamed. She looked like she'd just won first prize in the Publishers Clearing House sweepstakes. "So, you forgive me?" Her voice was full of hope and excitement.

"At first, I will admit, I was angry with you for telling me Andrea wanted to meet with me at that hotel, knowing full well she was there with another man."

Phoebe's expression turned to panic, so she tried to explain. "I know, Marc, and I'm so sorry, but I just—"

Marc held up his hand to quiet her. "But after I had some time to think about it, I realized that you really helped me see I'd never be able to trust her. I wanted to marry her, and that would have been a big mistake."

Phoebe tilted her head to the side. "You were going to marry her?" She knew he had been into Andrea, but she never imagined them being married.

"Yes, and when I marry, it will be for life," he said. His mind immediately went to Rose.

Phoebe moved closer, placing her freshly manicured hands on the desk. "I know it was painful for you. Are you sure you're not still angry with me?" she asked pitifully.

"I've moved on. Life is good to me now, and I'm happy," he said.

Phoebe sighed. "It's such a relief to hear you say you've forgiven me, Marc. When I found out you'd moved away, I didn't think I'd ever get the opportunity to ask you for forgiveness, which is very important to me."

She tried to make her voice sound as remorseful as she could. And she even made her eyes tear up for effect.

Marc reached over and placed his hands on top of hers. "It's okay. You don't have to worry about it anymore." He squeezed her hand to reassure her.

"I'm actually glad you came by, though, to talk to me about it. It says something about your character," Marc said, watching how the conversation was affecting her.

Maybe she hadn't meant to hurt him. She really had had his best interest at heart.

Phoebe had to control her expressions, because she wanted to smile at his words. She should have become an actor. She was doing really well playing the remorseful friend role.

She loved the feel of his hands on top of hers. She wanted him to touch her in other places, but she'd have to wait.

From the day her friend had introduced her to Marc, she had always wanted his attention. Phoebe had never thought her two-timing friend deserved Marc, anyway. If she played her cards right, she would get him to caress her body with his.

Phoebe stood and looked down at his desk. She noticed he had a monthly calendar, with writing inside the dates.

"Jackpot," she said to herself as she scanned as much as she could with his hands on top of it.

If he was one of those brothas that always wrote down their appointments and functions, maybe his calendar would be the key to tracking him.

Marc looked intently at her before reaching out to her. "Phoebe, are you alright?" He patted her arm.

Gradually, she lifted her head. She tried to memorize the two dates she saw on his calendar: the grand opening and a trip to St. Julian Winery in Michigan.

"I'm fine," she said, moving away. "I think I'll get going. I know you're busy," she said as she approached the door. Turning back to him, she said, "Thanks again for seeing me, Marc. I hope to see you around sometime."

Marc gave her a genuine smile. "It was good to see you, too, Phoebe. Take care of yourself."

Phoebe opened the office door and walked out. She quickly unzipped her Louis Vuitton handbag as she headed to the front door. She pulled out a slip of paper and quickly wrote down the information as she remembered it from his calendar.

Now she had to talk to Lance about going to Michigan and purchase a gown for the grand opening. She wanted to look good for her man.

* * *

Marc sat back in his oversized leather chair and went over the conversation he'd just had with Phoebe. He appreciated her coming to him to apologize.

He had hated running into her at Hearts and Flowers weeks earlier because he thought she'd cause trouble for him, but he was wrong. A burden had been lifted from his shoulders.

Today he saw a glimpse of another Phoebe, a more caring and mature woman. Not the troublemaking, spoiled one he knew in Boston.

He picked up the phone and dialed Rose's number at the shop, anxious to tell her about his day. He loved sharing his successes with her. He waited to be transferred to her line.

"Rose Hart speaking."

"Baby, I hope your day has gone as well as mine has because I feel like partying," Marc said enthusiastically.

Rose chuckled. "Sweetie, you want to party on a Monday? It sounds like the inspection went well."

"Oh, yes," he emphasized.

"Excellent. Now Ivy will be relieved. She was worried you guys would mess up all her hard work, and the grand opening would have to be postponed."

"Oh, no, everything will proceed as planned," Marc said as he rested his head on the back of his chair. "Baby, you're not going to believe who came to see me today."

"Who?" Rose asked.

"Phoebe," Marc said plainly.

"Really? What did she want?" Rose asked.

"She wanted to apologize. Hey, let's have dinner at my place, and I'll tell you about the whole conversation."

"Okay," Rose said, wondering what had happened between the two of them.

"What time are you leaving the shop today?" he asked.

"Probably at five o'clock."

"Dinner should be ready by six-thirty. I want to prepare something really special," he said.

"I'll be there, sweetie," she said before disconnecting the call.

Marc didn't realize Rose had used a term of endearment several times until after they'd hung up. His day was getting better and better.

Chapter 17

Rose stopped at home first before going over to Marc's place that evening. She wanted to change out of her uniform and put on something comfortable for their special dinner.

She slipped on a mid-calf blue jean skirt and a red, button-down, long-sleeve shirt. As she dressed, she couldn't help but wonder what Marc was going to say about his conversation with Phoebe.

Rose brushed her loose curls and applied a hint of lip gloss to her lips before she grabbed her swing coat and headed over to Marc's.

After parking her car, she walked to the door and rang the bell.

Marc opened the door immediately and pulled her into his arms. "Umm, you smell good," he said, burying his face in her hair.

Rose wrapped her arms around his neck and savored the feel of his body against hers. She loved the physical contact between them.

She stepped away and looked up at him. "You sure are in a good mood," she said, stepping farther into the room.

Marc closed the door behind her. "I'm always in a good mood when I know I'm going to see you."

He walked back to the kitchen area, where he had been preparing their meal. "I did have a great day though, with the health inspector giving us the green light and Phoebe's visit," he said, concentrating on his task.

Rose slipped off her coat and hung it on the coat rack behind the door. She walked into the kitchen and noticed the pristine white linen and the beautiful place settings on the small table in the corner.

She decided to take a seat on one of the tall stools in front of the island.

"What happened between you and Phoebe that makes you so happy?" she asked.

Marc had just placed a tablespoon of butter into a heated pan. "Like I said on the phone, she wanted to apologize for what she did to me."

"What did she do?"

"I used to date her best friend, Andrea Walker, and we had gotten pretty tight," he said as he sprinkled a finely chopped leek into the pan. "Anyway, one day Phoebe calls me and says Andrea wanted me to meet her at the Doubletree Hotel in downtown Boston," he said, adding a tablespoon of white wine to the pan.

Rose got up from her seat and leaned over, so she could see. "What are you making?"

"Ballotine of Chicken," he responded as he busied himself with the next ingredient for his dish.

"I don't think I've ever had that before," Rose said, making herself comfortable in her chair.

"It's a breast of chicken wrapped in spinach leaves and filled with leek mousse."

"Sounds fancy," Rose said. "Why don't you go back to your story after you finish the dish?"

"I think that might be a good idea," Marc said as he opened the refrigerator to get the ingredients for the brandy mustard cream sauce that went with the chicken. "I bought a bottle of chardonnay to go along with our dinner. It should be chilled by now. And there's a salad already prepared for us, so can you get them for me?" he asked, mixing the components in a saucepan.

Rose got up and retrieved the wine bottle, placing it under her arm, and the salad from the fridge. "You must have left work right after you talked to me."

Marc removed the saucepan from the heat. "Yes, I did. I wanted to prepare something special. I even made chocolate mousse cake for dessert." He smiled at her. "Why don't you have a seat, baby. Dinner is almost ready."

Rose placed a salad at each place setting and set the wine on the table before taking her seat.

She loved the burgundy taper candles nestled in the crystal holders on the table. There was a small matchbox lying close by; she picked it up and lit the candles.

Soon after, Marc came over and retrieved the plates. He expertly placed a piece of chicken on each plate, then spooned the cream sauce around it, topping it off with fresh tarragon.

Marc carried both plates back to the table, placing one in front of Rose, then the other at his setting.

He went over to the sink to wash his hands and then picked up a clean cloth to dry them before taking his seat at the table.

Marc reached across the table and grasped Rose's hands. They bowed their heads as he blessed their food. He picked up the wine bottle and opened it before filling her glass, then his.

Rose stuck her fork in her salad. "Marc, I've never had shrimp on a Caesar salad." She lifted a forkful to her lips.

"It's called Caesar Salad Chiffonade. It's excellent with crab also," he said, sampling his own.

For several minutes they ate quietly. Rose didn't want to bring up Phoebe right away, but she wanted him to finish telling her about his conversation.

Marc took a sip from his wineglass. "Anyway, let me finish telling you about Phoebe," he said, placing his glass on the table. "Phoebe told me not to stop at the desk, gave me the room number and everything. So when I got to the hotel, I went straight to the third floor, Room 316. I knocked, and this guy opened the door. At first, I thought I had the wrong room, that is, until Andrea came to the door, with a petrified look on her face when she saw me. I knew I had been set up."

Rose's eyes widened. She laid her fork down, her salad forgotten. "What do you mean you were set up?"

"The guy was standing there in a robe. I was meant to see him," he said as he continued to eat his salad.

Rose had to control her facial expressions. She took a sip of wine, then pressed her lips together to make sure her mouth wasn't hanging open. "So…" she started, waving her hand for him to continue.

"He was some guy that worked with Andrea at the law firm," Marc said casually.

Rose's mind was going a hundred miles a minute. "Oh no, Marc. I'm so sorry."

"It's ancient history now. I'm over it," he said, taking another sip from his glass.

Rose leaned forward slightly. "So, Phoebe knew they both would be there and wanted you to catch Andrea with the guy."

"Precisely. I was so furious at Phoebe for deliberately sending me over there. And even more furious with Andrea because I had planned to ask her to marry me that evening. I had the ring in my pocket and thought that since she had set up a sensuous afternoon tryst, I'd ask her then."

"Did Andrea give you an explanation?" Rose asked curiously, picking up her fork, pushing the green leaves around on her plate.

"Baby, what could she say? The evidence was right in front of my face. How can you explain a man and a woman inside a hotel room with robes on and probably nothing underneath?"

"Point taken. So where was Phoebe when all this happened?" Rose wondered what Phoebe's motive was for telling Marc.

Marc hunched his shoulders. "I didn't care where she was. I had to get out of there before I committed bodily harm against someone."

"Well, did Andrea try to follow you or contact you to discuss the matter?" Rose asked, knowing the answer.

"Before I got to the lobby, she was blowing up my cell phone. I answered it a couple of times but got tired of hearing her weep, saying how sorry she was for not being honest. I turned the phone off and went home.

"When I got back to my apartment, everything started to sink in. I was so angry, not to mention the pain in my chest.

"Phoebe shows up at my door, trying to console me, but I was so angry at her. I just felt she and Andrea weren't best friends for nothing. They were two of a kind."

"How soon after this happened did you move back to Taylor?" Rose asked.

"Well, Jonathan and I were already in negotiations for the building. At first, I was only coming back to Taylor to help him get on his feet; then I'd go back to Boston. After this incident, I decided to move back to Taylor permanently. So two weeks later, I came back here." Marc cut into his chicken.

Rose reached over and grabbed his hand. "You needed a fresh start, huh, sweetie?" she said with concern.

"Something like that," he responded, squeezing her hand.

"So what did Phoebe have to say today?" Rose asked as she moved her salad plate aside and then sliced into her chicken.

"Like I said, she apologized and wanted my forgiveness," he said.

Rose twisted her mouth. "That's interesting. Maybe she had time to think about what she'd done."

"Baby, when I saw her sitting in the receptionist's office, the first thing that popped in my head was trouble. I was all wrong about her."

Rose picked up her wineglass. "Is that why you treated her the way you did the other times we ran into her?"

"Yes, I just didn't want to reopen old wounds. Andrea Walker and what happened that day at the hotel are dead subjects to me. And anything dead should be buried." He continued to eat his meal.

Rose reached across the table and grabbed his hand again. "Thank you for sharing that with me. I know it was a painful situation for you to deal with."

Marc lifted her hand, pulling it to his mouth. "I'm fine now because I have you." He kissed the inside of her wrist.

Rose smiled, slipping her hand from his.

"Now that's enough of that," Marc said as he picked up his fork. "Let's finish our meal, so we can kick back and relax."

"So you believe what Phoebe said today?" she asked.

"She seemed sincere, so, yes," Marc replied, placing the last bite of his chicken in his mouth.

Soon, he got up from his chair, picked up his plate, and carried it over to the sink.

Running the hot water, he squirted a small amount of liquid detergent inside the sink, causing bubbles to form.

Rose also got up with her plate. She hadn't quite finished her entrée, but now it was cold. She handed him her plate.

"How did you like it?" he asked, taking the dish from her.

"I thought it was tasty, but I waited too long to eat it," she responded.

Marc scraped the remainder of her food into the garbage disposal and then immersed her plate in the soapy water. He turned to her. "Baby, I forgot to tell you, I need to take a road trip to St. Julian Winery up in Michigan on Wednesday."

Rose blew out the candles and started to clear the table. "Why are you going up there?"

"I want to take a tour and see about getting an account with them for Magic Moments," he said as he rinsed the dish he held in his hands. "Why don't you come along with me? I would love the company."

"I don't know if I can get away on Wednesday. We're trying to finalize some things for Phoebe's sister's wedding," Rose responded as she picked up a plate and wiped it with a dry dishcloth.

"Do you think you can let me know by tomorrow evening?" he asked.

"I should be able to," she responded.

They finished tidying up the kitchen and went into the living room.

Marc sat down on the sofa and pulled Rose onto his lap. He wrapped his arms around her, and they rested there together.

Before either of them knew what was happening, they had both fallen asleep in each other's arms.

Rose opened her eyes, realizing they had fallen asleep. She maneuvered her body so she could watch Marc. He looked so peaceful.

Soon Marc awakened and then looked down at her. "Baby, I'm sorry for falling asleep on you." He kissed her forehead.

"I took a little nap myself," she said with a smile. "Are you ready for the grand opening?"

"I'm really, getting excited. I can't wait to get the feedback from the critics and the public. I only hope it will be a success," he said, his tone growing serious. "Are you ready?"

"Yes, I'm ready, and I'm sure it's going to be fantastic," she said, giving him a kiss on the lips.

Marc took over, deepening the kiss until they were both breathless.

"Umm, you taste so good," he mumbled against her ear as he hugged her.

"It's the wine," she responded before giggling as he played with her earlobe.

Rose sat up and Marc leaned toward her, kissing her on the neck. "You sure, baby? I think I taste chocolate right here," he said as he continued to explore her.

When he got to the opening of her blouse, he kissed her there. "See, right here is apple pie, and I love apple pie," he said, palming her left breast through her blouse.

Their lips touched once again, and Rose was lost in the kiss.

"We could always go and lie down," he suggested in a husky tone of voice.

"Let's," Rose said, getting up from the sofa.

Rose cleared her calendar on Wednesday to take the two-hour trip to the winery with Marc. Wednesday was usually the day she finished all projects for the week, but today she felt she could catch up later that evening.

She waited for Marc to come and pick her up. They were leaving at eight o'clock to be there by ten.

Rose had been up since six-thirty and had dressed in a pair of black slacks, a white top, and her red crocheted poncho. She slipped on her black ankle boots and went downstairs to make a quick breakfast.

She popped two pieces of wheat bread in her toaster and made a cup of hot coffee. As soon as she'd taken one bite from her toast, she heard the doorbell.

Rose poured the coffee into a Styrofoam cup and grabbed a napkin for her toast. She pulled out her leather coat, figuring it would be cold outside since it was November.

Opening the front door, Marc stepped inside.

"Good morning, baby," he said, rubbing his hands together. "It's chilly out there."

"Do you want some coffee before we head out?" she asked.

"No, I've had my share this morning already. Let's roll; the tour is supposed to start at ten-thirty." Marc opened the front door.

"I'm right behind you. Let me get my purse," she said, picking up her black shoulder bag from the chair.

The cold air hit Rose in the face as she pulled her front door closed. She decided to go back inside and grab her fur hat. "Shoot, it's too cold to be cute today," she muttered aloud.

After placing the hat on her head, she picked up her things and went to the car. Sliding into the passenger seat, she situated herself comfortably before securing her seat belt.

"Do you have enough music?" she asked him, pulling out her mini CD holder. "I brought some of mine, if you don't." She handed the black case to him.

Marc took it from her. "We can listen to some of yours, too.

That's fine with me." He placed the case on the backseat, pulled out of the driveway, and headed for the interstate.

They listened to old-school R&B, hip-hop, and some jazz on the way.

Marc glanced at Rose. "Baby, can I ask you a question?"

"Sure."

"You've created wedding memories for dozens of people. Have you ever given any thought to your own wedding and what it would be like?" he asked, wanting to know what her dreams were for her future.

Rose smiled. "Oh yes, I've always had dreams of my wedding day. Are you sure you want to hear them?"

Marc grabbed her hand and squeezed it. "Of course, baby, that's why I asked you."

"Well, it would be a weekend event," she said, laughing. "We would need Friday, Saturday, and Sunday to celebrate it properly."

Marc smiled. "A whole weekend, huh?"

"Of course," she chuckled. "And the colors would have to be red and gold. I wouldn't mind it being on Valentine's Day, with lots and lots of candles and flowers," she said. Her eyes sparkled with excitement. "Oh, and I would love to create a personalized aisle runner with 'and they lived happily ever after' painted on it in red script," she said, smiling as she described her wedding fantasy. "I definitely don't want to forget the horse-drawn carriage to whisk me and my Prince Charming away after the ceremony."

She glanced at him quickly. "I could go on and on, but I won't bore you any longer."

Marc looked at her for a moment, then back at the road. "Why do you think you're boring me? I'm listening to you," he said, squeezing her hand again. "No, baby, continue if there's more."

Rose looked at him curiously. "Why did you ask me about it?"

"I just wondered what would make you happy on your special day, that's all," he said, bringing her hand to his lips.

After he released it, Rose asked him a question. "You said that weddings were a waste of time. Was it because of your experience with Andrea?"

Marc hesitated before answering. "Yes."

"At any time have you ever thought about your dream wedding?" she asked.

"Whatever my bride wants would be what I want."

"Okay, that's usually the consensus of most men. It's really the woman who makes the plans. The man just wants the woman," Rose said, pulling her hat off her head as she looked out her window at the scenery along the highway.

"Rose, I want you to meet my aunt and uncle. Do you think you could come over to my Aunt Rachel's for Thanksgiving dinner in a couple of weeks?"

Rose smiled. "I'd love to meet them. Won't they be at the grand opening next Friday?"

"Yes, they'll be there, but it will be so hectic. I wanted something more laid back and family oriented," he responded as he approached the exit to the winery.

"Are we here already?" Rose asked. "It didn't seem like we drove for two hours. We got here quick," she said, looking at the road sign advertising the winery.

Rose watched Marc and couldn't help but think about his questioning her about her dream wedding. She wondered if there was a specific reason why he'd asked. Hopefully, she'd find out.

Marc parked the car in the first available space he could find. He got out and went to assist Rose.

They walked together inside and headed to the front office. There they were shown a video that gave the history of St. Julian Winery and some of the important facts about how wine, brandy, juice, and sparkling cider were made at the family-owned winery.

They were then greeted by Dennis, the representative for Marc's area, who explained all about setting up an account, ordering, and the delivery of the product.

The short, middle-aged man was very cordial and answered all of Marc's questions about the winery's line without hesitation.

Dennis took them into an area of the winery called the tasting center. The huge room had about fifteen round tables, half of them occupied with people tasting the product.

Marc and Rose took a seat near the back.

"Let me get you a sample tray," Dennis said before walking away.

"What would you like to try first, Rose?" Marc asked, watching the others.

"I think I want to try the Blue Heron, and that's only because they bragged about it being their number one seller. After that I would like to try the peach sparkling cider," Rose replied.

Dennis returned with samples of just about all the winery's products.

Rose lifted the small wineglass that contained the Blue Heron and took a small sip. "Wow," she said with excitement. She looked up at Dennis. "It has a fruity flavor."

"Blue Heron has peaches, melons, and citrus blossoms. There is also a pear and mango flavor mixed," Dennis responded proudly.

"Well, I like this very much. No wonder it's your best seller," replied Rose. She looked around and stopped suddenly.

Rose patted Marc's hand to get his attention, since he had started to taste some of the red wines they had to offer.

"Look who just walked in here," Rose said to him.

Marc turned in the direction Rose was looking and saw Phoebe and a tall, light brown–skinned gentleman coming toward them.

Phoebe stopped by their table. "Well, hello, you two," she said, holding on to her escort's arm.

Marc stood. "Hi, Phoebe," he said before offering his hand to her companion. "Marc Damon, pleased to meet you," he said to the gentleman.

Lance took the offered hand. "Lance Cooper, pleased to meet you."

Marc introduced Dennis to Lance as well.

Phoebe went around to the other side of the table, where Rose sat.

"How's it going, girl?" she said, smiling.

"Good," Rose responded, watching Phoebe.

"Do you guys come here often?" Phoebe asked.

Rose smiled. "This is my first time here. I've never had a reason to do a wine tasting, but it's fun."

Phoebe took the empty chair she stood in front of. "I've never been here before, either."

Marc offered Lance a seat next to him, and Dennis took a seat on the other side of the table, facing the two couples.

Phoebe leaned forward so she could see past Lance. "Marc, what would you suggest we try?" Phoebe couldn't help but notice how Marc's navy blue pullover clung to his upper body.

"Rose tried the Blue Heron, and I've tried some of the red wines, but that's as far as we've gotten," Marc said as he picked up a small glass filled with a white wine.

"Phoebe, if you like wine with a fruity taste, then try the Blue Heron," Rose suggested.

Dennis got up from his chair. "Let me go and get a sample tray for you two." He walked away.

Phoebe looked at Rose. "How long have you been here?" She wondered what Marc saw in Rose because she definitely didn't look like any of his usual companions.

"We've been here about an hour."

"What are you guys going to do after you leave here?" Phoebe asked, hoping Rose would give her the answer she desired.

"I'm not quite sure. I just came along because Marc asked me," Rose responded.

Dennis returned with a tray for Phoebe and Lance. They sampled every wine, juice, and sparkling cider offered by the winery.

"Dennis, I think I'm ready to place my order," Marc said, rising to his feet. "Do you think I can receive my first shipment before next Friday?"

"I'm sure we can arrange for you to have what you need before then," Dennis replied.

Marc turned to Rose. "Baby, I'm going to go back to Dennis's office. Would you like to come with me or stay here until I come back?" he asked her.

Phoebe touched Rose's hand. "Why don't you stay here with us? We can chitchat until he comes back. And maybe we can get a bite to eat together when Marc returns," Phoebe suggested, batting her eyes at Marc.

Marc looked at Rose for an answer.

"I can stay here until you return," she said, hoping she would get a chance to talk to Phoebe about her sister's wedding.

Marc gave Rose a quick kiss. "I'll be right back," he said before walking away with Dennis.

"Rose, how did the meeting go with my mother the other day?" Phoebe asked, sipping from one of the wineglasses.

Rose was glad Phoebe brought up the subject but didn't want to say the wrong thing, so she was careful how she worded her sentences. "I think it went okay. I just hate not getting much input from your sister."

"Cassie is a sweet girl. Very quiet and reserved," Phoebe said.

"Has she ever said anything to you about her dream wedding?" Rose asked.

"No, she hasn't said anything in particular, except for wanting to get married in Jamaica," Phoebe replied.

This information pleased Rose because it gave her a little more to go on about the bride, instead of the vision her mother portrayed. "Has she found a dress yet?" Rose asked.

"We're supposed to see your sister Violet in the morning about a gown."

Rose smiled. "Good. I'm glad," she said, watching Lance as he sat idly, not saying a word.

Rose decided to talk to him as well. "Lance, have you ever been to a place like this before?"

"Yes, I've been to several wine tasting events over the past couple of months actually," he lied. He'd never been to a winery.

Rose chuckled. "So you're an old pro." She suspected their winery visit was Lance's idea then. "What do you do for a living, if I may ask?"

"I'm an investment banker for Morgan Stanley."

Rose glanced over at Phoebe and nodded her head. "Impressive," she said.

Phoebe hugged Lance. "Yes, my baby is good at what he does, too." She kissed his cheek when she saw Marc coming back toward the table. "Here comes Marc," Phoebe said, getting to her feet.

Marc walked around to Rose's chair. "We're all set. Are you ready to go?" he asked, bending to kiss her temple.

"Would you all like to have a late lunch with us?" Lance asked, reaching for Phoebe's hand.

Marc looked at Rose before answering Lance. "Actually, I have some things I need to do when I get back to my office, so I'm afraid we're going to have to take a rain check."

Marc reached in his back pocket and pulled out a business card. He handed it to Lance. "I would like to invite you and Phoebe to the grand opening of my new banquet facility."

Lance took the card and glanced at the words. "When is this grand opening?"

Marc smiled. "I guess it would help if I give the date. It's next Friday evening at six o'clock. The address is on the card."

Marc turned to Phoebe and smiled. "It was good to see you again, Phoebe," he said as he stepped back so Rose could push her chair out from under the table.

Rose stood, then replaced the chair before turning to Phoebe. "I'll probably see you tomorrow at the estate."

"Yes, maybe I'll bring Cassie by your office to talk before we leave," Phoebe responded, knowing full well she had no intention of even mentioning to her sister that she'd seen Rose.

Marc placed his hand on Rose's back so she could lead him from the room.

Phoebe watched as the couple walked away. Her plan was moving along well. Both Marc and Rose bought the change in her attitude, but she needed to step up her game a bit. She wanted to be engaged to Marc by Christmas, and it was already November. Getting Rose Hart out of the way might not be as hard as she thought. The woman was too nice. They could become girlfriends fast; then Phoebe could get her man. Phoebe knew just how to do it.

Marc and Rose got back on the road at twelve-thirty.

"Baby, now do you see what I mean about Phoebe?" Marc glanced over at Rose.

"Yes, she acted the same way when I saw her at the mayor's house the other day."

Marc shook his head. "I remember when she was a spoiled, obnoxious young woman with a gold card."

"As we grow older and learn a few lessons in life, it changes us for the better. And she has a man, too. Remember what you said about Ivy?" Rose said as she made herself comfortable for the ride back to Taylor.

"You're right. I guess I was just shocked is all. Lance is definitely the kind of guy Phoebe would hang out with."

Rose rested her head on the headrest and closed her eyes. "He's an investment banker for Morgan Stanley," she said, opening one eye.

"He knows how to handle money, too. Oh yeah, Phoebe loves the ones with money," Marc commented.

"He seems nice, but very quiet." She wondered why he was so concerned about Phoebe's man.

After a couple minutes of silence Marc spoke.

"Baby, don't get silent on me. I only asked about Lance because I have never seen Phoebe out like that with a guy."

Rose sat up. "You haven't?"

"She always talked about her rich boyfriends, but every time she was supposed to double-date with me and Andrea, her date was always running late. Then he'd never show up. She would give an excuse about him having to work, so most of the time it would be just the three of us."

"Interesting" was all Rose could say. She lay back once again and closed her eyes.

Marc patted her hand. "Go to sleep; I'll wake you when we're almost home."

"Will you be okay driving while I'm asleep?" Rose asked, concerned.

"I have my music and the CDs you brought, so I should be fine."

Rose rested while Marc drove them back to Indiana. She hoped Marc wasn't unconsciously jealous of Phoebe and Lance's relationship. If he was, they definitely had a problem.

Chapter 18

Marc dropped Rose off at home before he headed to Magic Moments.

Rose went into her kitchen to prepare something to eat. She and Marc would share dinner later, but right now she was starving.

She opened her refrigerator to pull out the ingredients to make a turkey sandwich. As she spread mustard on the fluffy wheat bread, her phone rang.

She picked up the cordless from its cradle. "Hello?"

"Where have you been?"

"Dez, I haven't heard from you since last Saturday," Rose said before her cousin could start an argument.

"I thought you'd at least call me back Sunday morning after your night with Marc, but noooo, you couldn't even call me and give me the lowdown."

"Why didn't you call me?" Rose asked as she got back to making her sandwich.

"I've been busy myself," Destiny defended herself.

"Okay, we've both been busy," Rose said, cutting her sandwich in half.

"What's up for the weekend?" Destiny asked.

"I don't have any plans at the moment," Rose said. She took a bite of her sandwich.

"Why don't we try one more time to go stepping?" Destiny suggested. "We don't have to go to the Fifty; we could go to Mr. G's instead."

"I'll ask Marc later tonight," Rose said.

"Are you eating?" Destiny asked.

"Yes, I'm starving," Rose said, going over to the cabinet, pulling a glass out, and filling it with tap water.

"Look, you go on and finish eating. Don't forget to call me back later to let me know if you guys are going to come," Destiny said before she ended the call.

Rose laughed as she placed the phone back on the cradle. She knew chewing over the phone annoyed Destiny, but she didn't want to go into detail about Marc. Destiny could ask twenty thousand questions back to back, and Rose wasn't up to it.

Rose placed her sandwich on a napkin, picked up her glass, and carried it into her family room. Since most of the day was over, she decided to finish her sandwich in front of the television.

Saturday, Rose and Marc joined Destiny, Nicholas, Vanessa, and Richard at the Fifty-Yard Line, which was a sports bar, lounge, and dance club all in one. It was a great place to drink, dance, and mingle.

During the week there was an older crowd, and the weekends were for the younger ones. They dressed to impress, and some of the women wore everything from leather to spandex.

The men dressed in jeans and designer sweaters, and some even had on colored suits with matching hats.

Rose thought most of the people were there to see and be seen. The usual crowd was in attendance. Those who frequented the place knew each other by name, and the men outnumbered the women.

Rose watched as an assortment of multi-colored lights flashed to the beat of the Temptations's "Stay" as the couples hit the dance floor, spinning their partners to the rhythm of the music.

"Vanessa, get out there, girl, so we can see if you're wasting your money on those lessons," Destiny teased.

Vanessa jumped up, pulling Richard along. "Come on; let's show them."

"Wait, baby, I haven't finished my drink yet," he protested, trying to take one last gulp of the scotch in his glass.

"I didn't know Vanessa and Richard were seeing each other," Destiny said to Rose.

"Everybody doesn't have to tell you everything, Dez," Rose said with a chuckle.

Marc stood, reaching for Rose. "Come on, baby; let me see what you've got."

Rose grasped his hand and removed herself from her seat. "The dance floor is so crowded; I hope we can find a spot," she said loudly over the music.

Marc weaved his way through the crowd, with Rose, Vanessa, and Richard following him.

As they danced, Rose couldn't believe how smooth Marc's steps were. Whenever she had visited the popular establishment in the past, she had never really had one partner, so she didn't know what to expect dancing with him.

Being with him in this manner seemed natural, just like

their relationship. Rose enjoyed being on the dance floor with Marc, and he even showed her a few moves she hadn't seen before.

"Look at Vanessa," Rose said to Marc.

Marc turned to his right, where Richard had just spun Vanessa. "She's keeping up really well. That's good."

The crowd was lively, and everyone seemed to be having a great time.

After several turns on the dance floor, the couple decided to go back to their table.

Marc pulled out Rose's chair and then took the one next to her.

Rose leaned over to her cousin, who sat on the other side of her. "Dez, why didn't you and Nick get out there? This was your idea."

"I need more room," Destiny said, scanning the room. "It's really crowded in here tonight," she added, checking out several different areas. "Hey, isn't that Phoebe Hawkins coming this way?"

As Phoebe came closer, Destiny leaned forward as if she was trying to see better. "Girl, who is that fine brotha with her?"

Rose looked up. "That's her boyfriend, Lance."

"Umph," said Destiny as Phoebe approached the table.

"Good evening, my people," Phoebe said, smiling, trying to sound hip.

Marc stood and shook Lance's hand. "Great to see you guys again," he said before retaking his seat.

Lance nodded his greeting to the other men as well.

Marc introduced the couple to everyone else, then said to Lance, "Man, I would invite you guys to join us, but we don't have any extra seats."

"We'll find a spot," Lance said, pulling Phoebe to his side.

Phoebe placed her dainty hand on Lance's chest as she hugged him. "Thanks for the offer, Marc. We'll check you guys later. It was good to meet you all," she said to the others.

"Don't forget the grand opening next Friday evening," Marc reminded them.

"We'll be there," Phoebe said before they turned to leave the table.

"Rosie, I thought you said Phoebe Hawkins was stuck up," Destiny said, watching the couple walk away.

"That was what I thought after I met her the first time, but I'm beginning to think she's actually a decent person," Rose said, reflecting on the differences in Phoebe's attitude.

Rose watched the couple until they were in the midst of the sea of people in the club. Phoebe seemed to be very happy with Lance. Rose wondered if *he* was the real reason for the change in her attitude.

Marc kissed Rose on the cheek. "What's on your mind, baby?"

Rose leaned into him. "Love," she said, twisting her lips before kissing him on the cheek.

After Lance had found them a table, Phoebe sat. Her thoughts were jumbled. She couldn't believe her luck, running into Marc, but her horoscope this morning had said that she would come in contact with an important person from her past.

Lance leaned over to her. "What would you like?"

The huskiness of his voice and the feel of his breath against the side of her face made her abandon her thoughts for a moment, and she looked into his grey-tinted eyes.

"Sex on the beach," she replied.

"Hmmmn," Lance said in a sensuous tone of voice.

Phoebe frowned. He had misunderstood what she'd said.

"No, no, sex on the beach is a drink; vodka, peach schnapps, orange juice, and cranberry juice," she explained.

Lance moved his head up and down. "Oh, that sex on the beach."

"You knew what I was talking about in the first place," Phoebe said, hoping he didn't think their public display of affection would become private.

Lance smiled and winked before leaving the table to get their drinks.

Phoebe's thoughts went back to Marc and Rose. She had no idea she would run into them this evening, but it was a good thing she had. It would just drive home the point she was trying to make that she was into Lance. She didn't want either of them to figure out her plans for Marc.

Phoebe couldn't help but admit that Lance was a great guy. They'd had a lot of fun together, but he wasn't Marc. Anyway, he was being paid handsomely to play the loving boyfriend, so she wanted to get her money's worth.

Phoebe believed in her heart she and Marc truly belonged together. And together they would be, if it was the last thing she did.

Lance came back with their drinks and joined her at the table. Soon the music slowed down.

"Why don't we dance, Phoebe?" he said, getting up from his chair.

At first Phoebe was going to say no, but when she saw Rose and Marc on the dance floor, she agreed.

Lance led her to the dance floor, then pulled her into his arms.

Suddenly Phoebe was lost in the moment, and the sensuous love song caused her to move closer to him.

Lance enveloped her in his embrace even more as they moved to the music.

Phoebe rested her head on his chest and relaxed. She'd worry about getting her man after the song ended. Hopefully, he was watching.

Monday morning, Rose received confirmation for all the supplies and equipment she'd ordered for Cassaundra Hawkins's wedding. The wedding of the century, as Dianna Hawkins had titled it, would be in less than five months.

With all the ruckus surrounding the wedding, Rose didn't want any mishaps or any products missing, so she made sure to obtain everything she needed.

She called Dianna Hawkins to give her an update on the progress after she entered the information into Cassaundra's computer profile.

To her relief, Dianna didn't ask a lot of questions and didn't have any problem with the amount of money they were paying for the expensive décor.

Rose attributed that to just being a show-off, which was fine with her. This was a business, and a client's personal reasons for doing something were just that…personal.

She reminded Dianna that there were no refunds, cancellations, or exchanges. Even though this was printed on the receipt she'd already given to her, Rose emphasized it again, because people conveniently forget.

Rose scrolled through Cassaundra's file to see if she'd finally chosen a wedding gown. She still had not done so. Rose questioned the delay, but then thought it was probably due to Dianna Hawkins's fickleness and not Cassaundra.

As she was about to close the file, Ivy walked into the workroom.

"Rosie, I see you've had Cassaundra's file open. Are you done?" Ivy asked.

"I was just about to close it," Rose responded, saving the information just in case before exiting the file.

Ivy walked over to Rose's desk. "We started out shaky with this one, but I think it's coming together fine."

"Vee, the girl still hasn't purchased a wedding gown," Rose said.

"Maybe they purchased it someplace else," Ivy suggested.

"True. I spoke to Dianna today about the whole floral décor order, and she agreed with everything. There are going to be so many flowers there. I hope we'll be able to see the couple standing at the altar." Rose couldn't help but laugh.

Ivy didn't laugh, causing Rose to grow silent.

"Rosie, did you remind her that there are no refunds, exchanges, or cancellations on her order?" Ivy asked. "All we need is for these people to cancel on us. What would we do with all that product?"

Rose sighed. Ivy always asked her the same question. They'd been in business together for years, and she was still reminding her. "Of course, Vee, I went over the cancellation policy with her. It's also printed on the receipt I printed for her the other day."

Ivy was relieved. "Good. I need to update the reception information in the file, so I'll talk to you later," she said before walking to the door. Ivy turned back to Rose. "Don't forget to go to Magic Moments early Friday, so you can get started on decorating for the grand opening."

"I'd already planned on doing just that, but thanks for reminding me," Rose said. She didn't feel like going back and forth with Ivy.

"Okay, if I think of anything else, I'll buzz you," Ivy said as she left.

"Please don't," Rose said to herself.

Chapter 19

The big day had finally arrived, and Rose went over early to decorate for the grand opening of Magic Moments.

She placed a large silk floral centerpiece with lilies and orchids on the round glass table with an antique bottom in the lobby.

White silk flowers and tulle adorned the railings of the staircase leading from the lobby to the bridal suites.

In the Royal Ballroom, where the actual dinner would be served, she coordinated her centerpieces and decor with the champagne color theme.

The staff had already set up the tables and placed the tablecloths on them. They still had to put on the white chair covers and gold sashes.

Rose liked Ivy's idea of having a wedding reception theme for the grand opening.

The Embassy Ballroom, which was the smallest of the four, had been set up with ten different table linen selections, china, colored napkins, and flatware.

Rose even created ten different floral centerpieces for the customer to choose from.

The other two ballrooms were empty but open for viewing.

Marc and his brother hoped the setup would give the food critics, the media, guests, and potential clients a realistic view of what Magic Moments had to offer.

They even had Lili create a towering wedding cake as a showpiece for the evening.

Rose was placing floral centerpieces on the tables in the Royal Ballroom when Marc walked in.

He came over to her. "Hey, baby, I didn't know you were here already."

She received his kiss with anxiousness. "Yes, I like to get started early. I've been here since ten-thirty. I had planned to come to your office after I was done. I know you'll be very busy today."

Marc stared at her in her company uniform and then gently pulled her into his arms. "I'm never too busy for you. Remember that," he said sincerely. Marc snuggled against her, reveling in the warmth of her body. "You are going to be my date this evening, aren't you?" he asked as Rose stepped out of his embrace.

"I figured you'd be too busy to have a date," she said, taking another centerpiece out of the box she had on a rolling cart.

"What did I just tell you, woman?" he said, smiling. "I'm never too busy for you. As a matter of fact, why don't you and your sisters sit at my table?"

Rose smiled. "Okay." She continued to the next table.

"Come back here," he said, holding his arms out. "I need a kiss, and I'll let you get back to work."

Rose walked into the circle of his arms, and soon after his head descended. The kiss was so sensuous, Rose could barely stand up.

Marc caressed her back as their tongues did a dance to a beat of their own.

After Marc released her, Rose had to wait until the foglike state she was in lifted before she could move.

"Do you want me to pick you up?" he asked.

"I had planned to come with Violet," Rose responded, still imagining his lips on hers.

"Okay, I'll see you later," Marc said, kissing her one last time before he left her in the ballroom.

Rose still had several tasks to complete before she could go home and dress for the evening's festivities. She began to hum as she completed her tasks.

The town of Taylor needed another elegant banquet facility for special occasions. The two existing facilities were always booked and didn't accommodate over three hundred people.

The capacity of Magic Moments was up to seven hundred, and the building had four ballrooms, which meant they could have four functions going on simultaneously.

Rose was so proud of Marc and Jonathan and hoped tonight would be a success for them. She knew from experience that running a business wasn't easy and that they needed as much moral support from other entrepreneurs as they did clients.

Rose took care in dressing for the evening. She sat at her dressing table and applied her makeup. She decided to wear a red, off-the-shoulder sheath dress with a sheer shawl, shimmery hose, and her matching red pumps.

She pulled her hair up in big pin curls, with wisps of curls hanging from each side. Admiring herself in the mirror, she could hear the blare of her sister's car horn signaling her arrival.

Rose picked up her shawl off the bed. It wasn't cold enough

yet for her fur coat, so Rose pulled out her long leather coat from the closet and headed for the stairs. By the time she got to the side door by the kitchen, Violet was pulling open the screen door.

Rose opened the oak door. "Hey," she said, stepping back to allow her sister to enter.

"Wow, Rosie, you look pretty," Violet said as she walked into the house.

Rose opened her sister's brown wool coat. "Thanks girl, you do, too," Rose said as she admired her sister's lanky figure in an ivory gown with scattered beads along the front. She looked out the door. "Where's Lili?"

"She's over at Magic Moments, setting up the cake. She's going to change over there."

"Do you think she needs any help?" Rose asked. "The cake is supposed to be really tall. The picture she showed me kind of reminded me of the cake Whitney Houston and Bobby Brown had at their wedding."

"It's supposed to be, but Desire went to help her," Violet said, walking up the stairs to the kitchen. "And you know Vee is there, too."

"She's probably giving Marc and Jonathan hell if everything isn't going exactly the way she planned it," Rose chuckled.

"And you know this," Violet said jokingly.

Both sisters laughed as they thought about their oldest sister's by-the-book lifestyle.

"Well, I'm ready, so we can go now, too, just in case Lili needs extra help." Rose grabbed her purse and keys and followed Violet out, locking the door behind her.

They climbed into Violet's late-model Lexus sedan. Violet turned on the radio to a preset station before she backed out of the driveway and onto the street.

Violet looked over at Rose. "Rosie, did it bother you the way Mama acted the other day at dinner?"

"Girl, Mama is a trip," Rose chuckled, thinking about her mother. "She doesn't mean any harm. I'm just not quite sure why she's tripping so hard now because none of us are married."

"I know. I wanted to ask her why, but I didn't feel like hearing one of those stories about yesteryear," Violet said.

"I don't think all of those stories are true. Sometimes I think Mama is just a good storyteller," Rose said.

"I guess you're right. She probably doesn't mean any harm, but I think she kind of overdid it with Marc and his brother, don't you think?"

Violet gave her attention back to the road.

"I think she would have been worse if Daddy hadn't said something to her when they went into the kitchen."

"Daddy to the rescue," Violet said, her volume increasing. They both laughed.

Rose thought about what her sister had said. They had never been a family that liked to keep up with the Joneses, and their mother raised them to be their own persons, so when she started on the marriage trip, they were all surprised.

It had gotten so bad that at the end of the year, they made her make a New Year's Resolution to not mention any of them getting married for one whole year.

Violet pulled into the portico of Magic Moments. They spotted both Ivy's BMW and the Hearts and Flowers delivery van Lili used in the nearby parking lot.

Violet eased out of the driver's seat and handed her key to the valet and waited for Rose to join her.

Rose and her sister walked side by side into the facility. They checked their coats, placing the tickets the young man gave them in their compact purses.

As they entered the Royal Ballroom, they spotted Lili completing the cake setup. It was a beautiful confection of sugar and creativity.

There were food stations being set up in various locations throughout the room. It was a good idea to get the people mingling and walking around as they dined. There was a live band setting up as well.

"Wow, Lili," Rose said as she stood before the six-foot-tall cake.

Lili beamed with pride. "This is my best work yet. But to get this baby up was a lot of work."

Desire patted her forehead with the bottom of the apron she wore. "You're telling me. I didn't know cake could be so heavy."

Rose looked up at the towering creation. "Well, it's beautiful. You really should be proud of yourself. I bet you'll get more cake orders after tonight." Rose looked around. "I'm surprised Vee isn't over here supervising you," she commented.

"Vee has gotten on my nerves *this* day," Lili said, with a look of exhaustion on her face.

Violet shook her head. "Don't start on my sister. I honestly don't think she can help herself. She's just a perfectionist."

Rose leaned closer to her sisters. "I think maybe she doesn't realize she behaves the way she does. I've even tried to talk to her about it. Didn't do any good though."

Lili waved her hands. "Girl, please, Vee knows she's domineering and sometimes obnoxious. She really hides it good; she's such an angel with the customers and a monster to us."

Rose couldn't help but giggle as she looked around the room. "Uh, oh, here she comes," she whispered quickly.

Ivy walked over to them in a long, navy blue fitted gown

with a bolero jacket. As always, she looked beautiful with her hair pulled back in a perfect chignon.

"Lili, I think you need to clean up your mess now and go get dressed. The guests should be arriving shortly," Ivy said without speaking to the others.

"Good evening to you, too, Vee," Rose said.

Ivy looked at her sisters, then at her silver bezel watch. "You guys should have been here," she said as she assessed Violet's outfit. "You look nice." Then, looking Rose up and down, she said, "Why do you have your arms exposed like that?"

If Rose could have stared a hole in her sister, Ivy would have several at that moment. "They look good, don't they?" Rose said sassily, shaking her arms toward Ivy. She turned around so Ivy could see her entire outfit.

Then Rose walked away before Ivy could respond and the night turned ugly before it got started.

Her oldest sister was asking for Rose to kick her butt. Instead of hitting her, Rose decided to go and find Marc. Just as she was about to walk out the double doors, Destiny and Nicholas strolled in.

"Hey, cuz, you look really pretty," Destiny said, giving Rose a kiss on the cheek.

"Thanks, girl. You two look nice. Do married couples dress like twins now?" Rose said with a smirk on her face. She was happy to see Destiny, so her mind wouldn't be on Ivy.

"Shut up. You just wait until you're married. I'm going to remind you of this evening," Destiny said, looking around the room. "As a matter of fact, here comes your husband now."

Rose's head jerked to her left, and she saw Marc strolling toward them. As usual, he looked so handsome; his hair was trimmed to perfection, and the diamond in his ear only enhanced his good looks.

Marc reached out to Rose, giving a low whistle. "Look at my baby," he said, twirling her around.

Pulling her to him, he gave her a wet kiss and continued to hold her as he greeted his cousin and Destiny.

Rose loved the way his black, one-button tuxedo fit his muscular frame. "How are things going for you, baby? Are you nervous?"

Marc smiled. "I'm doing great. Henry is working with us tonight, and so he's going to take over the kitchen, helping Thomas while I'm handling things out here." His expression grew serious. "Your being here with me makes me feel good all over," he said, kissing her once again.

Rose broke the contact to catch her breath. "I love you," she said, wiping the remnants of her lipstick from his lips.

Marc took her hand and placed it against his chest. "My heart belongs only to you, baby." He then brought her hand to his lips and caressed the inside of her palm.

Rose smiled. "I'm so happy for you, sweetie," she said.

Marc looked around the room as guests entered. "All the prep work has been done, so everything should go relatively smooth. If I get the chance, I want to have a drink with you."

"I'll save a seat for you at the table then," Rose promised.

Marc kissed her on the lips. "Okay, baby, I'm going to check on Jonathan. He's still in the office with some last-minute stuff." He walked away.

Destiny stepped forward closer to Rose. "You two are going at it, girl."

Rose's face reddened. She looked at her cousin. "I really do love him, Dez."

Destiny hugged Rose. "I know you do, girl, and it looks like he loves you, too." She smiled with tears in her eyes. "I told you your prince was coming."

"Yes, you did," Rose replied, with unshed tears in her own eyes.

"Why don't we take our seats, ladies?" Nicholas suggested, walking over to the table in the front.

As the evening got into full swing, people began to fill the ballroom. The lights had been lowered, and the flicker from the candles nestled inside the high centerpieces Rose had created fit in very well, giving the room a very romantic ambiance.

"Marc told me he found a condo in Shaker Village," Nicholas said, making small talk.

"Yes, he's on the other side of where Ivy lives," said Rose.

Destiny leaned forward. "Does she know he moved out there by her?"

"No, I haven't told her. Marc and I have been busy decorating the place," Rose replied.

Destiny's right brow lifted. "Oh, so you've been helping him decorate." She sighed. "I asked you to give me some decorating tips and you couldn't do that. I see how you are, Rosie."

Rose ignored her cousin's last comment. She knew Destiny was rubbing in the fact that she had been spending a lot of time with Marc.

Nicholas stood up. "Would you two like something to drink?"

Rose nodded. "I'll have a Sprite or 7UP."

Destiny shook her head. "I want something a little stronger than that. I think I'll have a glass of wine."

"I'll return shortly," Nicholas said, walking away.

Destiny glanced around the room. Both she and Rose were quiet. Then she saw Violet and Lili coming over to their table.

"I hope you guys saved us a seat," Violet said as she pulled out the chair on the other side of Destiny.

"Where's Desire?" Destiny asked.

"She went to the washroom. She's coming."

Rose glanced at Lili. "Baby girl, you look tired."

Lili dropped herself in the chair next to Rose. "I am." She let out a deep breath.

Rose patted her hand. "I have some of our business cards, so if you want to go on home, you can," Rose offered, sympathetic to her sister's needs.

"No, I'll be fine. I just need to rest a little. And anyway, did you see the tall, cute guy in the band." She shifted her head toward the front.

Rose looked up at the five-member group on stage. They had been playing instrumental pieces and a few R & B selections.

"Which one?" Rose asked, looking at each one of them carefully.

"The one that looks like a piece of caramel," Lili responded, turning her head in the other direction.

Violet smiled. "Oh, you mean the one that's coming over here?"

Lili sat up straight in her chair and quickly patted her hair.

"Excuse me, ladies," the stranger's voice boomed.

He held his hand out to Lili. "I was wondering if I could have this dance," he said just as the band began to play another song.

Lili looked up at the mountain of a man, then down at his outstretched hand. Slowly, she put her hand in his and stood.

As he escorted her to the dance floor, Lili turned around to her sisters, making a funny face.

Violet looked around. "I'm glad Mama's not here, 'cause she'd be acting just like she did when you and Marc were dancing at Destiny's wedding."

"Why didn't she come? Marc invited her," Rose said.

"Daddy said he had plans for them this evening, so that's probably why," Violet replied.

Rose and Violet looked at each other. "Daddy to the rescue again," they both said together.

Nicholas returned with their drinks. "I see Lili's found a dance partner already, and the night has just started," he said, placing their drinks on the table.

Nicholas looked at Violet. "I'm sorry, Violet, I didn't know you were going to be sitting over here. I would have brought you something from the bar as well."

"It's okay, Nick. I don't want anything right now anyway," she responded.

"You sure? I don't mind going back."

"Yes, I thought I saw a waiter walking around with champagne," she said, scanning the room for a server.

Rose sat wondering where Marc was. She couldn't help thinking of him. He was always on her mind. It seemed as if she'd conjured him up, because a few minutes later, he came back into the ballroom, with an older woman on his arm and a gentleman beside him. They were headed over to her table.

Marc placed his hands on her bare shoulders and squeezed gently.

Rose put her hands on top of his and leaned her head to the side, against his arm.

Marc bent to kiss her. "Baby, I had a minute and wanted to come over." He stepped back so she could get up.

Rose pushed her chair back and stood. She turned toward Marc and the older couple.

"Rose, I'd like you to meet Isaiah and Rachel Damon," Marc said.

Isaiah was a tall, handsome, dark brown–skinned man with

broad shoulders. Rose could tell that in his heyday he probably turned more than a few heads.

Isaiah stepped forward and lifted Rose's hand. "So you're the beautiful Rose Marc spoke about." He kissed her knuckles.

Rose blushed before saying, "It's a pleasure to meet you, sir."

Isaiah waved his hand quickly. "Call me Zeke," he said.

Rose nodded. "Okay," she said before extending her hand to the tall woman standing beside him. "Hello, Mrs. Damon, Marc's told me a lot about you," Rose said to the older woman.

Rachel Damon had to be almost six feet tall. She was a thin, chestnut brown–skinned woman with short, salt-and-pepper hair, which was expertly done. She was very classy and reminded Rose very much of Ivy.

Rachel smiled and then looked at Marc. "He did? I hope it was all good."

"Yes, ma'am, it was," Rose responded, admiring the older woman's champagne-colored cap sleeve gown.

Isaiah and Rachel greeted everyone else at the table.

Marc pulled out one of the chairs at the table. "Auntie, you can have a seat here," he said.

Rachel took her seat, and Isaiah joined her.

Marc sat in the chair next to Rose that Lili had vacated. "I invited Rose to Thanksgiving dinner," Marc said to his aunt and uncle.

Rachel smiled. "That's fine. We'll have plenty," she responded, looking around the room.

Rose smiled. "Looks like the night is a success."

"Yes, there were about twenty people in the tour group we were in," Rachel said, staring at Marc, her eyes getting teary.

Marc got up from his seat and went to her. "Auntie, don't start crying on me this evening."

Rachel lifted her hand and palmed the side of his face.

"Oh, your mother would be so proud of you and Jonathan." She allowed a tear to run down her brown cheek. "I want you to come by the house. I have something I want to give you."

Marc nodded. "Okay, Auntie, now stop crying," he said.

Isaiah pulled his wife to him briefly to help her control her emotions. "Baby," he whispered, "don't get all worked up; the boy has to work."

Marc wiped away her tears with his thumb.

Rachel picked up his hand and looked into his eyes. "I'm filled with so much pride. I can't express it in words," she said before Marc kissed her on the forehead.

"Where is that brother of yours?" Isaiah asked, scanning the room for Jonathan.

Marc went back to his seat. "The last time I saw him, he was talking with a reporter from the *Post-Tribune*. He wanted a tour of the facility, so Jonathan handled it." Marc paused. "Have you guys had anything to eat yet?" he asked everyone at the table.

"We were just about to go over and get something," Destiny replied.

Marc got up from his chair, grabbing Rose's hand. "Come on, baby, I really want you to try the jumbo three cheese–stuffed pasta shells."

Rose went along with him to the pasta food station. He grabbed two plates and placed several pasta shells on them. They went to several other stations, filling their plates with salmon salad, carved beef, and vegetables.

Marc even had a chocolate fondue fountain. One of the supply distributors had told him about it. He thought it was a wonderful idea, and the other facilities in the area didn't carry it yet.

The five-tiered fondue fountain flowed with Belgian chocolate and was surrounded by lots of strawberries, pineapple chunks, cherries, grapes, pretzels, marshmallows, biscotti, piroulines, Vienna Fingers, and caramel squares.

Marc and Rose drenched several pieces of fruit in the flowing chocolate and placed them on a separate plate.

Rose looked down at the two plates she held and over at the two he had. "Are you going to have time to eat all this? I know I won't be able to do it alone."

"We'll do the best we can," he replied as they went back to their table.

After the others returned, they sat comfortably and dined on the selections they'd made.

"Look who's coming this way," Destiny said, biting into a chocolate-covered strawberry.

Rose looked up to see Phoebe and Lance coming their way. She couldn't help but notice that Phoebe looked like she had been poured into her silver beaded gown.

"Good evening, everyone," Phoebe said cheerfully, grasping Lance's arm as they stood right behind Marc's chair.

Placing her hands on Marc's shoulders, Phoebe bent to whisper in his ear. "I've been looking everywhere for you."

Marc looked up at her and picked up his linen napkin to wipe his mouth. "Good to see you again, Phoebe," he said.

Phoebe stepped back in order for Marc to push his chair back and stand.

Marc shook Lance's hand. "I'm glad you could make it. Won't you join us?" he said, offering them the two remaining chairs at the table.

"I wanted you to give us a tour of the facility," Phoebe said softly.

"We have four different tour guides showing the guests around," Marc said.

"Aw," Phoebe said, disappointed. "I had hoped you could show an old friend around yourself." She tried to snuggle closer to him.

Violet leaned over to Rose. "I thought her sister was getting married at the mayor's house."

"She is," Rose whispered in return. "Maybe she and Lance are thinking about getting married."

Rose gently grabbed Marc's hand. "Baby, go ahead and show them around. I'll be here when you get back," she said, turning to Phoebe, giving her a smile.

Marc looked deeply into Rose's eyes. "Are you sure?" he whispered.

Rose nodded. "Yes, this is business."

Marc excused himself from the table.

"Thank you," Phoebe said, quickly positioning herself between Marc and Lance. She grabbed both their arms, but she leaned closer to Marc as they walked away.

Rose had to catch Destiny's hand before she got away.

"Where do you think you're going?" she asked her cousin.

Destiny pointed in the direction the trio had headed. "I don't like her. Prissy little heifer thinks she can just come over and get what she wants."

Rose patted her cousin's hand after she sat back down. "She and Marc knew each other when he lived in Boston. She's an old friend. No harm done," Rose said, picking up her glass, taking a sip of her soda. "Anyway, didn't you see the fine brother she was with?"

Destiny leaned closer to Rose. "Yeah, I saw him. I wonder where she found him."

"We ran into them last week up in Michigan at the winery. He's an investment banker," Rose said in return.

A tiny voice of doubt inside Rose tried to raise its ugly head, and she was determined not to let it get to her. She trusted Marc and knew he loved her, and that's all that mattered.

The evening was a hit, but Marc never returned to Rose's table, neither did Phoebe and Lance.

Rose tried her best not to read something into the situation that wasn't there. After all, the night belonged to Marc and his brother. There could have been a number of reasons why he hadn't returned.

Most of the guests had left. Isaiah and Rachel Damon had left sometime ago. Lili and her new gentlemen friend were sitting in the back of the room talking. Destiny and Nicholas had already gone home.

Rose and Violet prepared to leave. When they got to the lobby, Marc spotted them.

"Rose," he called out.

Rose stopped until he could reach her.

"Baby, I'm so sorry. I got tied up in the kitchen."

"It's okay; I think the night went well. What did Phoebe have to say about your new business?" she asked.

"She was enthusiastic about it, actually. She and Lance both said they would spread the word among their friends. I think that's great," Marc said with excitement.

"What happened to them? They never returned to our table after the tour," Rose said.

"Lance said they had another engagement they had to get to, so they left right after the tour," Marc responded.

"It was nice of them to stop by," Rose said, switching her purse to her other arm.

"Let me take you home, Rose," Marc said, looking at the two sisters. He turned to Violet. "I promise to get her there safely."

Rose turned to her sister. "You can go on."

Violet hugged Rose. "I'll talk to you tomorrow, Rosie," she said before turning to Marc. "Everything was really lovely, Marc. I wish you and your brother much success with your new business."

Marc lifted Violet's right hand. "Thank you so much. It really means a lot to hear you say that." He shook her hand firmly.

Violet handed the valet her ticket and waited for him to bring her car around. Violet winked at Rose before she walked out the door.

Marc grabbed Rose's hand and pulled her toward the office. Once inside, he closed the door behind them.

With his back against the wall, he pulled her into his arms, kissing her senseless. After he released her, he said, "Baby, I couldn't wait to do that again." He placed his forehead against hers, trying to catch his breath. "I don't know how to thank you for your support. You and your sisters have been so kind to us."

Rose retreated, pulling his hands from around her waist so she could hold them. "We were glad we could help. Business people have to work together. That way we all win." She gave him a kiss on the cheek.

Marc took two steps forward so he could open the office door. "You don't mind waiting for me, do you? It shouldn't take me too long. I need to make sure everything is set in the kitchen. I also want to make sure your crystal vases are packed properly."

"I could help you with those," Rose offered. "Jonathan had the empty boxes placed in a storage closet down the hall," she continued, following him out of the office. "I could have someone come by and pick them up on Monday."

"No, I want to bring them back to you myself," Marc said.

They walked down to the storage closet and retrieved the cart she'd left her boxes on. Marc pushed the cart into the ballroom, and Rose began to place the vases back into the boxes.

She looked up from her task and saw her sister Lili still engrossed in conversation with the guy she'd met earlier. Rose wondered if the couple had noticed the guests had left and the band was packing up.

When Rose made it to their table, she glanced at her sister's facial expression. "Could it be?" she said aloud and shook her head in disbelief. She had no idea what Lili and the gentleman had been talking about, but she could have sworn Lili was mesmerized by him.

Rose smiled as she continued her task, pushing the now heavy cart to the next table. She didn't say anything to Lili; she wanted her to enjoy her time without any hassle.

Just as Rose was packing the last box, she saw Marc walk over to the couple. He said something to the young man before he stood to his feet.

The tall stranger pulled a card out and gave it to Lili before he walked away.

Rose saw Lili scanning the room until she spotted her. Lili walked excitedly over to her.

"I guess you two forgot you weren't the only two people in the room all evening," Rose said.

Lili laughed, flicking her wrist to check the time. "We've been talking for hours," she said in amazement.

"Did you even get something to eat?" Rose asked.

Lili put her finger to her chin as if she were thinking. "Yes, we did get a little something." She smiled, remembering her conversation.

Rose moved in a little closer. "What's his name?" she asked.

Lili had that same mesmerized look on her face again.

"Lili," Rose said a little louder.

"Yeah," Lili said as if she was thinking about something else before her name was called.

"I asked you his name," Rose repeated.

"Dominic Ballard," Lili said in a dreamy tone of voice.

Rose tried not to giggle. She understood the way her baby sister felt. She had those same reactions to Marc, if not worse.

"Rosie, I'm going to head out," Lili said, turning to walk away.

"Wait, sweetie," Rose said, stopping her. "Don't go out alone. I know you're driving the delivery van, so why don't you let Marc and me drop you off. We can come get the van in the morning," Rose suggested.

"Cool. Let me ask Marc if I can leave my supplies here, too, until tomorrow." Lili walked over to where Marc was standing with the band.

Rose had completed her task, but the cart was entirely too heavy for her to move it now, so she waited for Marc.

The staff had cleared everything from the ballrooms and had left for the evening. Lili had put away her supplies, and soon everyone was ready to leave.

As they approached the business offices, Rose noticed Ivy was still there. She turned to her baby sister. "I didn't know Vee was still here," she said to Lili.

Lili looked around her sister at Ivy, who was standing in the doorway of Jonathan's office. "I'm surprised. She couldn't be scolding him. The evening was grand."

Rose smiled. "How would you know? The only person you saw was Dominic."

Lili chuckled. "Why do you think I said the evening was grand?"

Lili took a step forward before Rose stopped her. "Where do you think you're going?" Rose asked.

"I feel so good; I feel like aggravating Vee," she said as she continued to move toward her oldest sibling.

Rose followed, and at that moment Marc approached her. "Baby, let me tell Jonathan we're leaving. He should be ready to go himself, so we can all walk out together," Marc said, walking around her and toward his brother's office.

The sisters stepped outside the office door. Lili was the first to speak. "Vee, we thought you'd left already."

Ivy began walking over to the coatroom. "I was just about to leave when I remembered something I had to tell Jonathan," Ivy responded, pushing the door to the coatroom open.

Lili stood in front of the opened door. "You sure Jonathan isn't the reason you haven't left yet?"

Ivy's eyes shifted disapprovingly to Lili. "How are you getting home?" she asked, totally ignoring Lili's comment.

Rose laughed as she watched the exchange. She decided to say something herself. "Vee, Marc and I are taking Lili home. We'll come back tomorrow for the van. But, you didn't answer Lili's question."

Ivy grabbed her long, white, cashmere hooded coat from the rack and walked out of the coatroom before turning back to her sisters. "I'm not going to answer her, either."

Ivy slipped her coat on and stood there as if she was waiting for another remark from her sisters.

Marc and Jonathan both had their trench coats on when they approached the women.

Marc wrapped his arm around Rose's waist. "We can all walk out together," he said.

Jonathan armed the alarm system, then walked Ivy to her car and watched her drive off.

Chapter 20

Marc, Rose, and Lili got into his Lincoln, and they waited for Jonathan to get in his automobile. "Lili, what's your address?" he asked.

"3817 Pleasant View Road," she replied. "If I had been thinking, I could have left with Violet."

Rose waved her hand over her shoulder. "Girl, please, the only thing you were thinking about was Dominic."

Lili smiled, then pulled herself forward to get closer to Rose. "I think Jonathan's got a crush on Vee," Lili said from the back-seat, changing the subject to anyone other than herself.

Rose had noticed Jonathan's mannerisms when he was around Ivy. She hoped her oldest sister didn't hurt the younger man's feelings too bad, but after working with her over the past several months, Jonathan should have gotten used to Ivy's ways.

"I know he does," Marc said as he headed down Broadway Avenue.

Rose stared at Marc, but before she could reply, Lili laughed and said, "He's got to unthaw her first."

Marc looked over at Rose. "When the right man comes along, he doesn't have to do anything but be himself," he said loudly over his shoulder.

Lili sat back in her seat. "True," she said, thinking about Dominic, whom she'd just met that evening.

Everyone was quiet, and the only sound was the music from the radio.

Rose broke the silence. "I know I could be wrong, but I think Vee likes him, too. But that's just my opinion," she clarified.

"I guess we'll just have to see what happens, then," Lili said, crossing her legs as she looked out into the night.

Rose looked straight ahead, but her thoughts were actually of all of her siblings. She wanted them to be as happy as she was with Marc.

Marc pulled into the Polo Club apartments, and Lili directed him to her building, where he put the car in park and got out.

"I see Violet came straight home," Lili said as she pulled the door handle.

Marc held the door open for her as she climbed out of the vehicle.

Lili moved to the front, where Rose had rolled the window down. "I'll talk to you tomorrow," Lili said, giving Rose a kiss on the cheek.

"You did a great job today, sweetie," Rose replied as she watched her sister walk to her building.

Marc jogged around to the driver's side and hopped in. Once he secured his seat belt, he turned to Rose and said, "My place or yours?"

"Mine," Rose responded.

The Monday after the grand opening, Ivy entered Rose's shop with the *Post-Tribune*, the town's biggest newspaper.

"Rosie, did you see the article in the paper about the grand opening?" she asked.

Rose laid aside the project she had been working on to see it.

Ivy handed her the paper, and Rose scanned the 1fi-page article. She smiled as she read the reporter's praise about the ambiance, food, and spacious facility. He had even mentioned Hearts and Flowers, with their names, address, and telephone number printed below Magic Moments. It seemed everything Marc wanted came true.

Rose handed the paper back to Ivy. "Well, Vee, your plan of partnering with them might come true," Rose said.

Ivy had taken a seat at the worktable. "Oh yes, just like I knew it would." She smiled as she accepted the paper. "While we're on the subject of partnering, I have Cassaundra and Dianna Hawkins on the schedule for today," Ivy said.

"I saw that. Hopefully, they're coming in to buy a gown," Rose said as she picked up the bouquet she was creating.

"Dianna said they're going out of town for the Thanksgiving holiday, and she wanted to go over everything they'd accomplished so far. That's fine with me," Ivy said, thumbing through the rest of the newspaper.

"Thanksgiving is next weekend," Rose said, looking at the wall calendar.

"I know. So the sooner we get things done for her, the less Dianna will bug us to death," Ivy responded.

Rose picked up the floral tape. "I can show them the detailed sketches I've drawn for the décor, and I'll show Dianna the containers I want to use for the centerpieces. I have to wait on the topiaries, ribbon, and other little things."

Ivy closed the paper. "That should be good enough. I just want to keep this woman happy." She got up from the chair and walked to the door. "I'll buzz you when we're on our way."

Rose wanted to ask Ivy about Jonathan but thought better of it. Today Ivy seemed to be in a good mood, and hopefully, she would stay that way for the rest of the day.

Later that afternoon, Rose decided to rearrange her bouquet display in the showroom. She'd taken everything down and had begun replacing the bouquets by collection. She gave them names like Elegance, Charming, Bliss, Victorian, Romance, and Passion. She had almost completed the task when her intercom buzzed.

Rose walked to the desk and picked up the phone. She figured it was just Ivy telling her the Hawkinses had finally arrived.

"Yes," she said into the receiver.

"Rose, Cassaundra Hawkins is here to see you," the receptionist said.

Rose frowned. "Okay, send her down," she said before hanging up the phone.

Rose quickly put the last bouquets in their proper places before Cassaundra came down the hall.

She heard the chimes in the front, but before she could make it out there, her sister Lili came into the showroom.

"What's up?" Lili asked.

"I just finished rearranging the flowers. I'm waiting for Cassaundra Hawkins," Rose said, picking up the rag she used to dust the display case.

"That's what I'm talking about. Charmaine buzzed me and said Cassaundra asked to speak to me." Lili raised her shoulders to emphasize her confusion.

Rose raised her brows. "There is no telling what Dianna Hawkins is up to now."

"Maybe she wants the bride to fly in over the ceremony site

and have her enter that way," Lili said, trying to make light of the situation.

Rose put her things away. "Well, we'll find out shortly; she's on her way down now."

As soon as the words came out of Rose's mouth, they heard the chime once again.

When Rose walked into the receiving area, she expected to see Dianna hovering over her daughter. To her surprise, the only person she saw was Cassaundra.

"Hello, Ms. Hart," Cassaundra said meekly.

Rose went over and hugged the young woman, and Lili did the same.

"Where is your mother?" Rose asked.

"She had some errands to run for my dad, so…" Cassaundra's voice was almost as low as a whisper.

"Let's have a seat," Rose said, moving over to the sofa.

Lili sat beside Rose, and Cassaundra took a seat across from them in the armchair.

"What can we do for you today?" Lili asked, folding her arms over her lap.

Cassaundra stared at the two women. Then suddenly, like a dam about to break, tears began to slip down the young woman's caramel-colored cheeks.

Rose went to her immediately. "What's the matter, sweetheart?" she said, getting down on her knees, pulling Cassaundra's head against her chest.

Cassaundra moved away, wiping the tears that ran down her face. "I can't take anymore of this," she said loudly.

Lili went into Rose's office and pulled several pieces of Kleenex from the box. She returned and handed them to Cassaundra. "Of what?" she asked with concern.

Cassaundra dabbed her eyes with the tissue. "My mother,"

she all but screamed. "This morning I heard her on the phone with my fiancé's mother. They were arguing about the reception menu."

Rose and Lili looked at each other.

"Sweetie, why would that upset you?" Rose asked.

Cassaundra jumped up from the armchair and walked over to the threshold leading to the display area. "I didn't want a big wedding in the first place. Reginald and I wanted to go to Jamaica and have a quiet ceremony with our parents and a few friends."

Neither Rose nor Lili said anything. They saw Cassaundra's need to vent, so they allowed her to continue.

The young woman began to pace back and forth. "I don't want to upset my mother, but this is my wedding. Instead of her asking me what I want, she tells me what's going to happen. It's so unfair." Cassaundra stopped for a moment and looked at the two women. "I feel like a puppet, doing everything she tells me to do. You know what I mean?" The tears started all over again.

Rose walked over to her and led her back to her chair. "Have you talked to your sister about how your mother's been treating you?"

"Phoebe can't do anything about my mother, either. That was one of the reasons she moved to Boston several years ago," Cassaundra replied, the tears steadily coming.

"Cassaundra, everything is going to be alright." Rose gently rubbed her flowing black hair.

Cassaundra glared at Rose. "She won't even let me pick my own dress," she cried harder.

Lili came over to Cassaundra and hunkered down beside her. She lifted her chin. "You're a grown woman. What are you going to do about it?" she asked, then looked up at Rose, who was shaking her head in disagreement.

Rose didn't want Lili filling Cassaundra's head with thoughts that would make her situation worse.

"Reginald and I talked about it right before I came over here. We've decided to elope on Thanksgiving weekend."

Both Rose's and Lili's mouths dropped.

"I thought your family was going out of town for the holiday?" Rose recalled.

Cassaundra dabbed the now disintegrating tissue on her cheeks. "We are, but they think I'm going to be spending the holiday with Reginald's family, and his family thinks he's going to be with us."

Lili patted her shoulder. "Good for you, Cassaundra. I would do the same thing."

Rose nudged Lili.

"Well, it's the truth. I would," Lili said without remorse.

Cassaundra stood once again. "I need you two to help me."

Rose and Lili went back to their seats on the sofa. "Okay, what can we do for you?" asked Lili.

"I want you to swear to secrecy about this."

The two sisters looked at each other before Rose responded. "We wouldn't say anything to your mother, but what about all the things she's ordered and paid for?"

"Don't worry; Reginald will repay my mother for everything. He says my happiness is his primary responsibility." She smiled.

"I like him," Lili commented. "Does this mean we can't tell Ivy?"

Rose shook her head. "Oh, no, and not because she would tell Dianna, either. I just don't think she should know," Rose said, imagining the lecture Ivy would give them if she found out the bride was eloping.

Lili turned her attention back to Cassaundra. "Now, is there anything else?"

"I need a wedding gown. I would like your help in choosing one," Cassaundra said.

Rose smiled and then glanced at her sister, who was smiling also. "Of course. Let me buzz Violet to see if she has some time this afternoon," Rose said, walking over to the telephone.

The three women left the flower shop and went to the wedding boutique located on the second floor. After they briefed Violet on the situation, they got to work on finding the perfect gown.

Violet was very helpful in finding Cassaundra an elegant, white, V-necked chiffon sheath gown with spaghetti straps. It had scattered beads, pearls, and sequins throughout and a handkerchief hem. She looked so beautiful, and the gown fit her perfectly.

Because the couple had planned to get married on the beach, she wouldn't wear a headpiece.

For the first time since Rose met Cassaundra Hawkins, she saw her face glow. Now she looked like the bride to be.

Violet steamed and bagged the gown before giving it to Cassaundra.

Cassaundra hugged each woman before she left to meet Reginald.

"Dianna is going to hit the ceiling when she finds out that girl got married already," Lili said, then smiled.

Rose sighed. "Yes, she will, but her daughter will be happy."

"That's our goal, right?" Violet said. "The slogan is 'Hearts and Flowers, where wedding dreams that last a lifetime begin,'" Violet recited.

"Yes, and I think we just made a dream come true for a deserving young woman," Rose said.

Rose hoped when the couple's families found out about their hasty nuptials, they would see their happiness and not cause them any trouble.

* * *

Marc was very curious as to what his Aunt Rachel wanted to see him about. He took the newspaper article about the grand opening over to her house to show her. But knowing his Aunt Rachel, she had already seen it. She always kept up with all of Marc's and Jonathan's accomplishments.

He got out of his car after parking it and went into the house.

"Auntie," he called out as he walked through the hallway that led to the kitchen. "Auntie."

Rachel was on her knees in the pantry. She backed out before trying to get up, so she wouldn't hit the shelf above her head.

Marc helped her to her feet. "Woman, what are you doing on your knees like that?" he asked.

Rachel patted her hair. "I know I canned some peaches, preserves, and cha cha. I wanted to pull them out to use them for Thanksgiving dinner," she said, moving around the Ball glass canning jars on the shelves.

"You said you wanted to give something to me," Marc said, helping her look for the things she wanted from the pantry.

Rachel pulled a jar of peaches off the shelf. "Yes, I did want to see you," she said casually. "See if you can find the cha cha for the greens, because I don't want to hear Freddie's mouth about me not having any."

Marc continued turning jars around, glancing at the labels. He found the jars she'd been looking for, pulled them out, and handed them to Rachel.

Rachel sat all the jars in the middle of the kitchen table and then washed her hands. "Let's go down to my room for a minute," she said as she snapped a paper towel from the dispenser on the counter.

Marc didn't say anything; he washed his hands and followed her to the bedroom. His mind was running a mile a minute. He couldn't think of any reason she would want to talk to him, unless there was something wrong with her, and she wanted to tell him herself.

Marc headed for the window seat in the bedroom, but Rachel stopped him. "Sit over on the bed, son. I need to get something out of there," Rachel said, lifting the cushion on the window seat and retrieving a locked box.

She brought the box over to the bed and sat down next to Marc.

Marc looked up at his aunt, and for a reason he couldn't put his finger on, he knew whatever she had to talk to him about was serious. "Auntie, what is this all about?" he asked.

Rachel reached for the box. "Just give me a minute, and I'll tell you," she said as she pulled the top off.

Marc looked inside at the many papers that filled the box. "Is this about your and Uncle Isaiah's wills?" he asked, his patience running thin.

"No," Rachel said softly as she continued to sift through the various items in the box.

Finally, Rachel removed an envelope from the box and handed it to Marc.

Marc glanced at the writing on the front, which had his name on it. He turned the letter over before he looked up at his aunt. "Is this from Mom?" Marc asked, trying to blink back the tears that rushed into his eyes.

Rachel nodded, trying to keep her composure as well.

Marc hesitated. He wasn't sure if he wanted to open the letter. All this time he hadn't even known of its existence. He did know, however, that whatever was written on the pages inside would change his life forever.

"Why are you giving this to me now?"

Rachel wiped the tears that had escaped from her eyes. "It's time," she said as she reached out and gently rubbed his back. "Go on, son, and open it," she suggested.

As Marc peeled opened the flap, he could no longer hold back his tears. He allowed them to quietly slip down his dark brown face.

Grasping the white paper inside, Marc finally removed it from its envelope. His heart began to pound as he unfolded the paper. Before reading the words, he just stared at the penmanship and began to wonder when his mother wrote the letter.

Rachel sat quietly wiping Marc's face from time to time. She wanted him to absorb this experience in his spirit.

The letters her sister Ruth wrote while she could still hold a pen were precious, and Rachel knew how important it was to Ruth that Marc and Jonathan received them when the time was right.

Marc took a deep breath before he began reading.

> *My dearest Marc,*
> *I asked your Aunt Rachel to keep this letter until she feels you're ready to handle it. I know my leaving you and your brother while you're still so young will be very difficult, but please know I love you both with all my heart. Take care of your father for me. I know this is going to be hard for him, so help him as much as you can.*
> *I tried to do all that I could to prepare you for life, and I hope you feel I did a good job. I know both you and Jonathan will grow up and make me proud.*
> *My prayer is that you find sheer happiness like your father and I had. When you find her, Marc, love her with all your might, hold on to her, cherish her, and treat her like a queen.*

> *Your Aunt Rachel has my wedding ring, and I asked her*
> *to give it to you to give to your bride when the time comes.*
> *I know it's not much to leave you, but I leave with it*
> *my love, blessings, and faith.*
>
>
> *Yours Forever,*
>
> *Mama*

Rachel walked over to her dresser and opened the top drawer. She retrieved a white box and brought it back over to the bed. Placing the box gently in Marc's hand, she sat and waited for his response.

Marc slowly opened the box and stared at the antique-looking diamond ring nestled inside. He wiped his face with the palm of his hand. He took the piece from its cushion.

"Wow" was all he could say.

Rachel put her arm around his neck. "I saw the way you looked at Rose the night of the grand opening, and that's when it hit me that it was time for you to get your letter," she told him carefully. "It may not seem like much, but your mother was adamant about writing the letters to you boys before she had to become more dependent on the pain medication."

"I understand," Marc said, still eyeing the tiny piece of jewelry. He couldn't form the sentences he needed to express the way he felt inside.

He repositioned himself on the bed so that he faced his aunt. "Aunt Rachel, when did you know that Uncle Isaiah was the man you'd spend the rest of your life with?"

Rachel smiled as she remembered how adamant Isaiah was about courting her. "Your uncle told me that I was going to be his wife the first day I met him outside a neighbor's house."

Marc's eyes widened. "Really, what did you say?"

"I told him to go to hell. I didn't know anything about Isaiah Damon. He was a smooth talker, and I just felt he was talking trash," Rachel said.

Rachel put her hand on top of Marc's. "Was I correct about what I saw between you and Rose?"

Marc nodded. "Yes, I think I've wanted Rose to be my wife ever since Nicholas and Destiny's wedding reception. She has captivated me in a way that I've never experienced before."

Rachel squeezed his hand. "Good. Now you have a very special person to wear this special heirloom," she said, pointing to the ring.

"Do you know what Jonathan's letter says?" Marc asked curiously.

"No, I don't know what his letter says. I left the room when your mother wrote those letters to you both. Because she was already in a lot of pain, I didn't want to distract her. I wanted her mind to be as clear as she was able." Rachel stood. Sometimes remembering those months she had to watch her sister suffer got to her. "Jonathan will receive his letter as soon as I think he's ready," Rachel said, moving to the door.

Rachel beckoned for Marc when she got to the doorway. "Come on, so you can help me set up the tables downstairs. If you can, I want you to help me with some other things," she said, walking from the room.

Marc sat on the bed a few moments longer. He couldn't help but look at the ring that had once graced his mother's hand. Now it belonged to him, and there was no other person on earth he'd rather give it to than Rose Hart.

Receiving the precious gift made him realize even further how much he wanted Rose in his life permanently. The thought of marriage had been floating around in the back of his mind for the last couple of weeks, but now he knew with all certainty that Rose would be changing her last name to Damon soon.

Chapter 21

Thanksgiving at the Hart household was always a special time, but this holiday would be different from any other. Today Rose would meet Marc's family.

She only got to say a few words to Rachel Damon at the grand opening, but from their meeting, Rose could tell Rachel and her husband were great people. She also knew the couple loved Marc and Jonathan very much.

When Rose told her mother that she would be coming late for dinner, since Marc had invited her to his family's house, Louvenia decided for the first time ever to have Thanksgiving dinner at six instead of the usual one o'clock in the afternoon. She made Rose promise to bring Marc with her.

Rose told Marc that she could drive her own car, since she had to go back to her parents' house, anyway, but he insisted on picking her up and dropping her back off later that evening.

Rose wore a red, three-quarter sleeve, ribbed, ballet neck sweater with a buckle detail, black slacks, and black high heel mules. She'd curled her hair and brushed it so the curls would lie around her nape.

She was ready to walk out of the house by the time Marc came to pick her up.

When she slipped into the passenger seat of the car, she sighed.

Marc reached over and grabbed her hand. "What is it?" he asked, bringing her hand to his lips.

"Nothing," she replied, pulling the seat belt across her chest with her right hand.

Marc released her hand and began to back out of the driveway.

"Baby, my aunt is excited about you coming to dinner. I hate to tell you that she called all my aunts and uncles to tell them."

Rose panicked. "Oh no," she exclaimed. "She told everybody?" She looked over at Marc. "How many people are usually at Thanksgiving dinner?" she asked.

"Oh, about twenty-five or thirty," he responded. Marc watched Rose's facial expression change. "Don't worry, baby; you'll fit right in."

Isaiah and Rachel Damon lived in a brown brick, ranch-style home on Baker Street. Most of the homes on the tree-lined street were owned by families that had been there for more than thirty years.

Marc had to park at the end of the street because there was no more space in the driveway or right in front of the house.

Rose took a deep breath as she climbed out of the car.

Marc came around to her side of the car and offered her his hand.

Rose grabbed hold of it, and they walked hand in hand to the front door.

Marc pressed the latch on the door handle and pushed the door opened.

When they walked into the home, it sounded like a crowd at a football game.

Marc stopped and took off his coat, then assisted Rose out of hers. He walked down the hall to the first bedroom and placed their coats on the bed with the rest of them.

When Marc returned, Rose followed him through the throng of children that had gathered on the floor in the hallway.

Rose's family had nothing on this one. There were people everywhere. Her family had never had this many people together in one house before. With so many folks, Rose wondered how they would all sit at a table together.

There was a crowd in the living room, family room, and kitchen, and in each room, Marc introduced everyone to Rose.

They found Rachel in the kitchen, with two other older women, who were busy getting the feast on the table.

"Looks like we got here just in time," Marc said as they entered the kitchen.

Rachel's face glowed. She wiped her hands on a towel and walked over to the couple. She hugged Marc. "You're late," she said.

"Did you need my help?" he asked with concern in his voice.

"We've been cooking long before we even put diapers on your behind, boy," an older woman said as she continued to peel potatoes with a small knife.

"Auntie Anna, I know that, but I just wondered if you needed my expertise," he teased.

"Expert! Boy, just because you learned how to scramble an egg and sprinkle some vegetables over it doesn't mean you're an expert," his Aunt Bertha said as she stirred her potato salad.

Rachel moved over to Rose and embraced her as well. "I'm glad you could make it today"

Rose moved out of the older woman's grasp. "Thanks so much for having me."

"I'm sure your family is preparing a big dinner as well," Rachel said as she went back to check on the food in the oven.

"Yes, they are. I promised my mother that we would stop by later," Rose said.

Rachel looked up at Marc. "Aren't you going to introduce Rose to the rest of your aunts?"

Marc laughed. "I thought you did that already."

Rachel swatted him with her dishrag. "Are you playing the part of comedian at this year's dinner?"

Marc couldn't help but laugh again at himself; then he tried to get serious before he answered her. "No," he said, pulling Rose to his side.

Extending his arms, he said, "Aunt Bertha, Aunt Anna"—he pointed at each of them—"this is the love of my life, Rose Hart. Rose, these are my mother's two other sisters."

Rose waved. "It's so nice to meet you, ladies."

Anna came over and assessed Rose, looking her up and down as she continually pushed up her cat-eye glasses, which kept slipping down on her nose as she walked around her.

Rose had to hold in her laugh at the animated faces the older woman was making. She could tell Anna was the oldest and funniest of the three women.

Anna glanced over at Marc, who was also trying not to laugh at his aunt.

"Well, at least this one's got some meat on her bones," she said, staring at Rose. "'Bout time, too," Anna said as she went back over to the table and retook her seat. "Them others looked like skeletons. Shucks, man needs sumpin to hold on to."

"Auntie," Marc exclaimed before turning to Rose and murmuring, "Baby, she didn't mean any harm."

"Don't Auntie me," Anna retorted. "How do you think your narrow behind got here? I didn't get this old and not know nothing. Now, the truth is the light."

Marc shook his head and looked to his other aunts to help him out, but they were busy with their own tasks.

Rose moved her hand forward. "It's alright, Marc. I'm not offended, really." Rose tried to reassure him.

Marc walked over to where Rachel stood. "Auntie, seriously now, do you need any help in here?"

"Well, if you don't mind, you could carve the ham and make it presentable," Rachel said.

Marc went to the sink to wash his hands. "Where's Jonathan?"

"He's downstairs playing with Buster's twins' video game," Bertha replied.

"Okay, I didn't see him in the family room with Booker and his crew," Marc said as he pulled out a large carving knife from the drawer.

Rose walked over to the table, where Anna was still peeling her potatoes, and took the chair across from her. "Ms. Anna, would you like for me to help you with these?" she asked.

Anna looked over her glasses. "See, this one even has manners," she said before turning back to Rose. "Do you know how to peel white potatoes, baby?"

Rose smiled. "Yes, ma'am, I do." Rose picked up a potato and the extra knife on the table and got started.

"What are you going to make with these?" she asked.

"Mashed potatoes," Anna responded.

The group worked diligently together, and soon dinner was being placed on the table.

Because there were so many people, the family had put a system in place so that everyone could eat at the same time.

The food had been placed on three banquet tables so that it could be served buffet style.

There were three other tables for the guests, and then they had separate tables for the children.

As Marc's Uncle Chester said grace, Marc whispered in Rose's ear. "I hope you don't fall asleep or starve to death before Uncle Chester gets finished."

Rose pressed her lips together to keep from laughing just in case someone was watching her. Since she'd stepped foot in the Damon house, it seemed someone had always been watching.

Finally, Chester finished his long, drawn out prayer, and they were all ready to eat.

Rose and Marc prepared their plates and headed over to a table to sit down.

Anna waved them down. "Come on over here, you two. Sit with us; we need to talk to you, anyway."

Marc rolled his eyes.

Aunt Bertha waved her fork at him. "Boy, get over here," she said.

Rose couldn't help but laugh. Marc's aunts were so funny, and he acted like a little boy around them. She thought it was so cute.

Marc pulled out a chair for Rose, then one for himself across from his Aunt Bertha and Aunt Anna.

For a while they all sat quietly and ate their food.

Anna picked up her water goblet and took a sip before breaking the silence. "Now, when are you going to get married?" she asked Marc.

Several seconds passed before he answered. "When I decide my family will be the second to know."

His aunts exchanged glances, and everyone went back to their meal.

Rose thought Marc's aunt acted just like her mother... always trying to get somebody married.

After the meal, Rose assisted the women in cleaning up. Rachel insisted that she take some dessert home with her, even though Rose explained that they were stopping by her parents' house.

Soon, Marc and Rose were saying their good-byes and were on their way to the Harts'.

By the time Rose and Marc arrived at the Hart residence, it was filled with more people than ever before. Rose was surprised, but suspected her mother invited them because Louvenia told them Marc was going to be there.

After being there for a while, Marc noticed that each time Rose would announce they were leaving, her mother would find a reason for them to stay. By the time they finally left, it was very late, and Marc could tell Rose was getting tired.

In the car, Rose leaned her head against the window. She was exhausted. All she wanted to do was go home, take a hot bath, and go to bed.

Marc looked over at her. "Baby, you're not falling asleep on me, are you?"

Rose lifted her head and looked in his direction. "No. I hadn't realized how tired I was until now." She yawned and lay back against the head rest with her eyes closed.

Marc reached over and massaged her thigh. "You'll be home in a minute, baby."

They were both silent the rest of the way to Rose's house.

Marc pulled into her driveway and cut the motor. He got out of the car and walked around to Rose's door.

"Thank you, sweetie," Rose said after he opened the car door. She got out of the car.

Marc pressed Rose against the car as he captured her lips in a soul-stirring kiss. "I just can't get enough of you," he whispered, resting his forehead against hers.

"Do you want to come inside?"

"No, you go on in and get some rest. If I come in, we'll probably be up the rest of the night."

Marc followed her to the door and watched as she disengaged the locks. He waited until she was safely inside before going back to his car.

As he climbed in, he shook his head at the thought of continuing to leave her. He wanted to be with her…only her. He looked at the house once more before he put the car in reverse, backed out of the driveway, and headed home.

Chapter 22

Rose and Lili sat in her office on Monday discussing the floral decorations for the cake table of a wedding that coming weekend.

They were going over several sample photos given to them by the bride, who wanted her cake table to reflect the décor captured in the photos.

At first, Rose thought she was hearing things when suddenly she heard voices. She got up from the table and turned down the volume of her CD player, so she could hear more clearly.

"Shh," she said to her sister.

Both she and Lili listened closely. They heard the voice of Gwen, their receptionist, along with several others. The voices grew louder and louder as they neared the shop.

Rose moved swiftly to the front, with Lili following her. They almost collided with Dianna and Phoebe Hawkins.

"Rose," Gwen called out breathlessly. "I'm sorry, but I tried to stop them until I contacted you about their arrival, but they ignored me and kept walking," the young woman said in defeat.

Rose glanced at Dianna and Phoebe. She could see fire shooting from Dianna's eyes. She knew then that Cassaundra had succeeded in getting married over the Thanksgiving holiday weekend.

"It's okay, Gwen. We can handle things from here," Rose said.

Gwen frowned as she stared at Dianna and Phoebe before turning her attention to Rose. "Are you sure? Do you want me to call security?" she asked.

"Call whomever you like, young lady," Dianna spat, jerking her neck.

"Mrs. Hawkins, what can I do for you?" Rose asked Dianna with a smile, ignoring her comment.

Rose then turned to Gwen. "Go on, sweetie, we'll be fine," she tried to assure the young woman.

Keeping an eye on Dianna and Phoebe, Gwen backed out of the room and into the hallway and walked away.

Rose turned her attention back to Dianna.

Dianna Hawkins pulled out her receipt from her designer bag and threw it at Rose. "You can give me all my money back," she demanded.

Rose watched the paper sail to the floor. She waited a few moments, all the while thinking this confrontation could get ugly.

Lili picked the white sheet up from the floor and handed it to Rose.

Rose took it and glanced over it for several seconds before looking up at Dianna. "Mrs. Hawkins, if I recall, we went over our cancellation policy, not once but twice. It's also printed on this receipt in red." She pointed at the red print on the receipt.

"I don't give a damn what that receipt says," Dianna fumed. "I want my money back," she yelled louder.

Rose tried to ignore the indignant way Dianna spoke to her. She always wanted to keep a professional attitude, but she didn't know how much longer she would be able to take the woman's yelling.

"Why do you want to cancel your order, Mrs. Hawkins?" Rose asked in a normal tone of voice.

Dianna snatched the paper from Rose's hand. "We are no longer in need of your services." Her voice modulated as she spoke.

"Mrs. Hawkins, why do you feel the need to yell at us?" Lili asked, tired of the nonsense the woman was spewing like venom. "There is no reason for you to yell at us. We're standing right in front of you."

Phoebe pranced forward, not stopping until she was standing toe-to-toe with Lili. "How dare you speak to my mother that way!"

Lili's eyes narrowed. "Getting in my face isn't going to get your money back any faster," she said as calmly as she could. "What you will get is your narrow behind kicked and quick," she said slowly, balling one of her fists.

Rose grabbed her sister's arm. She had had enough and didn't want the situation to get out of hand. "Mrs. Hawkins, what happened to make you so angry? When I spoke to you last, everything was going according to plan."

Dianna took several steps closer to Rose and pointed a finger in her face. "Don't act like you don't know what happened, Ms. Hart," she said, looking between Rose and Lili. "As a matter of fact, Cassaundra told me that she asked you both not to say anything about her and Reginald eloping." Dianna continued to point.

Rose couldn't deny that, but she wasn't going to admit to Dianna that her daughter confided in her. "Well, Mrs. Hawkins, I think Cassaundra is old enough to make her own decisions, and since you wouldn't listen to what she wanted, she took matters in her own hands. I think that's good for her," Rose said truthfully.

It was Phoebe's turn to confront Rose. She looked her up and down distastefully. "You don't know anything about my family," she spat.

Now Rose was tired of being nice. "Phoebe, I think you'd better heed my sister's warning."

"I want my money back!" Dianna said. "I'll sue you!" she added with squinted eyes.

"And you'll lose, Mrs. Hawkins." Rose took a deep breath and then released it. "For the fiftieth time, the cancellation policy is printed on the receipt. No refunds or exchanges." Rose tried to explain again, but this time her patience had run out.

"Your signature is on the receipt, Mrs. Hawkins. You agreed to the terms of the contract," Lili said, moving toward the door. "We're going to have to ask you to leave," Lili continued. "You can have your attorney contact ours. His name is Steven Holman, and he will be more than happy to assist you."

Rose nodded. "Yes, ladies, my sister is correct. There is nothing further for us to discuss. Let's have the attorneys handle things from here," Rose said, hoping that would end the discussion.

Dianna wasn't satisfied; she was so angry, she could spit fire. She'd been talking about her daughter's wedding being the biggest the town had ever seen, and now she'd be the laughing stock of Taylor.

Dianna looked to her right and spotted a vase on the table. She walked purposefully over to it and picked it up.

Rose watched Dianna carefully. "Mrs. Hawkins, please don't vandalize my establishment. It will only add to your expenses," she warned her.

Dianna let the vase slip from her fingers, and it went crashing to the floor. "Oops," she said, then covered her mouth with her hand.

Phoebe took note of her mother's action, and she decided to join in. She pushed the antique armchair over, then smacked her hands together as if she'd just done a full day's work.

She looked straight at Rose to make sure she had her attention. "You think Marc really wants your big behind? Sister, girl, let me *let you* in on a little secret. Marc is in love with me." She pointed to herself.

Rose lunged forward until her sister stopped her. "I knew you were a fake wannabe diva, Phoebe."

As Rose walked closer to Phoebe, Phoebe took two steps back. "With your Louis Vuitton carrying, Gucci wearing, no couth or home training, hungry-looking behind," Rose yelled.

Lili pulled on Rose's shirt.

Rose pushed her sister's hand away. "No, let me go." She moved closer. "I could care less if you *think* Marc is in love with you. You'd better check yourself 'cause you're delusional."

Rose gave Dianna a deadly look. "And how dare you two come in my shop and try to destroy it like you tried to destroy your daughter's life, Mrs. Hawkins."

When Rose got angry, she couldn't stop the words coming from her mouth, so she continued. "You want to make people think you're all that and a bag of popcorn. You are, but the popcorn is stale!" She pointed toward the door. "Now get out of here before I call security."

Phoebe stood to her full height. "Call security. I dare you."

Just as Rose went over to her desk and picked up the phone, Marc and Ivy rushed into the room.

* * *

"What is going on in here?" Ivy asked. She didn't know who to look at first for an answer. She looked down at the turned-over armchair and the broken glass on the floor.

Marc rushed over to Rose, who still had the telephone receiver in her hand. "What's going on?" he asked.

Rose started pressing numbers on the phone. "I'm calling security so they can come and get this trash out of here."

"You should be calling the garbage man, then, Rosie," Lili yelled as she stared Dianna Hawkins down.

Rose shook her head. "No, maybe the police would be better." She continued to dial until Marc pressed the button to cut the call.

She frowned at him. "Why did you do that?"

Marc took the receiver from her and placed it on the cradle. "Baby, don't you think calling the police is a little extreme?" he asked, attempting to calm her down.

Rose moved away from him. "You don't even know what happened here, so how can you come in and just take over like that?"

"Baby, I'm not trying to take over. I think if you tell me what happened, between all of us, we can figure something out."

Rose placed her hands on her ample hips. "Marc, do I tell you how to run things over at your place?"

Marc shook his head back and forth. "No."

"Well, what gives you the right to come in here and tell me how to run my business? I own this," she spat, pointing her fingers downward. "I'm responsible for this. It's my business, my reputation, that's on the line here." Rose's voice grew louder.

Rose looked over at Dianna and Phoebe, who were both talking at the same time to Ivy. "I'm not going to let these two hens come in and tear up my coop, which I've worked so hard to build, because they couldn't run someone else's life."

Marc realized then that he had walked in on what looked like the beginnings of World War III.

Rose glanced over at Marc. "Why are you still here?"

Marc gave her a long, penetrating stare. "I am not leaving." He enunciated each word.

He moved over to the empty chair behind the desk and sat down, folding his arms.

Rose glared at him. Her level of annoyance had increased with his presence. How dare he think she was taking things to extremes?

Rose walked over to where the other women stood. "Before we settle the controversy about the cancellation clause in the contract, I want to straighten out another matter."

She looked over at Marc. "I'm glad you decided to stay, because first, we're going to settle something with the daughter before we take care of the mother."

Marc straightened in his chair.

Rose stared at the skinny woman. "Ms. Phoebe Hawkins said, and I quote, and Ms. Phoebe please correct me if I'm wrong. 'You think Marc really wants your big behind? Sister, girl, let me *let you* in on a little secret. Marc is in love with me.'"

Marc rose slowly to his feet and the room was filled with a swollen tension. "Phoebe, you are wrong. I do happen to love all of her, big behind included. What you see standing here which embodies Ms. Rose Hart, that's whom I love."

He looked at Rose. "Baby, when you're finished with this, call me. I'll be outside." He walked out of the room.

Rose looked at Phoebe and almost felt sorry for her when the tears that filled her eyes rolled down her cheeks. She pulled herself out of her temporary shock with Marc's unexpected public declaration of love.

Rose shifted her gaze to Phoebe's mother. "Now, as for you,

Mrs. Hawkins. As the wife of an elected official familiar with hosting events, you should be more than knowledgeable about cancellation clauses in a contract. I will send you a bill for services rendered, and because I'm in a good mood, I'm not going to bill you for the destruction of my vase. If there is any further dialogue, it should be between your attorney and ours."

Dianna puffed up her chest, reminding Rose of a hen settling down on her nest. Dianna looked at her daughter and said between clenched teeth, "Let's go."

Rose, Lili, and Ivy bit their bottom lips to keep from laughing. After Phoebe and Dianna walked out, Lili was the first to burst into laughter.

They all were doubled over laughing.

Lili snapped her fingers over her head in a circle. "Welcome to the Hart Sisters' Chicken Coop."

Rose and even Ivy were truly cackling like hens.

Marc walked into the office to find the Hart Sisters laughing hysterically. All he could do was shake his head, pleased they were able to defuse the situation without involving the police.

He closed the distance between him and Rose, cradled her face between his hands, and brushed a light kiss over her mouth. "I will see you later tonight." He smiled and left.

Rose stood in the same spot stunned.

"Girl, what was all that?" Lili asked.

Rose looked at her sister and said, "When I find out, I'll let you know."

Ivy said, "You know what? Mr. Smooth Talker really let the air out of Phoebe's inflated head."

"It worked because she didn't have anything else to say," Lili added.

They laughed all over again.

* * *

Marc was slightly nervous when he arrived at Rose's house later that evening. He knew after speaking to her that his life would be forever changed. He patted his pocket to be sure the ring he'd placed there was secure. He pressed the doorbell and waited for her to answer.

"Hey, baby," he said once she opened the front door. He stepped inside the foyer.

Rose smiled. "Hey, yourself." She closed the door behind him.

Marc shrugged out of his jacket and handed it to her. He followed Rose down to the hall closet and then into the den. He'd noticed how exceptionally quiet she was tonight.

Marc stood in front of the sofa and stretched out his arms. "Come here, baby."

Slowly, Rose stepped into the circle of his arms. She loved the way she felt when he held her. After several seconds, she stepped back. "Thanks so much for helping me defuse the situation with Phoebe today. It actually took the wind right out of Mrs. Hawkins's sail."

Marc lifted her chin so he could gaze into her eyes. "As long as I live and breathe I'll always be there for you, baby."

Rose smiled. "It was nice of you to say what you said. You didn't have to say you loved me in front of everybody. You made it sound so real."

Marc glared at Rose as he held her hand and pulled her close once again. "Woman, how many times do I have to repeat myself? I say what I mean and mean what I say."

He sat down on the sofa, pulling Rose down onto his lap. Wrapping his arms around her, he snuggled close to her, and they sat quietly for a few moments.

Rose turned to face him. "Marc," she whispered, trying to find the words to say what she was feeling.

"Shh," Marc said, placing a finger over her lips. "Baby, I love you so much."

Tears began to form in Rose's eyes and were threatening to fall.

Marc wasn't finished telling her everything he had in his heart, so he continued. "First I want you to know what I'm about to say is not a joke or a game, so I want you to listen to me carefully."

He held her tightly. "Rose, every time I think about what my life was like before that Saturday night when we met, it makes me sad." He lifted her chin. "You want to know why?"

Rose's tears had broken free and were running down her face. She nodded slowly to his question.

"The reason is you weren't a part of it. You are the one, the one I've been looking for all my life. I don't want to see anyone but you, I don't want to smell anyone but you, and I don't want to taste anyone but *you*." Marc pointed to her chest.

He lifted her slightly and placed her beside him. He reached down into the pocket of his brown slacks and pulled out his mother's ring.

Rose's hands flew to her face.

Marc chuckled. "Baby, I need you to look at me if I'm going to do this the right way."

Rose was speechless at first. "Oh my God," she finally said, removing her hands from her face. She was so excited; she didn't know what to do with her hands, so she began to trace his neatly trimmed hairline with her finger. "I love you so much, sweetie."

Marc pressed his lips against hers. When he retreated, he just looked at her. "Rose, I want to live and not just exist. The only way I can do that is if you'll become my wife."

Marc glanced down at the ring he held in his hand. "This ring belonged to my mother." He looked at Rose once again.

Rose stared into the dark pools of his eyes. Her heart fluttered at the smoky gaze she saw there. Marc Damon was her Prince Charming. Deep down she had known he was the first time she'd watched him walk toward her at her cousin's wedding reception.

Tears leaked from her eyes and Rose waited before answering him. "It would be my pleasure to spend the rest of my days on this earth with you, Marc."

Rose moved her head from side to side as she watched the man she loved slip the antique piece on her finger. "I'm honored you feel me worthy of something so special to you."

Marc kissed her after securing it. "I don't know another woman more worthy than you."

He lay back, pulling her with him. He kissed her forehead. "Now you can have that dream wedding you wanted, complete with the horse and carriage. Since you love the color red, what do you think about getting married on Valentine's Day?"

Rose looked up at him, her eyes brimming with tears. She wiped away a lone tear that ran down her cheek.

As quickly as Marc could wipe her tears away with his thumb, another one rolled down her cheek.

Rose jumped up from his lap. "I'd better get started."

Marc caught her hand before she could get away. "Wait just a minute." He lay back on the overstuffed pillows, Rose rested against his chest. He stroked her hair, whispering his love and her importance to him in his life.

Rose lifted her head, gazed into his eyes, and then shifted to his moist lips. Her head descended, and Marc immediately deepened the kiss.

Their desire began to blaze like a forest fire; it kept spreading.

Marc groaned as Rose slipped her tongue in his mouth. She soon retreated, stood, and reached for his hand.

Marc knew the action was an invitation. He gently grabbed her hand and stood up.

They walked silently to the staircase and Rose stopped. She turned and wrapped her arms around his neck and repeated what he'd said to her earlier. "I don't want to see anyone but you, I don't want to smell anyone but you, and I don't want to taste anyone but you."

Rose turned and they continued up the stairs. An old O'Jays' song popped into her head. She knew they were about to climb the stairway to heaven.

Epilogue

Three months later…

On Valentine's Day, all the dreams Rose had had as a child were realized. She couldn't stop smiling as her sisters helped her into a beautiful white classic cap-sleeve, matte satin gown. The red embroidered lace and beading fell from the banded neckline. There were layers of lace falling from the split down the back of the semi-cathedral train.

Rose had her stylist give her the Audrey Hepburn look, just like in the movie *Breakfast at Tiffany's*, complete with the jeweled crown tiara as her headpiece.

All of her sisters, including Ivy, served as bridesmaids, and Destiny would stand beside her as matron of honor. They all wore simple yet elegant red strapless floor-length gowns with matching red shawls.

The men looked dashing in their black tuxedos with red ascot ties. Marc opted for a traditional white one.

Rose's mother couldn't stop the tears of joy from spilling

from her eyes. Today, Louvenia Hart walked down the aisle as the mother of the bride.

Rose felt there was no better place for her and Marc's romantic Victorian-themed wedding than the atrium at Hearts and Flowers.

With Destiny's help, Rose used lush flowers and gauzy fabrics with lots of candles to transform the all-glass indoor room into a stunning display of romance.

Topiaries of semi-tight white and red roses lined the aisle where the custom aisle runner Rose created would be laid to lead her to the altar. She hand-painted the long white carpet with the words "And they lived happily ever after…" in red script. She created a stunning nosegay bouquet for herself and simple presentation sprays for the girls.

One hundred friends and family would witness their nuptials.

Rose was relieved all the drama she'd encountered just months earlier had been resolved. Dianna Hawkins's attorney had informed her that she didn't have any right to a refund from Hearts and Flowers since she signed the contract. It was legal and binding.

Rose told Steven Holman, the family's lawyer, that she would give Dianna everything she'd ordered for her daughter's wedding. When Dianna declined, the attorneys settled, leaving Rose with extra product. She and her sisters decided to donate the product to a less fortunate bride who wouldn't otherwise be able to afford the wedding of her dreams.

The string quartet began to play the bridal march, and Rose was ready to take her walk down the aisle.

Holding her father's arm in a tight grip, Rose tried to steady herself as they stepped through the threshold of the door.

Jonathan stood next to Marc as they watched Rose make her way to the front.

"Who gives this woman to be wedded to this man?" the preacher asked.

Andrew Hart looked to his left at his wife and smiled, then dropped his arm to grasp his daughter's hand before he answered. "Louvenia and I give our daughter Rose Marie to Marc Damon to be treated with love and respect as she has been accustomed all her life." He kissed Rose on the cheek before placing her hand into Marc's. He then took a seat next to his wife.

Rose and Marc moved closer to the preacher before he began the service. They both decided on traditional wedding vows, repeating after the minister.

Rose turned to Destiny and took the plain gold band that she would place on Marc's finger. Marc took the gold diamond channel-set band from Jonathan.

Marc and Rose gazed deeply into each other's eyes. As they slipped the golden tokens of their affection on each other's hands, they spoke softly together.

"With this ring…"

Dear Reader,

I hope you enjoyed Marc and Rose's story.

You can't put love in a box, and you never know who you'll fall in love with. I guess the point of this story is to follow your heart. Let love lead you, and if it's right, you'll know. It can be a beautiful surprise.

Remember, it's not your physical size, but the size of your heart, that matters. Won't you open your heart and let love in?

I love hearing from you. You can contact me at http://www.seandyoung.com or seandyoung@comcast.net. My snail mail address is P.O. Box 14143, Merrillville, IN 46410.

All Good Things,

Sean D. Young

Wedding Tip:

When choosing a floral designer, make sure they understand you and the vision you have for your wedding. They should be able to come up with exciting ideas that incorporate your color, style, and theme within your budget to make your wedding day fantasy come true.